My Sweet Cory

My Sweet Cory

Pat Gillespie

iUniverse, Inc.
New York   Bloomington

iUniverse books may be ordered through booksellers or by contacting:

iUniverse
1663 Liberty Drive
Bloomington, IN 47403
www.iuniverse.com
1-800-Authors (1-800-288-4677)

ISBN: 978-1-4401-6843-7 (sc)
ISBN: 978-1-4401-6844-4 (ebook)

Printed in the United States of America

iUniverse rev. date: 01/18/2010

I would like to dedicate this book, and all my others, to my mom and dad, Roy and Virginia Gillespie, and the rest of my family for their belief in my ability to write my stories.

❧ *Chapter One* ❧

"Cory," her mother called out from the kitchen, while washing the breakfast dishes, "you know you don't have to sit around the house, waiting on your friends to get here. Why don't you go out and get some fresh air. Maybe go down to the park and walk around some."

"That does sounds good after all the shopping we did yesterday for the cabin. And since I've been home, we've hardly been down to the park at all!" the twenty-four year old, ghost story writer commented, having come home to Cedar Rapids to recuperate after a vicious attack on her innocence. Meantime, getting up from the couch to head out, she stopped to get herself a lightweight jacket due to the chilly May weather. "Mom," she turned back, "if I'm not back when the girls get here..."

"I know." she replied, when coming to stand in the kitchen doorway, while drying off her hands. "Tell them where to find you," the forty-eight year old widow smiled.

Smiling back, Cory headed out for her walk, while enjoying the brisk morning air. "Boy, how I have missed being here," she cooed, while walking down the street toward the park.

Getting there, she saw the swings she used to spend hours on as a child, clear through high school. Laughing, she walked over to sit in one, and began thinking back to other happier times. Times like when she, Angela and Jenny use to sneak off to watch the guys drive by. One particular guy was Max Brummet, the son of her parents' best friends, who had eventually went off to college.

After her own graduation, she too went away, but to New York, to work on her writing. Today Cory Hall is known in the publishing world as Cory Spencer. That's when her nightmare started, after meeting Ted Harden.

Taking in a cleansing breath, she tried her best not to think about that horrible experience of her attack, when feeling the breeze catch her long brown hair, as she swung higher. Unfortunately, with each pass of the swing, what led up to that day did seep in. 'The death of her father'. As it went, going off to New York to work on her book, she started dating a man she met, while at a boarding house. One day, four years later, she received a call from home, concerning her father. Having been warned of his bad heart, Bob Hall, a local farmer, was told if he didn't slow down he wouldn't last out the year. However, that didn't seem to stop him, when getting help from his best friends' son.

Meanwhile, back the park, dealing with her own memories, the very person she came to love, since childhood, was having a difficult time dealing with his own memories, that, being the loss of her father.

While parked along the country road, near the field where it all took place. Thinking back to that day, Bob had just gone back to his truck to get out some tools needed for the tractor, as it had started to rain.

"Damn…!" Max recalled swearing. As if not already in a bad mood, the thirty-four year old, Cedar Rapids police officer, got down off the tractor, after setting the safety switch, to clear the plow blades of the caked on mud, with a pipe.

"Damn it anyway," he swore again, while banging away at a stubborn clump, when trying to break it loose. In doing so, the safety switch failed, causing the arms that held the blades to shift. At that moment, hearing the sound of metal rattling overhead, Max stopped to look up and see what was happening. "What the hell?" he yelled, seeing the arms swaying from side to side.

Turning, he tried to get out from under them before the blades could get to him. Sorry to say, his left foot had slipped in the mud, when one of the blades succeeded in landing hard across the back of his leg.

"Oh, God, no_____!" he screamed, feeling the searing pain, as the blade nearly severed his leg, just above the knee.

Seeing this, Bob, against all warnings from his doctor, went running back out into the field to try to save Max's life. "Hang in there, son…" he yelled, "I'll try to dig you out!"

"No… it's too late! You have to get some help!"

"Yes, and by the time they get here, you would have bled to death."

"But your heart…! What about your heart…?"

"I have to do something!" the man cried out, when suddenly feeling his heart shoot out warning signs that were telling him to slow down.

Meanwhile, while attempting to dig Max out from beneath the blade, blood had started gushing out from the deep gash.

"Ahhh…" Bob cried, feeling the sharp pains getting worse, as the warning signs he had been getting turned into a full-blown heart attack.

"Bob…?" Max called out questioningly in the ongoing rain.

"No… it's all right!" he called back. "It's nothing!"

"No, it's not nothing," he groaned, seeing the agony in the man's face, when at that very moment he knew Bob's heart was sending out sharp pains. "Oh, my God!" he cried, lightly across his chest. In doing so, she recalled him coming to, only to see a blurred vision of someone he hadn't seen in eight years, leaning over him.

"It's going to be all right!" she recalled, whispering angelically, while brushing her hand lightly over his cheek.

At that, he drifted back off to sleep, while still under the effects of the anesthesia.

Shortly after the funeral, Cory had to get back to New York to finish her book, which was about to become a movie. While there, the man whom she had been dating during the time she was working on her writing, stopped by to see her.

Having fallen asleep on her sofa that night, Ted Harden, a tall dark haired, brown eyed man in his late twenties was just about to leave when he overheard her calling out in her sleep to someone named Max. Having heard her, he went ballistic and tried to take what she had been saving herself for all those years, to have for himself. Doing so, in a fit of rage, he had nearly killed her in the process.

Meanwhile, at the present time, as the soft rain let up, unaware her two friends had just arrived. Spotting her almost right away, they were about to join her, when seeing the look of sadness on her face.

"She must be thinking about her dad," Angela commented.

"Yeah, maybe," Jenny agreed.

They couldn't have been further from the truth, when Cory felt a tug at her heart strings over going back to New York when she did. And again she cried quietly, while running her hand over the cold metal chain of the swing, before the two went up to take a seat on either side of her.

"If only I hadn't gone back when I did," she cried, sensing their presence.

Realizing then what she was thinking, Jenny, the shorter of the two, shook her strawberry blonde head, "You know, Cory, while you are back trying to recuperate, we are just going to have to keep you so busy that you don't find yourself thinking about Ted and all that he had done to you."

"Thanks, but that's not the only thing I was thinking."

"Thinking about your dad, too?" Angela, Cory's closest of her two friends, with light brown hair and blue eyes, asked.

"Yes. I can't believe it has been nearly a year now since he died."

"Yes, it is hard to believe," she agreed sadly.

Not thinking, Jenny blurted out, "Yeah, but what about Ted, and what he had done to her?"

"Jenny…!" Angela scolded. "How insensitive."

"No, she's right!"

"Oh, Cory, what he did to you was simply horrid," Angela cried.

"Yes, and thank God he has been put away for it," Jenny groaned. "Hey, why don't we go and get something to eat? After all that shopping we did the other day, I can't believe I am still hungry."

"Girl, you are always hungry," Cory and Angela teased, while getting up to head for Angela's van.

On their way over to what had always been everyone's favorite restaurant, Angela spotted Cory's mother's car as it pulled into the parking lot of Tony's Eatery.

"That's odd!" Cory commented to her friends while sitting outside the restaurant in her friends' maroon van.

"What is it?" Angela asked, while seeing both, Cory's mother, Rose, and Max's mother, Mary, walk inside.

Before she could answer, she spotted a tall, lean, sandy blonde haired man getting out of his black truck, while favoring his left leg. Seeing him, Cory couldn't shake the feeling she knew him. Yet, having seen Max in the hospital nearly a year ago, this man looked as though he had the weight of the world on his shoulders. That still didn't matter any, this beautiful young woman, with her long wavy brown hair, and green eyes, was now sitting outside the restaurant, watching, as their mothers went to take their seats at a table near the window.

"Cory," Angela spoke up again, seeing the look of puzzlement on her friends' face, "what is it?"

"It's that guy…!" she cried.

"Which one?" Jenny asked, while sitting forward in the back seat to get a better look out the front window.

"The one getting out of his truck!" she pointed.

"What about him?" Angela grinned, knowing full well what was about to go on inside.

"He looks…" She stopped suddenly, when noticing his eyes, as he turned back to look around before going inside. "No, it can't be."

"It can't be, what?" Jenny asked, when the three got out to walk up to the restaurant together, once the man went in.

At that time, Cory shook her head.

Once inside, the trio looked around for a secluded spot to sit while watching Cory's mother, with hair lighter than her daughter's, sit with her friend, another widow, though, slightly older, about to have lunch.

Meanwhile, looking around, Cory hadn't seen the man who had gotten out of his truck.

"Whatcha lookin' for?" Jenny asked absentmindedly, when all she could think of was food.

"That man! I don't see him, do you?"

"No!"

"Yes, well just the same," Angela spoke up hurriedly, "let's find a table before we are spotted."

Seeing one, the three headed for the rear of the restaurant, where Cory and her friends could sit quietly and watch the two women chatting away.

"Oh, look, there he is!" Jenny cried, grabbing Cory's arm.

To Cory's surprise, the man joined her mother after getting off his cell phone.

"I wonder what's going on?" she asked.

"Who knows," Angela continued to grin at the two of them. "They sure look intense though, don't they?"

Being Cory's best friend, Rose and Mary brought Angela in on their plan to carry out a dying man's wish, knowing his daughter had been in love with Max since childhood. One problem though. He hadn't seen her in years and had no clue what she looks like now.

Meanwhile, after having given their order to the waitress, Cory grumbled with mounting frustration, "I wish he would just turn around a little so I could see his face one more time."

"Any clue as to who he could be?" Angela asked, knowingly.

"Possibly!"

"He sure looks unhappy though, sitting there," Jenny noted. "What do you think they're talking about?"

"Why, Cory, of course!" Angela said, scolding her friend.

"Me...? Why me...?" she asked, while caught off guard by Angela's statement.

"I don't know!" Angela bit down on her lip nervously. "Maybe he's the one taking care of the cabin!"

'Darn, of course he would.' Cory thought to herself. *'After all, Max would be the one doing that, since it is his family's cabin that I will be staying in!'*

"Sure," Jenny was just saying, while breaking into Cory's thoughts, "after all, the cabin could have been sitting there all this time unused!"

"Perhaps, but I wonder what it looks like now?" she asked, while thinking back to happier days when she and her father used to go fishing at their favorite spot.

"Well you'll find out soon enough!" Angela exclaimed, while taking a bite of her food after the waitress had brought their order out to them.

"Mmmm... this is good!" Cory commented, while taking her mind off her mother for a while.

"It sure is," Jenny agreed, thinking to herself.

In her little girl-like voice, Cory teased, "Whatcha' thinkin' about?"

"I bet I know!" Angela laughed. "The time we spent at the park eating Rose's fried chicken and hot apple pie!"

"Cory, your mom sure did know how to cook," Jenny smiled, while rubbing her tummy.

"She sure could!" Angela agreed. "And still does!"

After lunch was over, the man got up to go to the restroom.

Taking that moment, Cory went over to talk to her mother, while Jenny went up to pay the bill.

"Cory, what are you girls doing here?" Rose asked worriedly, while the two watched for the man to return.

Seeing their growing concern, Cory explained while watching them closely. "Jenny was saying how she was still hungry after all the shopping we had done the other night for the cabin. I had even gotten a beautiful old rocking chair, too. You really should see it, since it was so late when we got back."

"Oh, I'll see it when I get home, dear. I shouldn't be too much longer. Why don't the three of you run along now, and have some fun? It's still early yet!"

Running her tongue along the inside of her mouth, Cory looked back at the restrooms, wondering what would make her mother act this way. Turning back, she asked, "Mom, who was that guy sitting here with the two of you? Was that…" She stopped once again, thinking back to the hospital.

"Oh, him!" Mary spoke up, catching Cory off guard, with a warm smile and a wave of a hand. "He's just the caretaker of the cabin I had to hire. You will be seeing him later, when you go up there to stay for the summer."

"But I had thought…" She stopped once again, and just shook her head. "Okay you two, just what is really going on here?"

"Now, Cory, we are just here having lunch and talking over some business with him," her mother spoke up, a little edgy at first. "Why don't you girls scoot along now like I said and have some fun. I'll see you back at the house in a little while."

"All right, fine, don't tell me." She sounded disappointed when she and Angela turned to walk away. But then she stopped to thank Mary for the use of the cabin. "It'll be nice to see it again after all these years."

"Yes, I imagine it would," she smiled. "Yes indeed I imagine it would," she repeated more to her and Rose, when the two girls walked away.

Meeting up with her friends, Jenny asked, "Are we ready to go?"

"Yes," they replied.

But just as Cory turned to look back one last time, she nearly ran into the caretaker while on his way out of the restroom.

"Pardon me," the man said gruffly, when passing them by.

Not really looking at Cory as he had the others, there was something about him that kept nagging at her. But then, turning to look back at him, as he returned to the table, she saw the look on their faces, which had nearly given them away. Just then, Cory felt the old familiar pain of sadness, as she became so acutely aware of his limp. '*The limp…!*' she cried to herself, having occurred in a farming accident, when he lost his leg. "Max…" she continued softly under her breath, at the thought which was crossing her mind.

"Do you remember him now?" Angela asked, taking Cory by the arm.

"It has to be! It's that limp of his, along with that voice!"

she exclaimed, while looking at her mother for some sort of sign. "Oh, God, Mom, just what are you and Mary up to?"

"Maybe she doesn't want you to know just yet," Jenny suggested, while taking Cory's other arm to pull her out to the van. "Besides, just when was the last time he had seen you anyway?"

"It's been awhile, and he wouldn't have remembered seeing me at the hospital. He was still out of it after his surgery, when I went up to see him." At that, she thought back to the day she had said goodbye to her father, and the promise she had made him. Turning then to Angela, she added in disbelief, "I can't believe you don't remember him."

"Well...!" She had to think quickly, or Cory's mother would surely have her hide. *'This has to come natural,'* Angela thought to herself, while thinking what to tell Cory. *'They have to fall in love on their own. This is what Cory's father wanted for his little angel.'*

"You're kidding me, right?" Cory nearly shrieked, when seeing the look on Angela's face.

"Well, I have been kind of busy with the store and all. And he has been staying to himself a lot lately, since all this has happened to him!"

"It could be him!" Jenny added to take some attention from Angela.

"What do you say we get back to your house and start making plans for your trip to the cabin?" Angela suggested, changing the subject, while walking back to the van.

"Sure."

But then, no sooner had she said the word, Max looked up from the table and out at where the three were now standing.

"Cory, what is it?" Jenny asked, seeing the connection between the two, when their eyes met for the first time.

"That has to be him!" she cried, while still feeling sad at seeing the pain in his eyes just then. "I can't believe it, why didn't she just tell me it was Max? Why the big secret?"

"Well..." Angela started, "perhaps it is him!"

"Yes, and maybe he doesn't recognize you after all these years. You have been gone a long time!" Jenny exclaimed, while going on to get into the van.

"Hmmm..." Cory thought out loud, while doing the same.

After Angela had pulled out onto the main road, a sly grin came to Cory's face as she looked at her friends.

"Oh, no..." Angela laughed, when turning to see it, "I know that look."

"You should...!" she smiled.

"What...?" Jenny asked, while sitting forward once again in her seat.

"If that is Max," Cory grinned, "I just might have an idea."

Pulling into the driveway at her mother's house, she went about filling them in on her plan, while getting out to open the rear door. Stopping for a moment, she asked, "I wonder just why mom hadn't said something to me before now?"

"Who knows?" Jenny began, unaware of Angela's part in all of this. "Unless..."

"Unless, she and Mary are up to something?" she concluded.

Smiling, Angela commented to her friend, "This could be one very memorable stay at the cabin for you, Cory!" she grinned.

"It sure seems that way," she and Jenny both smiled, just as they finished getting what they needed out of the van before going inside.

❧ *Chapter Two* ☙

That evening Rose and her daughter talked about her trip up to the cabin. Careful not to mention Max's name during their conversation, Rose looked worried, thinking her daughter may have recognized him at the restaurant. At the same time, Cory wondered if he had, too.

'If so, my plan is useless,' she thought, flipping through an old issue of Cover Girl that had been sitting out on the kitchen table while her mother finished the dishes.

"Well," her mother went on to ask, while breaking into her daughter's thoughts, "how was your day?"

"It was fun! What did you think of the rocking chair and curtains I bought the other day for the cabin?"

"They're very nice!"

"Do you think the curtains will fit those old windows?"

"You'll be finding out the day after tomorrow!" she exclaimed, while going over to hang up the dishtowel, before heading into the living room to get comfortable.

"Mom?"

"Yes?"

"I meant to ask," she began, while watching her mother's

expression closely, "how was your lunch today with Mary and that…that guy, the caretaker…?"

"Oh… it was nice!"

"Oh…?" She sounded a little disappointed, just then. "Then I guess this means everything is set for Friday?"

"I hope so! He'll be there when you arrive."

"Good, I'm looking forward to meeting him," she commented, while secretly smiling to herself.

"I should warn you, though, he is a little hard to get along with at first, until he gets to know you, that is."

"Oh…?"

"Yes, he's been through a rather bad divorce, and he's still very bitter about it."

"Oh, all right, I'll keep my distance," she replied, while pondering over the news, when turning away to hide her ornery smile. *'For now, Max Brummet, I'll leave you alone, but not for long. You are about to get what you deserve after all those times of tormenting me. Just you… wait.'*

Not knowing what was going on at that time in her daughter's head, Rose concluded, "Just give him some time, Cory, he'll come around."

"All right," she replied. But then, not able to hold back any longer, she had to know if he recognized her. "Mom," she went on, while trying to hide her real feelings, "does he know who I am?"

"No, we didn't tell him," she replied sadly. "However, you bumped right into him at the restaurant."

"Oh… was that him?" she asked, while pretending not to know.

"Yes!" Rose sounded surprised that her daughter didn't recognize him.

Even Cory had her own thoughts of Max not recognizing her. *'Perhaps Jenny was right, I have been away too long like she said. Now how am I going to get him to recognize me without just coming right out and telling him who I am? He would only laugh if he knew! No,'* she thought sadly, *'he must remember me on his own.'*

"What is it, dear? You look as though you have just lost your best friend!"

"Oh, I'm just tired. I think I'll go to bed early tonight after going out for a walk. That's if you don't mind!"

"All right, but don't stay out too late."

"I won't," she returned, when getting up to head out the front door.

After Cory left the house, Rose called her friend.

"Mary is it safe to talk?" she asked, while looking out the front window to see her daughter walking toward the park.

"Yes, Max is in the garage working on his truck. Does Cory know?" she asked, taking a seat on her couch.

"No."

"Good. Where is she now?"

"She went out for a walk, before going to bed."

"This is going to be pretty tricky getting the two of them together."

"I know, but they need each other, especially now!" Rose was telling her friend fearfully. "Oh, Mary," she cried, "Ted has been calling here, making threats!"

"Oh, no… you were afraid of that. And yes, they do need each other. They just don't know it yet."

"Mary…?" Rose called, getting concerned when Mary had gotten quiet.

"I'm still here. I just wanted to see if Max was still under his truck."

"Is he?"

"Yes. Now tell me, how did Cory react when she learned that Max was the caretaker?"

"Hopeful, but disappointed when learning he doesn't know she's the one going to rent the cabin out for the summer!"

"I do hope we're doing the right thing here!"

"This is what Bob wanted for them. So yes we are."

"But that was before Karen did what she had to him. Now he doesn't believe any woman would want him after having lost his leg."

"Oh, but Cory isn't just any ordinary woman," Rose smiled.

"You're right about that!" Mary was saying, when Max walked in on their conversation.

"Mom, who are you talking about?" he asked, from the kitchen doorway.

"Oh, no one you would remember!" she explained, while trying to hide her surprise.

"You mean Cory?" he asked with a broad grin, thinking back to earlier days when he had gotten a kick out of tormenting her back at the same cabin, belonging to his parents.

"You remember her…?"

"Well I wouldn't know her now if she were standing here in front of me! She must be at least, what, twenty?"

"Twenty-four!" she corrected.

"Oh!" he said, stuffing a rag down into his back pocket. "Well, I just came in to let you know I'm going to take the truck out for a test drive."

"Okay!"

Just as he was about to turn and walk away, she called out, stopping him, "Hey, are you staying here tonight?"

"Yeah, if you don't mind, I'm pretty tired."

"Sure, that's all right with me!"

After Max had gone back out to the garage, Mary went back to Rose. "That was close!"

"Did he hear anything?"

"I had thought so, but he didn't let on if he had!"

Meanwhile, while the two went on talking, out in the garage, Max was gathering up his tools, before getting into his truck to take it out and see if he had fixed the misfiring problem. Whereas, down the street, Cory was getting ready to cross over to the park when he pulled out of his mother's driveway, unaware that he was about to hit her.

"Oh, God…!" she shrieked, jumping back out of his way, when he slammed on his brakes.

"What the heck…" he nearly yelled, throwing the gear shift up into park, before getting out to see if she was all right. "Are you out of your mind? What the heck were you thinking…" he continued, while glaring down at her with what little help the dimly lit street light had to offer, "crossing the road without first looking where you were going? Are you crazy? I could have hit you just now."

"I did look where I was going, you big jerk! You were the one tearing out of that driveway without looking!" she yelled back, while pointing back in the same direction he came from. Stopping, she suddenly looked back at the truck, remembering it from the restaurant, not to mention, that very driveway he had just pulled out of. *'Oh my gosh…! It is Max…!'* she cried silently, while backing away.

"Are you sure you're all right?" he asked, seeing the expression on her face change drastically.

"I…I'm fine," she replied, staring into his eyes for a moment.

"Wait a minute! You're the one I bumped into at the restaurant, aren't you?" he asked, while looking at her strangely.

"Uh huh…" she returned nervously.

With a slightly baffled look, he smiled, "We do seem to have a way of running into each other, don't we?"

"Yes, it seems we do!" she replied softly, while turning away to avoid being recognized just yet.

"Yeah, well, where were you heading just now?"

"Just over to the park for some fresh air!"

"Oh, isn't it a little late to be out?"

"Oh…" she flared up, when turning back to face him, "I am not a child."

"No, I guess you're not," he mused, thinking back to someone else who had a temper a lot like hers.

"Besides," she went on to smile up at him sweetly, "I'm not alone now!"

"No, you're not at that," he laughed, shaking his head, while looking down at her sweet face. "As for me, I was just checking out my truck."

"Oh? What's wrong with it?" she asked, looking over at it.

"It's been sounding a little rough."

"Hmmm, really?" she asked, hearing the problem right off, while it sat running roughly.

Walking up to the truck, she told him to pop the hood.

"What?" he asked, while going over to do just what she had asked of him. "What do you know about these things?"

"More than I want to!" she exclaimed, looking over the motor. "Okay!"

"Okay, what?"

"Turn it off for a moment," she smiled.

Going around to the driver's side, Max reached in through his open window to turn off the key. Coming back around, he stood by quietly at the front, while she pulled one plug wire to switch with another, and then another. Shaking his head, he grinned at what she was doing.

"Okay," she began, while reaching over to secure the last plug wire, before taking a step back. "Try it now."

"You're sure about that?" he asked, getting back in to restart his truck.

"Yes."

After getting it started back up, hearing the smooth sound of the engine, he looked out at her in total amazement. "How did you know to do that?"

"It was simple," she explained, while walking up to stand near his door, "you just had the wiring sequence all wrong. The guy who had helped teach me would have never made that the mistake."

"Well, he must have known what he was doing!" he laughed, shaking his head.

"He did, back then! In fact, it was my father who had taught him everything he knew."

"Your father...?" he asked, looking puzzled, as he went to shut off his truck. "Yes, well he is a smart man!"

"H...he was," she returned, while having to fight back the tears. "H...he died a short while back."

"I'm sorry to hear that," he replied, seeing a few tears slip down her cheek, when he reached out to wipe them away.

Taking that moment, she closed her eyes to feel his hand alongside her cheek. His touch was so warm and gentle. So much so, she wanted to reach out and touch his hand, but knew better than to try it at that time.

Shattering the moment, he spoke up startling her, "I can't help but feel as if we know each other. Do we?" he asked, just when his mother called out.

"Uh..." Pulling away, she chose not to answer him, when he got out to close the hood, before getting back in to start up the truck again.

"Well, I had better be going. Can I offer you a ride somewhere?"

"No, I think I'll just walk a little while longer. The air feels pretty good right about now."

"Are you sure?" he asked, reaching out to her.

"Yes, I'm sure!" she smiled back.

"Well, okay, maybe we'll see each other again!"

'Oh, I'm sure we will!'

"Hey! Just who are you, anyway?" he asked, over the sound of his motor, only to get a wave of her hand, when she simply walked away to leave him wondering.

That night, Cory slept peacefully, thinking of Max and the warm gentle touch of his hand alongside her cheek, until the bad dreams returned to haunt her.

Tossing and turning in her sleep, she was so full of fear,

when she began to cry out, hearing the man laughing his eerie laugh, as he went on chasing her.

"You won't get away from me this time, Cory...!" he laughed over and over again.

"Why are you doing this to me, when I don't love you anymore?" she cried, while feeling the chilling effect of his laughter going up her spine.

"What do you think...?" he asked, when then his voice became eerie. *"I'm... coming for you... Cory...! I'm coming for you soon...! And when I catch you..."*

"No...! Stay away from me...!" she cried, nearly waking herself out of her dream.

"Never...! You hear me...? Never..." he sneered, chasing her down a long and dark corridor, while reaching out, attempting to grab at her shoulder, when he had gotten closer and closer than before, while nearly closing the gap between them.

Suddenly, feeling herself falling back, back, back into the darkness, she woke, screaming into her pillow. "No_____! Oh, God, no_____!" she continued to cry, while rocking herself back and forth for the rest of the night. "No_____"

When morning arrived, her mother walked into her daughter's room to wake her. "Cory," she called out, going over to open the curtains, "are you going to sleep in all day?"

Not getting an answer, Rose turned to see her daughter huddled down into her blankets. "Oh, no..." she cried, taken aback when seeing her tear-dampened face and puffy eyes. Going over to sit by her, she asked, while brushing her hair from out of her face, "The dreams again?"

"Y...yes...!" She stifled a cry.

"Oh, Cory...!" she cried, wishing to take the pain away. Instead, getting up, Rose turned to her daughter, "Honey, I wish I could just say it will pass, but for now why don't you just get yourself up, grab a shower, and then come on down to breakfast."

"What time is it?"

"It's almost noon! Didn't you get any sleep at all last night?"

"No," she replied, getting up to go over to her vanity to pick up her brush. "Mom?"

"Yes?"

"How long is it going to take before these dreams do go away?"

"I don't know! Perhaps while you're up at the cabin, you might be able to get your mind off them for awhile."

'The cabin...' she thought back on her father, while brushing her hair. At that time, the thought hit her, when her father had died, leaving her totally heartbroken. "Oh Mom, I haven't been up there for so... long. It just wouldn't be the same without daddy there."

"I know, but it'll be good for you to get away."

"Hey," She turned back to her mother, when a thought hit her, "why don't you come with me?"

"Oh, honey, I wish I could, but I have got the church bake sale to do with your Aunt Mary!"

"But you will come up and see me, won't you?" she asked, looking worriedly.

"Oh of course I will. But first I need to get in touch with Mary to see if the cabin is ready for you." She smiled secretly.

"Will she let me fix it up some?" she asked. But then saw the look on her mother's face. "All right, Mom," she asked suspiciously, "what is it? What's really going on here?"

"Just finish getting ready, and then come on down to breakfast. I'll fill you in then," she suggested, with another smile, before leaving the room.

"Mom...!"

"Downstairs, Cory!" she waved, walking out.

"Great," she grumbled, while going off into her bathroom to get a shower.

Coming down the back stairway of their old home, Angela looked up from the kitchen table. "Is she coming down soon?"

"Yes, just as soon as she gets a shower," Rose returned, while going over to call Mary.

Looking over at Jenny, Angela turned back to Rose and smiled.

"Angela," Rose whispered, "you didn't tell her, did you?"

"No," she fibbed, not wanting to ruin Cory's little surprise she had in store for Max, "but she isn't happy that you haven't told her!"

"I know, but you know why?"

"Yes," Angela was saying, when Cory came walking in.

"Hi!" Jenny piped up, greeting their friend.

"What? When did you girls get here?" she asked, while sounding surprised to see them.

"Since your mom went up to get you," Jenny replied, while the three went over to get a plate of food, before taking a seat.

"Good, I'm glad you both are here, because I have an idea."

"Oh…?" Angela started in, when Rose walked back in smiling.

"Yes, but I will tell you both all about it in just a minute," she replied, turning to her mother.

"She said the cabin is almost ready."

"Great. How much is she wanting for it?"

"Well, I think she's been asking two hundred dollars a month."

"Wonderful, and now for my idea," she turned excitedly to her friends.

"Well…" they both cried out anxiously.

Laughing, she asked, "Why don't the two of you come with me?"

"When?" Angela asked.

"This Friday! Tomorrow in fact."

"Sure, I can hardly wait!" Jenny exclaimed cheerfully.

"Well, okay, but for how long?" Angela asked.

"For as long as you want!"

Thinking a moment, Angela smiled, "All right, just let me call and get things squared away at the flower store first."

"Sure!" she smiled, while Angela went off to make her call.

"Boy, this is going to be great getting away together," Jenny cried, while taking a hearty bite of her pancakes smothered in maple syrup.

"It sure is!" Cory added. "And just like old times too."

"Yeah, just like old times," she lit up, smiling.

Finishing her phone call, Angela returned to eat with the others, while Cory went on talking about their trip to the cabin, where as a child, she used to go with her family to spend the summers. While there, she knew she would someday come back and marry the boy who had captured her heart. It's just too bad Max had never known it.

Having been away for a while, she returned home to recuperate and try to recapture some of her happier memories, before she had gone. Unfortunately, during that time Max had gone off to college, gotten married, and then gone on to the police academy years before she graduated from high school, and gone on to pursue her writing career.

And now, she has gone and grown up from that little brat Max had always known, into the woman she is today, who is about to knock him for a loop, when he finally comes to realize who she is after all this time.

❧ *Chapter Three* ❧

After breakfast, Rose went over to Mary's while Cory and her friends went off to the park to talk. Upon their arrival, Cory went over to sit on a swing near the picnic shelter, while the other two picked a swing on either side of her, just like before.

"I'll always love coming here," she commented wistfully.

"Yeah, you're right, this place has been a lot of fun," Jenny smiled.

"Sure..." Angela put in, laughing, "up until the time you left that is. Since then, it just hasn't been the same anymore. Although, now that you're a successful writer...!"

"Yes..." Jenny teased. "And now that you have decided to come back to this little hick town and reclaim your friends...!"

"I know I should have come back long before now, but..." She broke off at the thought of what had happened to her, while fighting back the tears.

"Cory," Angela reached out to put a caring arm around her, "it wasn't your fault. He had no right to take something from you that wasn't his to take."

"I keep telling myself that, but those dreams just keep

coming back!" she exclaimed grimly, while getting up to walk over to the slide.

"Well, I've got an idea," Jenny announced. "Let's go back into town. There are a few new shops that you haven't seen yet, since you've been…" Stopping, she saw a look come over Cory's face.

"Cory…?" Angela asked, while seeing the same look, when she too looked up, hearing the familiar sound of Max's truck, as it began to pull out of his mother's driveway.

"Oh, my God…!" they all cried, seeing it heading their way.

Grabbing onto Cory, as if they really had too, everyone ran for the shelter to hide.

"Great!" they all cracked up laughing, while peaking over the side wall to see if he went on by.

"I wonder where he's going now," Jenny wondered.

"I don't know, but…" Cory broke off, looking back at her friends.

"Cory…?" Angela laughed, seeing the look of mischief on her friends' face.

"Oh, no, are you thinking what I think you're thinking?" Jenny asked, while getting up.

"Well…!"

"Well, let's go then," Angela suggested, while they all headed back to Cory's to get Angela's mid-sized red sports car.

Once again, arriving at an intersection, they saw Rose's light blue sedan drive through.

"Wasn't that your mom and Mary?" Jenny asked.

"Sure was!"

"Good, let's just see where they're going," Angela suggested, while turning to follow behind at a safe distance so as not to be noticed.

After a few minutes, they saw Rose turning into the same restaurant.

"Well, I'll be, they're going back to Tony's for lunch!" Cory commented, as a warm smile came to her, when thinking about what happened the other night with Max.

"Yep, and there's Max's truck, as well," Angela laughed, when seeing it pull up to the front door.

"I wonder what's going on now," Jenny commented, while Cory went on to study the hardened expression on Max's face, just as he got out to go inside.

"They're probably still going over the details on the cabin. What else could it be?" Angela asked.

"Yeah, you're probably right," Jenny agreed, looking to see Cory's expression. "Cory," she asked, "what are you thinking?"

"Oh, nothing!" she fibbed, just as Angela pulled away so they wouldn't be seen sitting across from the parking lot.

"All right, any idea on what we should do now?" Angela asked, while driving aimlessly.

Sitting quietly in the front seat, since leaving the restaurant, Cory had been thinking of her father and what all the doctor had said before he passed away. *"I'm sorry, Mrs. Hall,"* he whispered, seeing the look on her daughter's face, *"we simply did everything humanly possible to save him. It's just a matter of time now."*

"Time..." she repeated.

"Cory?" Angela looked over at her.

"I was just thinking about daddy. Mom said he was out working in the field that day."

"Do you want to go out and see it?" she asked sympathetically, when Jenny spoke up.

"I'll just bet the barn is still standing! What do you say, we go check it out?"

"Cory, it's up to you."

"Yeah, sure, let's do it."

Remembering Cory's little black diary, Angela smiled, "If

I recall there is something still hidden up there, that's if you didn't take it with you, did you?"

"No. Although, I had almost forgotten about it."

"Well then, let's go!"

Heading out south of town, it didn't take them all but ten minutes to get to where they were going. When pulling off the road adjacent to the side of the old weather-beaten barn, Angela shut off the car and got out.

"Why did we park here?" Jenny complained, while working her way through the tall thistles that had grown up all around the place, making it look as though the place had been half forgotten by man.

"Because, silly," Angela spoke up, "what if someone sees us, and calls Rose?"

"Or worse, Max?" Cory added.

Giggling, the three girls headed for the side door and made their way into the open area where the old Ford tractor sat collecting dust.

"Wow, there it is…" Cory cried, running her hand over the seat where her father used to sit for hours working out in the field.

"Those were the days," Angela smiled. "Just think of all those rides your dad used to give us, while plowing the field."

"Yes," Cory turned to fight back more tears, when there in front of her, she saw it, the old wooden ladder that led up into the hayloft. "Hey, girls!" she called out, taking a firm hold on the fourth step.

Having gone on ahead of them, she waited at the top for a moment to get her bearings.

"What is it?" Angela asked, arriving next to her.

"Nothing," she returned, "I just can't see much. It's too dark up here!"

"Isn't there a window up ahead there someplace?" she pointed, when Jenny had finally brought up the rear.

"Yes," she replied, going slowly so as not to fall over anything in her path.

Finding what she was looking for, with the help of her friends, she tried as hard as she could to slide the wooden bar over to one side so that she could open the large double doors that were keeping out the light.

"Boy, this is heavier than I remembered it to be!"

"Can you get it?" Angela asked, while trying to give her a hand.

"Ye...ah, here it goes now!"

And so it did. While stepping over to one side after removing the bar that had held the doors closed, both Cory and Angela took hold of a stud and began pushing the double doors open, while allowing in some more light to see by.

"Wow that was really heavy!" Angela exclaimed, turning back to her friends.

"What now?" Jenny asked, while fanning away some cobwebs from overhead.

"Well," Cory thought, looking around, "somewhere around here I remember an old loose board that I had put my old black book under."

Joining in the hunt, all three of the girls went looking, kicking, and had even gotten down on their knees to look for the mysterious board that would surely move, showing them where Cory's little black diary had been hiding.

"Here..." Cory cried out happily, "I found it!"

Carefully lifted it out with her fingernails, breaking only one, she finally got the board up to move it off to one side.

"Is that it?" Jenny asked excitedly, while going to sit next to her friends as Cory went to take out a small gold key to open it.

"Yes," she returned, seeing her old familiar handwriting, as she went to read one of the first passages she had written in it when she was only eight years old:

July 17th 1985

It's Saturday and Max just got the news he had been waiting for.

"News…?" Jenny asked puzzledly.

"His acceptance to Minnesota State," she replied, while reading the next few pages quietly.

Seeing a smile coming over her face, Angela looked over her friends' shoulder, while Jenny sat squirming around impatiently.

"What?" she asked.

"The following day, when Max was just about to leave, we were all still up at the cabin celebrating his acceptance to M S U, when I threw an egg at him, hitting his car by mistake."

"What did he do?" Jenny asked, while laughing at the whole thing.

"He turned and acted as though he were going to come after me."

"But he didn't though, right?" Angela put in.

"No, that didn't come until later, when he had thrown a worm at me down at daddy's old fishing hole. And boy was I ever so mad at him."

"That had to have been awful. What did you do then?"

"I ran off into the woods crying!"

"God…" Angela shook her head recalling that day.

"What?" Jenny asked.

"Daddy had gotten worried when I didn't return after an hour had gone by. By then a storm was moving in and…" Suddenly, she stopped when everyone stood, hearing a truck pulling up out front.

Knowing the familiar sound of its motor, she cried quietly, "Oh, my God…"

"What?" Angela asked, while seeing her face go white.

"It's Max…!" she cried. "We've got to get out of here, before he sees us!"

Taking the little black book with her, Cory hurried to

replace the board, before rushing off to climb back down the ladder.

Reaching the bottom, all three girls froze, hearing the lock on the front door being turned.

"We're too late!" Jenny cried out quietly.

"No…!" Cory cried, while looking frantically for a way out of their dilemma. "Here!" she announced, grabbing each of her friends' arms to lead the way just as the oversized door began to slide open to reveal Max's tall, handsome frame standing in its opening.

No sooner had they gotten clear of the large opened area, he walked in, staring at the old tractor that had taken his leg, and ended the life of one of the best men around.

"Damn you," he swore, growling at the heap of metal sitting in the middle of the barn, looking back at him.

"What was that about?" Jenny asked quietly.

Looking puzzled, as well, Cory tried hard to listen in on the rest of Max's self involved conversation, as he walked around, glaring at the old Ford tractor.

Picking up bits and pieces of his conversation, she sat back shaking her head, "I can't make any of it out!" she complained puzzledly.

"Well, then, we had better be getting ourselves out of here while the getting is good!" Angela suggested, while looking over the four foot wall, which they were hiding behind.

Just then, as the three girls got ready to make their break, there came a noise from the upper level. Recognizing its sound, Cory cringed.

"What is it?" they asked, while hearing Max's footsteps heading their way.

Sitting frozen once again, they watched as he went up the rungs to the upper floor.

Looking to Cory, Angela recalled the large double doors that they had opened a short while ago. "Oh, no!" she cried quietly.

"We have got to get out of here," she cried, looking over to the side door they had used to come in. "Come on!" she whispered, taking the lead.

Meanwhile, up in the hayloft, Max saw the open doors. Going over to check on them, he tripped on the loose board Cory had replaced, before going back down to the lower level. "What the hell?" he yelled, stopping the girls dead in their tracks.

Thinking he had caught them, they turned slowly expecting to see him standing there. However, coming from upstairs, they heard his deep voice going on, as he leaned down to pick up the loose board.

"What the hell is this?" he yelled again, holding the board in his hand.

Seeing the hole just beneath it, he bent down on his left knee to check it out.

"Cory?" Angela asked.

"It's the hiding place where I had the diary kept!"

"Well let's talk about it later, shall we?" Jenny cried, pulling at Cory's arm.

"You're right!" Cory agreed, clearing the short distance to the side door, while heading for Angela's car.

Thinking they had made their getaway, they were unaware that Max had climbed up to stand in the open doorway to look out over the field below.

Seeing the car pulling away, he became acutely aware of the make and model, as he tried to catch the license plate, as well. Again he growled, taking out his cell phone to call his old partner to report the trespasser.

Meanwhile, reaching the highway back to town, Jenny exhaled a heavy sigh of relief, "Boy that was close!"

"Too close," Cory cried, running a shaky hand through her hair. "Way too close."

"Do you think he saw us?" Angela asked.

"No, how could he?" she returned. "He was too busy

looking over the hole I had kept this book in," she pointed, while looking down at the book in her hand.

"Yes, and it's a good thing we went back to get it," Jenny added.

Meanwhile, back at the barn, Max was getting off the phone, when he looked back out at where he had last seen the car, as it pulled out onto the country road. "I'll find out who you are," he growled, before closing the doors. "And when I do…"

Getting back down, he stopped at where the loose board was to replace it, while wondering what was there before it had come loose, when he noted how there was no dust where there should have been. Thinking to himself, Max wondered if at some time Cory had been back to visit the old barn.

Now, looking down at the hole, he saw something odd staring back up at him. As there in the darkness of the hole was some dust, but not over the whole area as there should have been. While in the center was a shape. "What…" he asked, while looking closer to the centralized area, *'A book…?'* he thought quietly, while running his hand over the interior. Grinning coyly to himself now, he shook his head. "Well, well, well, you little brat, what did you have here?" he laughed. "And just when did you come back to take it out?"

Putting the board back in its place, he got up to go downstairs. Getting there, he stopped to see the side door open.

"Now what?" he growled, going over to check it out. Getting closer to it, his cell phone began to ring. "Damn…" he swore, turning away from a half hidden set of footprints leading out of the barn to answer his phone.

"Max?" his mother called out, not getting an answer right away.

Holding onto the phone after having opened its line to the caller, his thoughts flew back to Cory, as he stood staring at the old tractor again.

"Max…?" she called out again.

"Yeah, what?" he answered gruffly on his end.

"I was just wondering if you'd left to go on back to the cabin yet."

"No, I had some loose ends to tie up first."

"Oh?"

"Mom," he turned his attention away from the old tractor, "have you heard from Cory lately?"

"Where did that come from?" she asked surprisingly.

Looking back at the tractor, he shook his head sadly at the last thought that had crossed his mind. "It's nothing. What did you want?"

"I was just wondering if you were going to be coming back here tonight, that's all."

"Yeah, if that's all right with you?"

"Sure!"

"Yeah, well, if you don't mind I need to get out of here for awhile."

"Where are you?" Hearing his hesitation, she shook her head sadly, "You're at the old barn, aren't you?"

"Yes, but not for long."

"Okay, I'll see you back here later?"

"Yeah," he returned, "just as soon as Mike runs a make on a car that was here earlier."

"Oh, is something wrong out there? Should I get in touch with Rose?" she asked, while not giving any thought to Cory and her friends out running around.

"No, Mom, leave Rose out of this. I'll take care of the trespasser myself."

"Okay, dear," she went to hang up.

Forgetting what he was about to do before he was interrupted, Max headed back out to his truck, locking up the barn behind him.

Later that night, Cory had ventured back over to the park alone to think, while feeling the air blowing softly through the trees.

Unaware that she wasn't alone, Max, at the same time was sitting on the edge of the picnic shelters' wall, deep in his own thoughts.

"Why did all of this have to happen, Lord?" he cried. "First my marriage, then Bob, my leg... and now, Cory...! How the hell am I supposed to know what she even looks like now?" he growled, propping his right foot up on the ledge, while leaning back against the center post.

Meanwhile, at the other side of the park, crossing over to the playground, Cory was in her own deep thoughts, while looking up toward the heavens. "Daddy..." she cried out softly, "I saw him! I saw Max, and he looked so... sad! But then again, last night when he touched my cheek, I felt as though I would melt. Oh... Daddy, I love him so much. I don't think I could have ever stopped," she continued, while unaware that her soft sweet voice had reached out to the one man she loved across the way.

Sitting quietly in the shelter, Max bolted upright, when hearing the sound he had heard before. "That voice," he cried, looking around the darkened park from where he was sitting, "it sounded so much like..." He stopped for a moment, thinking back to the hospital. *You're going to be all right,* she had smiled. Recalling the whole episode in his head, he continued to strain his eyes over the area, hoping to pick up where it had come from. "Damn..." he swore, not able to see very much, because of some fog rolling in. As he continued looking, his thoughts played back to that smile of hers, and those eyes. But then it hit him, when he stopped. "That's it!" he cried, getting to his feet. "It's that voice of hers!"

Having no sooner made it to the opening of the shelter, he saw her. While crossing back over to the other side of the street, she was just about to walk out from under the street lamp, when he caught a glimpse of her. "Cory…?" he called out, slightly audible enough for anyone to hear, let alone, Cory, as she had then disappeared into the night. "No… how could it be…? I would have known she was coming home," he questioned, when going after the woman who had just vanished before his own eyes.

Just as he reached the street, his old friend, and former partner on the police force cut him off. "Hey… where you off to in such a hurry?" the tall, dark haired man called out, while getting out of his truck to come around to talk to Max.

"Mike, did you see her?" he asked, peering through the darkness, as well as the growing fog along the small town street.

"See who?" he asked, while looking in the same direction Max was.

"That lady!"

Barely catching a glimpse of what was left to see of her, Mike shook his head. "No, besides, she's too far away, and it's just too dark and foggy to make her out. Why?"

Since she hadn't taken the direct way home, Max had no idea this lady was his little brat.

"Max, are you all right?" he asked worriedly.

"Yeah, she just looks familiar, is all," he turned back, shaking his head miserably.

"Cory, you mean?" he smiled, having just been told by Max's mother of their plans to get these two together.

"Yes, but I have no idea what she even looks like now!"

"Have you been over to her mother's to ask yet?"

"No, not since…"

"Max, the guy had a bad heart. You couldn't have saved him!"

"No, but if I hadn't gone out to the field that day he would still be here."

"Or he would have gone out there alone. And Max, you would have still been blaming yourself for his death."

"Well…" He stopped to adjust his left leg, while feeling the effects the night dampness was causing it.

"Is it giving you trouble again?" he asked, while offering a hand.

"Yeah, it's this damnable weather. But enough of that, what brings you out at this time? Does it have to do with the car I saw out at the barn earlier?"

"Yes, and no. The numbers you gave me were not enough to get a clear ID on who it belonged to. Aside from that, I was just over at your mom's place looking for you."

"Oh?"

"Yeah," Mike smiled. "The transfer came in."

"State Police Department?"

"Yep, and I didn't lose my rank, either."

"Well, Captain Jones," Max teased.

"Yeah, well, you would have gotten your Captain's bars even sooner if only…"

"If only I hadn't lost my leg?"

"Darn it, Max…" Mike groaned, feeling really bad for his friend.

"Hey, enough about that, how about giving me a ride back to mom's. I need to get my truck and go back out to the cabin. I forgot I still have some work to do, before that lady writer gets there tomorrow."

"Who is this lady writer anyway?" he asked, while hiding his amusement.

"Are you ready for this?" he laughed. "Her name is Cory Spencer."

"Cory? Your Cory?"

"No, this lady is much bigger."

"But I had thought that Cory was…"

"Yeah, she writes, but from what mom tells me, this lady is really going somewhere. Her book is about to become a movie of sorts."

"And she wants the cabin for what?"

"Peace and quiet, mom says. But I can't help but feel that there is more to it than that."

"Oh…?"

"Yeah."

Getting into Mike's truck, Max just shook his head.

Chapter Four

The next day, Cory and the others were rushing around getting things ready.

"Now, you do have plenty of food, don't you?" Rose asked, while Cory and her friends were packing up the van.

"Yes… I think so!" she replied slowly, while turning to look up at her mother on the front porch.

"Remember, Roger's Food Market is just down the road from the cabin."

"I remember! Does he still run it?"

"Yes, and he knows you're coming."

"All right. And now, how will I find the caretaker?" she asked, knowing full well who he really is.

"Oh, he'll be meeting you around noon at the cabin."

"Well then, we had better get going!" she announced, while going up to give her mother a hug.

"I'll call you as soon as we get finished with the bake sale," she added, while trying to hide her sadness.

"Don't forget to bring us some of your goodies from the sales!" they all laughed, while calling out their goodbyes.

As they were about to pull away, Mary walked up to wave goodbye.

"She's going to be fine, Rose. The stay at the cabin will be just what she needs after what happened to her in New York."

"He should have gotten life imprisonment after what he did to my baby girl."

"You're right about that! When is he due to get out?"

"Sooner than we thought," she announced, when turning to Mary, looking worried.

Seeing this, Mary became alarmed. "When?"

"In two to three weeks."

"What?"

"You heard me!" she exclaimed, going back in to refill her glass.

"Oh, my, that doesn't give us much time!"

"I have a feeling that once Max realizes this is Cory, he will protect her from Ted. He will do it for Bob's sake," she replied, after getting her drink and going back to the table to work on the bake sale.

"He sure will. Come to think of it, he had always watched over her, when she was a little girl," Mary recalled fondly, while mixing the cookie dough.

"You're right, he did!" Feeling a lot better about things, Rose smiled, visualizing their reunion. "I have a feeling those two are going to get along quite... well, once they get reacquainted with each other," she said, looking to her friend with a warm smile.

"Yes, quite!" Mary chuckled.

Meanwhile, after being on the road for an hour, Jenny spoke up, seeing Roger's store coming up on the right. "How about stopping in here to get a few more things?"

"Good idea! Besides, I had just passed the road that would have taken us to the cabin."

"Oh…?"

"Yeah," Cory replied, smiling, while thinking about the look that would surely be on Roger's face once he sees his little lady again. "I just can't wait to see him after all these years."

Pulling into the small gravel parking lot in front of the store, they saw a black pickup pull out from around the side of the building, catching them off guard.

"Hey, isn't that Max about ready to pull out?" Angela asked, while getting out of her car to join the others.

"Yes, it is!" Cory exclaimed, while watching as he turned onto the highway, spinning his tires.

"I wonder what he was doing here," Jenny commented curiously.

"I don't know," Cory returned, hearing a familiar voice, coming out to greet her.

"Little Cory Hall, is that you...?" an older man in his fifties, with salt and pepper colored hair and blue eyes asked, while walking up to give her a big hug. "How are you?"

"I'm fine! How have you been?" she cried out with a bright smile on her face.

"Doing just great! Your mother said you were coming up for the summer!"

"Yes, and it's been a long time too!"

"I know, ever since your father last brought you up to go fishing. Do you still remember the spot?"

"I think so!" Cory thought fondly back to that summer, six years ago.

"Well now," he went on, changing the subject, "these must be the friends that are going to be staying with you for awhile."

"Yes," she turned to introduce them. "Angela, Jenny, this is Roger, our favorite grocer."

"Excuse me young lady," he laughed, "your only grocer."

At that, they all laughed while going inside.

"Now then, what can I get for you ladies?"

"Well now, I'm not sure! Do you know if the cabin has been stocked up yet?"

"Well, pretty much," he fudged a little.

"Roger, I know that Max is the caretaker, and that was him pulling out of here when we arrived, wasn't it?"

"Oh, now, was it? I didn't see anyone!" he lied, turning away.

"Roger… that may have worked when I was little, but not anymore. I know that mom and Mary are up to something. Are you a part of it too?"

"Those two would hang me out to dry if I told you anything."

"Oh, but you haven't. I'm telling you!"

"And…" Angela came forward to admit her part in this as well.

"Angela… you too…?" she cried.

"Well, yeah…"

"And yes," he put in, "that was Max leaving here. He has been working on stocking up the cabin for you, but all he knows is that he is doing it for a famous writer, who needs it for the peace and quiet. He has no idea that writer is you."

"Good, let's keep it that way," she suggested with a sly grin. "Now, what will we need for the cabin that Max hasn't already picked up?"

"Well he already has the firewood stocked up for the cool nights, and it does get pretty chilly up here at this time of the year."

"What else?"

"Food, toiletries, blankets, and kitchen supplies!"

"How about matches?" she asked, while walking around the store.

"No, I can't say that he has those!"

"I had better get some then. Oh, and Roger, one little favor."

"Sure, what is it?"

"Don't tell anyone that I'm here. It'll be our secret."

"You got it, little lady."

"Thanks."

"Hey! You might want to know that there's going to be a dance at the Corral Bowl tonight."

"How do we find it?" she asked, while placing their things on the counter.

"It's just about five miles down the highway. You can't miss it. It'll be on the right."

"Sounds like fun!" she began. "Will..."

"Yes, Max will be there, if I have to drag him all the way kicking and screaming," he laughed.

"All right, we'll see you there," she replied, while heading out to the van with her friends.

"Wow, this is going to be a lot of fun!" Jenny laughed.

"Yes, it is!" she smiled, just as the road came up on their left, leading them to the cabin.

Soon after, the cabin came into view.

"Well, here we are!" Cory sounded nervous as they pulled into the drive, seeing Max's truck parked at the side of the building.

"Yep, and it's just a little past noon, too!" Jenny added.

"It sure is."

"What are we going to do now?"

"Before or after I faint from fright?" she laughed nervously, while pulling out her sunglasses to put on.

"Cory," Angela called out softly, walking up to the van, "what's the plan?"

"I'm Cory Spencer, the novelist," she replied, after getting out to check herself in the side mirror. "Well, how do I look?" she asked, while turning back to her friends.

"You look fine!" Angela smiled.

"Yes, and those sunglasses really do the job," Jenny snickered quietly. "Max shouldn't be able to see your eyes now with those on!"

"You don't think they're too much, do you?"

"No, but they are sure to hide just how nervous you really are," Angela concluded, before taking her friends' arms to head up toward the front porch.

Upon getting there, the front door opened and Max walked out. "Oh, I see you made it all right. The lease is out in my truck. I'll just go and get it for you, Ms. Uh…?" he asked, while not really looking at her, as he headed out to his truck.

"Spencer," Jenny offered. "And we're her friends. I'm Jenny and this is Angela."

"Will the two of you be staying with her?" he asked, turning to Jenny.

"No," Angela spoke up, "I have a shop in town that I have to get back to Monday. However, we were just invited out to the Corral Bowl for a dance tonight."

"Invited?" He looked at Angela puzzledly.

"Roger told us about the dance," Cory spoke up then, while still trying to remain calm. "I told him we would be there, provided that's all right with you," she then grinned quietly.

"Yeah, why would I care?" he grumbled, looking at her now, while studying her features a little more closely now, when it hit him. "Wait a minute," he laughed, remembering her voice from the other night, "didn't we talk a few nights ago near the park in Cedars?"

"You remember that?" she asked, while attempting to look away.

"Well, sure…! I almost ran you over!" he went on laughing, while going on over to get the lease out of his truck.

"He what…?" Angela asked, taking Cory's arm while Max was off doing that.

"I'll explain later," she whispered, seeing that he was about to return.

"Here you go," he spoke up, handing her the papers. "Read these and sign the back page, if it meets with your approval."

Upon handing the lease to her, their hands touched, and for a brief moment it was like an electrical shock between the two.

"Sorry," he spoke up, feeling the warmth of her hand next to his.

Smiling, she went on reading the lease, while he couldn't help but watch her even closer now. And yet, even with the use of her sunglasses, she could still feel his growing curiosity to know who she really was.

"This is going to sound strange," he went to ask, "but are you sure we don't know each other?"

"Well, I uh..." she looked to her friends, feeling trapped just then.

"Perhaps," Jenny jumped in, seeing what this was doing to her, "it'll come to you when you least expect it."

"Yeah, maybe," he commented, while staring at her for a moment longer, while she went over to take a seat on the front porch to read the rest of the lease. *'Yeah, just maybe,'* he continued thinking. Then seeing her reach into her purse to take out a pen, he cleared his throat. "Here, use mine," he offered, handing her a pen.

"Thanks, Max," Cory caught herself a little too late, when she looked up, only to see his expression change.

"How did you know my name?" he asked, looking at her even more suspiciously now.

"I heard it the other night, remember?" she responded quickly, while handing back the lease and his pen, once she had signed it.

"Oh, yeah, I had almost forgotten. Well, I've got to get going. If you need anything else, here's my cell phone number."

"All right!" she smiled, taking his number, before going over to help unpack the van.

Turning to see what she had brought with her, he shook

his head, frowning. "Do you need any help with that?" he called, going to his truck.

"Not unless you want to hang some curtains," Jenny suggested, when pulling them out of the van.

"Jenny…" Angela yelled. "We don't need any help!"

"Give me those," he laughed, walking up to take them. "I don't want you to tear the place up before I get it back."

Watching him walk back to the cabin, Angela took Cory by the arm once again, "You did sign the lease in your pen name, didn't you?"

"Yes," she replied, before taking in a load of their things.

"Thank God," she returned, walking into the living room behind her.

Looking around, remembering the old place, she immediately turned to her friends. "Why don't the two of you take the bedroom for now, I'll just take the sofa for the weekend."

"Are you sure you want to do that?" Jenny asked, while coming back into the living room.

"Yes."

Hearing her offer to give up the only bedroom, he turned to tell Cory how the sofa folded out into a bed.

"Oh…?" she said, knowingly.

"Yeah," he finished, getting down to pick up his things, "you'll be comfortable there."

"Thanks!" she smiled warmly.

Ignoring the feeling her smile had caused, he just grinned, shaking his head. "Well, I'm sure you can handle the rest of your things from here. I'll just be going now," he turned, heading out to his truck.

"Thanks, again!" she called out, walking over to the front window to watch him.

Reaching his truck, he turned back to see Cory standing at the window, looking out. Seeing her, the look on his face turned to one of disbelief. *'No... that can't be,'* he thought, as she turned to walk away.

Seeing Max's face, Angela cried quietly, taking Cory's arm.

"What...?" she asked.

"Max...!"

"What about him?"

"He nearly recognized you," she whispered, while watching him get back into his truck to leave.

Looking back up at the cabin, he was still somewhat puzzled over what he had just seen. "Damn it, Max..." he scolded himself, while going on to start his truck, "get a hold of yourself, man, that isn't your Cory!"

Meanwhile, back inside, Cory was asking, "What did you see?"

"One very confused guy," Angela laughed, while nodding her head toward his truck, as he backed down the driveway.

As he did, he caught a glimpse of Angela's red sports car sitting in close to the van. With the license plate being somewhat hidden by the back door, it made it virtually impossible for him to see the numbers without having to get out.

"Could that be...?" he asked, while stopping his truck at the end of the driveway.

First, looking back up at the cabin, he thought twice, before making a move to check the license plate. By that time, one of Cory's friends had come to the door.

"No, this isn't the time," he commented to himself, knowing it would look too suspicious. "Besides, how could that be the same car? And if so, why would they..." he stopped, suddenly thinking back to the loose board and the hole it covered. Shaking off the thought, which had just crossed his mind, Max continued to shake his head, "No, our Cory is still in New York. Besides, Rose would have told me otherwise," he concluded.

Though this lady was pretty, like their Cory would probably be, he didn't think she would have done quite so well just yet.

Meanwhile, knowing he was starting to draw attention to himself, he went to pull on out of the driveway.

"Cory…!" Jenny called out nervously from the doorway.

"Yes?" she asked, while walking over to join her along with Angela.

"Max was just sitting out there looking at the cabin again."

"Oh…?"

"Do you think he has you figured out?" Angela asked.

"No," she returned.

"How's that?"

"I know him," she smiled. "He would have come barreling back in here if he had."

"Oh, no…!" Jenny cried.

"What…?" both Cory and Angela looked to each other.

"The car!" Cory suddenly remembered. "We used it to go out to the barn that day."

"What if he'd have seen us out there after all, when we left?" Jenny went on worriedly.

"Great!" Cory groaned. "If he did, my plans are useless now."

"Maybe not," Angela thought, turning back away from the door.

"Well…?" both Cory and Jenny waited patiently.

"Well, nothing!" she returned, smiling. "I just happen to know that there are two other cars just like it back in town! No," she shook her head, "he would have surely said something if he would have seen us out there at the barn that day."

"Yes," Cory agreed. "And one thing is for sure…"

"What's that?" her friends asked.

"He isn't stupid."

"Let's just hope you're right," they all agreed, when turning back to get their minds off what had just happened outside.

Chapter Five

After getting her things unpacked, Angela came walking out of the bedroom. "What are we going to wear tonight?"

"I've got my emerald green tunic and black belt!" Jenny announced, holding them up.

"Nice! And I brought my blue outfit," Angela put in, while going into the kitchen to put the rest of the groceries away. "What about you, Cory, what are you going to wear?" she asked from the kitchen doorway.

"I bet it'll be a sexy number!" Jenny laughed, while standing in the bedroom doorway, gleaming from ear to ear.

"Well, it will get his attention, at least," Cory turned to show them a long black, sleek dress, with long sleeves and a turtle neckline, that would no doubt accent her shape nicely.

"Hey, girl, that will do it all right. Yes indeed!" Angela whistled.

"Oh, yeah," Jenny agreed, "that will surely do it. But not to throw a damper on this party, what time is it getting to be?"

"Five thirty!" Cory announced. "Shouldn't we be getting ready?"

"No kidding!"

Once they were finished, they headed out for the Corral Bowl in Angela's car, while passing by Roger's store on the way.

Seeing a small light on in the front window by the door, indicating the store was closed, Angela commented, while driving by "Well, he's gone already!"

"Do you think he got Max to go?" Jenny asked.

"I hope so!" Cory replied hopefully.

Soon the time passed, and so did the miles, when they arrived at the Corral Bowl.

Looking around for Max's black pickup, Jenny asked, "Do you see it?"

"No, not yet," Cory returned, while feeling her heart begin to sink at the possibility he wasn't there at all, while Angela found a place to park.

Once they had, the three got out and headed for the front door.

"You don't think we're overdressed for this, do you?" Jenny asked, while looking around nervously.

"No, I don't think so. Look over there at those couples, and over there," Angela pointed.

"Good, I wasn't too sure what people wear to things like this."

"Me neither," Cory agreed.

"Well, you sure look pretty good to me!" came the sound of a familiar voice.

"Roger...!" Cory cried happily, while seeing his familiar face in the crowd. "Oh, please tell me, did he come with you?" she asked quietly.

"Yes. He's in the pool room now about to get a game started with a friend of his."

"Oh...?" she replied, looking in that direction.

"Go on in there and show him how it's done."

"Roger...!"

"Don't tell me you've forgotten how to play...!"

"Well... it has been awhile!" Cory tried to explain, as he took her by the hand and led the way.

"Come on, girls, who else wants to get in on this?" he asked. "It'll be awhile before the band starts up."

"Come on, Cory," Angela insisted, while pulling on her other hand, "it'll be fun!"

"Yeah, fun," she complained. "All right," she finally agreed, going into the poolroom with the others. Once inside, she saw Max across the way with a beer in one hand and a pool cue in the other. She could tell he wasn't in a very good mood.

"Hey, Roger, what do you have there?" a tall husky built man with light brown hair yelled out, while coming up to put an arm around Cory's waist, when Max looked up to see them standing there.

Noticing right away the look of sheer panic on her face, he put his beer down to walk over and greet them.

"Hey, Tony, what are you doing moving in on my woman?" he growled playfully, while going up to nudge his friend aside in order to place his own arm around her shoulder, hoping to calm her down some.

"Hey, sorry about that, Max," the man said, walking away.

After had Tony left, Max turned to Cory, "Are you all right?" he asked, feeling how cold her hands were to the touch.

"Y...yes. Thanks! I just don't like it when strangers put their arm around me like he did, is all."

"Sorry that had to happen," he offered when turning to his friend, "Gosh darn it, Roger, just why were you bringing them in here, anyway?"

"To play some pool!" he exclaimed, while turning to Cory. "I'm sorry, little lady!" His blue eyes paled, knowing what had happened to her.

"No, I'm all right, really."

With a reassuring smile, Roger took the others over to a table to start a game.

"Are you sure you're all right?" Max turned to study her expression.

"Yes. Thanks."

Interrupting the two, Roger called out, "Come on, you two! Let's play a game before the band gets started!"

"Well, are you game, lady writer?" he teased, lending her his arm.

"Sure!" she smiled up at him.

Coming over to join them, Roger turned, giving Cory a wink, "Max," he spoke up, looking as though he were up to something, "what do you say after one warm up game, this little lady here will beat you at the next two?"

"Roger...!" Cory cried out quietly in protest.

"You can do it," he smiled, while going over to get her a cue stick from the rack.

"Oh, and what's the bet?" Max laughed.

"Well...?" Roger turned, looking to Cory with a brilliant smile on his face.

"Roger...!" Knowing how he wasn't going to let it go, she turned back to Max with a warm smile of her own. "Okay," she conceded," if you lose, you owe me a dance. And if I lose..."

"You owe me dinner," he finished with a grin, while they shook on it.

"Fine!" she grinned as well, when seeing his gloating expression.

"Shall we get started then?" he asked, while gesturing a hand toward the table.

Feeling confident she couldn't play pool very well, with being a writer, Max stood back to let her take the first shot.

Taking the cue stick from Roger, Cory looked up at him for some sign of reassurance. "Roger..." she whispered nervously.

"You can do it. Just remember everything I taught you," he returned with a quiet nod of his graying head.

"Well...!" Max continued to grin, while standing back to watch.

"Ah..." she groaned quietly, while moving right in to take her shot. *'Don't mess this up, girl,'* she cried, feeling her hands and knees start to quiver.

In the meantime, leaning over the table while holding her cue stick at the ready, Max couldn't help but look her over. Starting with her long brown hair, as it fell softly over her back, to those luscious swells of hers, as she went on to take her first shot. With that, she sent two solids into each of the far corner pockets, scattering the rest in various directions.

"Way to go!" her friends cheered her on, as she moved right along to take another.

Meanwhile, standing just off to one side of Max, Roger couldn't help but see where his attention was going, and with a hearty grin, he cleared his throat, "Max...! Earth to Max...!" he laughed, interrupting Max's train of thought.

"W...what...?" he asked with a hint of embarrassment on his face.

"You're staring a hole right through her!" he teased.

"How can I help but not look? She's got a body on her that puts the most beautiful supermodel to shame!" he groaned, when turning back to give Cory one last glance.

'Oh, Max, if you only knew what you were saying, and about whom,' he thought with another laugh, while shaking his head.

Once the first game had ended, the time had arrived for the play off between Max and Cory.

"Can I get you something to drink?" he offered, laying his stick aside.

"Sure, an Amaretto and Cream would be nice!"

"Sure thing," he nodded, picking up his empty beer bottle to head over and get their drinks.

"No, allow me," Roger spoke up, stopping him, before he could refuse. "And while I'm gone, why don't the two of you talk?"

"Sure."

Turning back to set the table up for another game, he shook his head in amazement.

"What?"

"You play like a pro," he commented, grinning.

"Just luck!" she smiled, while watching him go around setting up the rest of the table.

"Luck, huh," he turned back once he was through. "That was some luck. Who taught you how to play?"

"Just an old friend of the family!" she replied sweetly, while going over to take her shot.

Putting the number two and number ten ball in the far right corner pocket, Max continued to shake his head.

Smiling, she ignored his puzzlement, when she moved around to take a shot that he knew couldn't be done, before going on around the table to take another clearer one. However, it went in slowly and with the greatest of ease.

"What...?" he cried. "How did you do that? I couldn't have made that shot, even with all the time I've spent on the table."

"You have to relax!" she explained, seeing how his confused expression only grew more baffled. "All right," she shook her head, smiling, "I've noticed that whenever you take a shot, you tighten up at the last minute."

"No, I don't!"

"Yes, you do," she laughed after fumbling her next shot on purpose.

Standing back to watch him take his, he scratched it badly while feeling her warm smile on him.

"Your turn!" he grinned sheepishly, when the others returned with their drinks.

Handing Max her drink, along with his own, Roger asked how things were going, as she went around to take her shot.

"She's beating the tar out of me," he laughed, when his turn came up.

"Your turn!" Cory announced sweetly.

Shaking his head, he handed Cory her drink, before going up to take his shot. At that time, everyone stood back quietly, while he made his aim more precise. This time, making it in one of the side pockets, along with another, and another, until he eventually missed, leaving the eight ball for her to finish off the game.

"Okay, lady writer, do your magic," he grinned.

Making it with such ease, Cory's friends cheered her on. "Well?"

"Ms. Spencer," he extended out a hand to wish her luck. "As though you even need it," he laughed.

With a warm smile, she returned the gesture, while Roger got the table ready for them this time.

Once done, he turned back to the two, "Well, folks," he gestured.

"Shall we?" she smiled, giving him the first shot.

"Sure." With a grin, he finished off his beer.

As the last game went on, he got a lot more serious about his playing, but still lost, when looking defeated.

"Well, it looks as though you owe me a dance," she informed him with a triumphant grin.

"So it seems," he bowed, before taking her pool cue to place it in the rack along with his. "Ms. Spencer, you realize what you are getting yourself into? I only have one good leg!"

"So," she replied, without a care in the world.

"Fine, don't say that I didn't warn you," he commented, while coming back over to offer her his arm.

"Warning well taken," she returned, with a small bow of her head.

With his own warm smile, Roger led the way out of the poolroom, announcing he had gotten a table earlier, while they were playing. Once they had gotten settled in, he went up to one of the female musicians and handed her a slip of paper.

"What was that all about?" Max asked when he returned.

"You'll see soon enough," he grinned, as the woman began to sing a soft melody. Hearing it, he smiled, "Well, Max, this is your song. Now it's time to ask the lady to dance, or I will."

Grumbling under his breath, Max got up and turned to Cory, who at that time looked pretty nervous. "Miss Spencer," he asked, while holding out his hand to her, "may I have this dance?"

Taking it, she followed him onto the dance floor. "I'm sorry if this makes you feel so uncomfortable," she began. "We don't really have to go through with it, if you don't really want to!"

"It isn't that," he offered, while looking into her beautiful eyes. "It's just that I haven't danced since the accident, and I'm not all that sure I still can!"

"Then let me help you!" she offered, placing her arms around his shoulders, as he followed suit by placing his around her waist to pull her in closer to him.

Meanwhile, feeling her body as it molded perfectly to his, he asked, "Who are you, Ms. Spencer, besides a writer, I mean? Who are you, really?"

"Someone who had fallen in love with an older man, years ago, while swearing to keep my innocence until I marry him."

"Why hasn't he married you yet?"

"He doesn't know I love him!" she exclaimed sadly, while

subconsciously laying her head against his shoulder. *'Oh, Max, I wish I could just tell you, but you would only laugh at me if you knew,'* she thought, while picking up the scent of his cologne, as the song was about to end.

'God why do I feel as if I know her, and yet she feels so familiar to me, as though…' Stopping as the next song began, he asked, "This guy, is he already married? Is that why you can't marry him yet?"

"No, not anymore," she returned. "She left him a year ago."

"Then what's stopping the two of you from going on with your lives?"

"He's still very bitter over her leaving him. Not to mention, he doesn't trust anyone right now."

"So you're going to just sit and wait for him?" he asked, looking down into her saddened eyes, heatedly. "For how long? Until he decides to come around?"

"Max…!" she cried, feeling the heat of his anger, as she looked away with tears flowing down her cheeks.

Realizing he had spoken a little too harshly, he turned her back to face him, while at the same time seeing her tears as he tilted her chin up to look into her eyes. "Oh, man," he swallowed hard, while offering his apologies, "I'm sorry, but you are so darn beautiful. Just how old are you, anyway?"

"Twenty-four," she replied, while unaware his mother had already told him.

Stopping for a moment to stare down at her, he asked again, "How old are you?"

"Twenty-four! Why?"

"My mother told me that a friend of hers' daughter is twenty-four."

"Oh…?" she asked nervously.

"It's just odd that you are the same age as she is."

"When was the last time you saw her?"

"It's been years. I wouldn't know her now if she were

standing right here in front of me. Heck, you could even be her and I wouldn't know it."

"Wouldn't that be funny if I were?" she asked, with a nervous laugh.

"What? Do that again," he ordered, hearing her laugh.

"Do what again?"

"That laugh!"

"Now you're making fun of the way I laugh!" she cried playfully, while backing away.

"Uh oh," Roger groaned, realizing their discussion was beginning to heat up, when he got up to walk over and interrupt them. "Excuse me, you two, but may I borrow this lady for the next dance?" he asked, while taking her hand in his.

Looking frustrated, Max simply shook his head. "Sure, I need to sit this one out anyway," he returned, while studying her for a moment longer. "Ms. Spencer," he glared, taking her arm, "I will find out who you are. And if you are playing some sort of a game with me, you will soon find out that you have picked the wrong man to mess with here."

"Max, take it easy on her," Roger put in, while pulling Cory back away from him. "She has her reasons for keeping her true identity a secret."

"Damn it…" he groaned, letting her go, "I'm sorry, Ms. Spencer, it's just that you remind me so much of someone, and it's really bothering me that I can't think of who," he explained with a great deal of frustration.

"It'll come to you one of these days. I'm sure of that," she replied with a soft touch of her hand to his, as he looked down on them.

"Sure it will. Now, if you will excuse me," he bowed his apologies once again, before returning to their table to drink another beer.

"Thanks, Roger. I wasn't quite ready to tell him just yet."

"Just when are you going to tell him?"

"Soon," she replied, looking over his shoulder at Max, who at that time was talking to Angela.

"You're really in love with him, aren't you?"

"Oh, yes! Ever since I was eight!"

"Eight is an awfully young age to be falling in love, don't you think?"

"Yes, but for some odd reason, I just knew in my heart he was the one."

"Yes, and you know there's not very many women out there who have gone as long as you have without a man taking her innocence."

"One man tried," she said, half under her breath.

"Yes, so your mother told me."

"What...?" She stopped dancing to look up at him in a state of shock.

"It's all right, little lady. It was some time after your father died. Your mother needed someone other than Mary to talk to."

"Yes, you're right, I'm sorry. I don't blame her for talking to you. Oh, Roger, you have known us for so long. Does Max know?"

"No, but he knows you have been through something pretty bad. He just doesn't know what it was, though."

"Good," she replied, just as the music stopped.

"Well, how about if we go and sit the rest of this out for now? This old goat can't handle you young folks anymore."

"Oh, Roger, you're not an old goat! You're just a goat!" she laughed at the corny expression on his face.

"I'll remember you said that," he laughed along with her.

Stopping just before they had gotten back to their table, he turned to her, "That reminds me, I have something back at the store that belongs to your father."

"Oh..." she cried at the mere mention of her father, "what is it?" she asked excitedly.

"It's his old fishing rod and reel," he whispered. "I'll come by tomorrow and drop it off, if you'd like."

"Thanks. Besides, I'd like to see our old spot anyway," she replied, smiling up at him, when they continued walking over to their table.

"Maybe you can get Max to go with you!"

"Go where with her?" Max asked, interrupting them.

"I'll let her tell you," he replied, smiling, as he made his excuses and explained that he had enough excitement for one night.

"I think I'm going to call it a night, too," she replied, while reaching for her purse to leave.

"Are you tired?" Angela asked, while not wanting to go just yet.

"Yes, I am. So if the two of you are ready to go, I'd like to leave now!"

"Oh, but we were just about to play darts with a couple of guys!" Jenny cried, sounding disappointed.

"I'll run you home," Max offered, while setting his half empty bottle down before getting to his feet.

"Thanks, but are you sure you really want to do that?" she asked, when looking at Roger.

"Yeah, I'm sure," he replied, going to put an arm around her shoulder. "Shall we go?" he asked with a warm grin.

Turning back, Roger smiled quietly, "Go with him."

Smiling, she conceded nervously, "All right."

Saying her goodnights, the two walked toward the front door.

"Max…" Roger called out, "drive carefully."

"I will!" he called back, going out to his truck to open Cory's door for her. "If you're tired, you can lay your head on my arm. I'll wake you when we get there."

"Thanks, I am pretty tired," she replied, sliding over to sit next to him, as he got in on his side, while closing the door after him.

The drive back though, was a quiet one, with Cory falling off to sleep almost right away, only to dream about Max and her father. That was when she began calling out to them.

Hearing his name being mentioned, he brought his truck to a slow stop at the side of the road to turn in his seat in order to listen a little more carefully. "What about Max?" he asked.

"Mmmm… he scared me…!" she cried softly as the dream went on.

"How?" he asked, while carefully turning even more in the seat to get a better look at her in the moonlight.

The answer she came back with really astounded him.

✿ *Chapter Six* ✿

"A worm?" he asked, when his expression changed, as he began to laugh. "What about..." Then he stopped and thought for another moment, *'Oh... my... God...!'* Looking down at her, he asked, while smiling at a sudden recollection of something he had done to a little eight-year-old brat, years ago. "Just what did he do with this worm?"

"Mmmm…" she moaned, as she began to wake up.

"Damn...! Not now...!" he swore under his breath, as she settled back into a sound sleep.

At that moment, she began humming a sweet little tune, while still leaning against his warm musk-scented arm.

"Just who are you?" he wondered, while pulling back onto the highway. "And just what are you so afraid of that you would be crying out to your daddy?" Looking out over the area, he thought even harder about why she would feel so familiar to him. "Lord, why is it that I can't quite place her?" he groaned miserably, while shaking his head.

After reaching the cabin, he went up to unlock the front door, and came back to get her. "Let's go, sleeping beauty," he spoke softly, while carrying her into the cabin.

Placing her carefully on the sofa, he removed her shoes

and covered her with a warm blanket from the back of the sofa, figuring her friends will help her later to pull out the sleeper.

Just before standing back up, he took a moment to study her soft features once again. "Oh, lady, why are you doing this to me?" he asked, shaking his head miserably. "Until you came along, my life was so much easier. Now it's..." He stopped just as she began to call out to him in her sleep. "What is it? Talk to me! Tell me who you really are," he whispered back, while kneeling down by her. At that moment, he couldn't help but take in the scent of her perfume, when then the urge to claim her gentle lips began to overpower him. "Why do you have to be so..." The words stopped there when he went on to claim her lips. As he did, the taste of her sweetness grew, as he wanted to press on even further.

Awakening to the touch of his lips to her own, she returned his kiss as it grew even deeper with every passing moment, until he lifted her up into his lean, muscular arms. "Oh, Max..." she repeated over and over again, while he went on to run his hand down the side of her dress where it had ended.

Bringing his hand back up under it, the thought suddenly hit him. *What am I doing? She is still a virgin, you dope!* he grumbled, when pulling away. "I...I'm sorry, I can't do this to you. Whoever this guy is, he's one lucky man to have your kind of love," he groaned deeply, while struggling to stand back up.

"Oh, Max, it's..."

"No, I don't want to know who he is. But I can say this, he's a damn fool for not realizing what he has here," he groaned, sitting down next to her.

Fighting back her tears, she closed her eyes, when he went to run a hand over her cheek, while wanting so much to kiss those lips again, but choosing not to.

"Cory, you mentioned earlier that you had never told him how you felt. Why?"

"Because he would only..."

"Would only what?" He stopped to hear what she had to say, when she finally looked up at him.

"He would only laugh if he knew!"

"What...? Why the heck would he do that?" he asked, while not intending for it to come out quite so harsh, when seeing the frightened look come over her just then. "Lord, I'm sorry. Please, tell me, though, why would he do that?"

"B...b...because..." she began hesitantly.

"Yes...?"

"He's ten years older than me. And... And well I have loved him ever since I was eight years old!" she blurted it out to get it over with.

"What...?" he asked, while looking at her puzzledly. "Sixteen years... that you have carried a torch for this guy? Not to mention, since you were eight! Wasn't that just a little bit young...?"

"Yes...!" she returned embarrassedly, while shoving him out of the way, to get up off the sofa, to go into the kitchen. Turning back, she cried, "I know how this must sound. But I can't explain it. All I know is that I have always loved yo... him," she corrected, "and..."

"Cory..." he began, when coming over to join her in the doorway.

"No, Max, I'm sorry," she cried, holding up a hand to cut him off, when finding it hard to go on. "Please, j...just go...!"

"Cory..."

"No...!"

Knowing he had upset her, he stopped. "Will you be all right here by yourself?" he asked, looking down into her tear-filled eyes.

"Yes, I...I think so." But all she really wanted was for

him to hold her until her friends returned. Instead, she tried putting a smile on her face. "They should be back soon, I...I'm sure of it."

"All right," he replied, brushing back the hair from one side of her face with a gentle touch of his hand. "But before I go," he whispered deeply, while bringing his lips closer to hers, "may I kiss you goodnight?"

Hearing those words was like music to her ears. "Yes, I would r...really like that," she stammered, as he pulled her up into his arms. Doing so, her own arms went around his neck, as their lips met. At which time, as the sparks ignited, it was like nothing they had ever felt before.

"Oh, Max..." she moaned, when feeling him lifting her up even closer in his arms, where her feet were no longer touching the floor.

"God, Cory, please... tell me who you really are!"

"I will, Max. I will. But for now, please be patient with me until then!"

"I don't know if I even have that much patience," he replied, kissing her once again, before hearing a car pulling in.

Letting her down easily, she grabbed onto his arm out of fear.

Seeing the frightened expression on her face, he spoke up quickly, "Hey, it's okay...! It's probably your friends coming back! I'll just go and see who it is!" he offered, just about the time Angela walked in.

"Are you still here?" she asked him teasingly, when not seeing the look on Cory's face at first.

"Yeah," he replied, still holding Cory in his arms.

"As for you," she smiled warmly at her friend, "I thought you would have been asleep by now!"

"No," Max offered in her place, "we were just talking."

"Oh?" she asked, when stopping short of the two of them, to see how pale her friends' face looked, before she went right up to put a friendly arm around her shoulder. "Hey, are you all right?" she asked, while taking her over to the sofa.

"Yes, you just startled me, is all," she explained, while fighting back a shiver when Jenny walked in.

"Hey, there!" she spoke up, just inside the door. But then seeing the look on Cory's face, too, she knew why it was there and walked over to join them. "Hey, it all right now, he isn't here! He's in jail, where he can't hurt you anymore!"

"I know he is, but…" Cory covered her face, when Jenny turned to Max, who was still looking puzzled over what was going on. Getting up to walk over to him, she asked, "What happened here?"

"I don't have a clue, but I sure as hell wish I did," he stated, while wondering what had happened to her that would have her so scared.

Before leaving the two to tend to her, he went over to the sofa and knelt down in front of her. "Cory, I don't know what this is all about, but I will do what you have asked of me. However, if your life is in danger, I won't hesitate to find out what the cause is, and do whatever I can to take care of it."

"Oh, Max… I only wish you could, but…" She broke off at that moment, to turn and cry into Angela's shoulder.

Looking at the two of them, he shook his head, as he got to his feet to walk over to the door. Getting there, he looked back once more. *'What madman could have done this to her?'* he wondered, angrily. *'Whatever happened to her in New York must have been pretty bad. And if it's what I think it might be, Lord help him if he ever tries it again here!'* Saying his goodbyes, he turned angrily and walked on out to his truck to leave.

As for the rest of the weekend, it went by pretty fast, as the time came for Cory's friends to say goodbye.

"I wish we didn't have to go yet!" Jenny cried, while carrying her things out into the living room.

"Me too! But…" Cory began, and then stopped, when she saw Angela carrying her things out as well. Seeing that had only made it that much harder for the two to say goodbye, since their friendship was closer than hers and Jenny's.

"Well, girl," Angela spoke up, while holding back her own tears, when walking up to give Cory a hug, "you know how to get in touch with me if you need me."

"Yeah, I sure do…!" she returned, crying, when no longer able to hold back her own tears.

"Hey…" She pulled back, when hearing her sobs, "I can always call the shop to put off going back in if you think you need me!"

"I wish I could just say yes, but that wouldn't be fair to the two of you. Besides, I have to start getting used to being on my own again sometime!"

"Yes, and it's not as if Ted is out there coming after you!" Jenny tried to sound cheerful, when two sets of eyes turned on her.

"No, but…"Angela began.

"But, nothing," Cory interrupted. "The two of you have a life to live. I'll call you if I feel I need t. I promise. Now go, before I regret having to say goodbye."

Giving their tearful hugs once again, Angela and Jenny went out to place their things in the car, before getting in to pull away.

After seeing them off, Cory was just about to go for a walk to think about her father and all the good times they had had, when she heard her cell phone ringing. Going back inside to answer it, to her relief, it was Roger calling to see if she was all right, knowing that her friends were leaving that day.

"Cory," he asked. "Are you all right?"

"Yeah, sure! I was just out seeing my friends off, is all. What's up?"

"Well, your mother had asked that I keep an eye on you in case you just might be needing something. And well…"

He stopped to take a breath. Not to mention, think of a good reason for calling her so that she wouldn't feel uncomfortable by his comment, just then. "I still have this old rod and reel of your dad's here that I wanted to bring by. In fact, what do you say, we go on down to the old fishing hole, and toss in a couple of lines, and just chat a little?"

"Sure, that would be kinda fun! Besides, I was just thinking about going for a walk anyway."

"Great! I'll be right over."

"Oh, and Roger?"

"Yes, little lady?"

"Max…"

"He is all tied up, doing something with his old buddy. So he won't be around for some time."

"Good. I just need some time to myself right now, is all."

"I kinda thought so."

Getting off the phone, Roger was over in no time, while bringing with him two folding chairs, some extra fishing equipment, and a small cooler loaded with all sorts of goodies, hoping to get in a good catch while there.

Walking out onto the front porch, when he pulled up in his old beat up pickup truck, Cory smiled, "Hey, Roger!"

"Hey there, little lady…" he called back, seeing her in a pair of worn jeans, old tennis shoes, and a t-shirt, with her hair pulled back, while carrying an old bucket out with her to greet him.

Coming to a stop, she suddenly recalled what it was that's been on her mind. *'It was Roger!'* she smiled inwardly. *'He had always reminded me a great deal of the old Quaker Oats man!'*

"Are we ready to get in some good ole fishing?" he asked, while getting out to reach around back to get, not only one rod and reel, but two, with some of the other equipment.

"Yep!" she smiled brightly, while joining up with him to offer her help.

Handing her the poles and net, he sat the cooler down

to go back and get the rest of the gear, before heading around behind the cabin to where there was a path leading down to her father's favorite spot.

"Do you remember the old spot?" he asked, while coming back to join her.

"That's all I could think about while I was gone!" she replied, while picking up one end of the cooler to help carry it down to their spot. "I sure have missed it here, and all the time we spent fishing."

Getting there, after setting the stuff aside, spotting her favorite boulder, not far from the water, she went over to sit on it, while he got everything set up.

"You know, your father would come down here, saying that he was just wanting to get in some fishing, before it got too cold. But I knew the truth of why he came down here."

"Oh…!" she smiled, while coming back over to join him. But instead of taking a seat in one of the chairs he brought with him, she squatted down on her heels to stir the sand around with a stick she had picked up.

Seeing this, he smiled, while recalling the days of seeing her as a child, doing the very same thing. "Some things never change, do they?" he chuckled, shaking his head.

"What?" she cried, smiling, while tossing the stick off to the side, before standing back up to brush off her pants.

"Oh, just that you used to do that very same thing when you and your father came down here to do some fishing. In fact, I would wager, you've even gotten bored a few times, while here."

"No, I didn't!"

"Sweetheart, remember who you're talking to, here. You… were… bored."

"Well, maybe at first, but not after I caught that big one!" she gleamed up at him.

"No, that's for sure. And boy was he ever so proud of his little angel, as he was that day."

Feeling her tears beginning to well up, she turned away quickly to avoid detection, but he knew he had brought up some sad memories of the two of them. Going up, he turned her back to face him, before bringing her into his warm fatherly embrace. "I'm sorry, little lady! I should be a little more sensitive, before I say anything."

"No, i…it's really okay," she sniffled. "I would really love to hear about daddy during the time I was gone. Please tell me more!" she cried, pulling back to wipe away her tears, while going over to take a seat, when he went on.

Getting her set up with her father's favorite fishing pole, having been considered good luck, since she used it to catch that very fish, Roger went on, "Well, as I was saying, when he first loaned you his pole, he never imagined on your first cast, you would catch anything right off, being your first time and all. But then, when the line took a hard pull, we all jumped up in surprise."

"In surprised…?" she cried. "It nearly took my arm off!"

"It sure did," he laughed, taking a seat, before casting in his line, when she did.

"Roger," she began sadly at first, "I miss him so… much!"

"We all do, little lady. We all do," he said, reaching over with a warm hand to pat her on the back. Then all of a sudden, her line took a hard jolt, as it did sixteen years ago.

"Oh, no…" she cried, "not again…!"

Getting to his feet, he burst out laughing, while she stood at his prompting so he could get in behind her to assist in bringing in her catch. "Just like old times, huh?"

"Yes."

With the pond being fed off a natural spring, after bringing in a five pound pike, the two had to quickly clear out the cooler, since the bucket was obviously too small to handle it.

"Boy!" she plopped herself down on her seat to catch her breath.

"Boy, is right! You sure have done it again," he laughed, while taking up his pole again.

"Oh… Roger, thanks for being here for me. I couldn't have gone on alone so soon after the others had left."

"No, I didn't quite think so," he agreed, while toying with his pole. "And while you're here, don't hesitate to call on me whenever you want. I'll be here for you."

"Careful, I may just do that," she laughed, when his line started going off in one direction, and then the other. "Oh, no…" she cried, seeing it going back and forth. "Ro… Roger…!" she continued, "Ro…Roger…!"

Turning, he saw it too. "Oh, boy," he laughed heartily, while getting back up to wrestle his catch, with her help, until bringing it in.

After all the work in doing so, the two opted to give up.

"What do you say, we call it quits," he suggested, while gathering up their things. "This old man is sure getting too old for this."

"Sure, besides, I still have some recouping to do."

"Sure thing, little lady," he smiled, while picking up their catch for the day. "How about I just take these babies on over to my place to get them cleaned up and ready for dinner this evening?"

"Oh, could we maybe do that tomorrow?"

"Sure, whatever you want. No hurry."

Taking his leave, she told him, she'd bring up the rest, when she returned to the cabin after a few more minutes of walking about the area. "I just want to soak it all in, before heading back, if you don't mind."

"No. I'll see you later."

Leaving Cory to walk casually around the pond, Roger headed back to his place, where he found Max's pickup sitting alongside the store. Getting out, he went inside to get help taking the fish down to his cabin, which was located back behind the store, while built on the side of one of Minnesota's beautiful valley walls, with all its breathtaking rivers and streams running through it.

Having gone inside, his hired hand looked up from the counter after their last customer paid for the things and left, while nodding at Roger on their way.

"Good day," he smiled warmly.

Seeing his puzzled expression, the clerk in his early twenties replied, "He's down at the cabin."

"Oh? And when did he get back?"

"Right after you left."

Wondering if he hadn't gone anywhere else, Roger went on to get Todd's help to carry the fish back to his place. "Do you mind?" he asked, heading for the door.

"No, not at all! It's been pretty quiet around here anyway."

Heading on back, he walked in ahead of his help, while picking up on the aroma of coffee brewing in the kitchen of his three bedroom cabin. "Well, what do I smell in here?" he asked lightheartedly, while stopping in the kitchen doorway to see Max standing at the counter, pouring himself a cup.

"Coffee. You want some?" he asked, while looking up in time to see the young man lugging in Roger's catch. With eyes wide open, he moved around to take a better look at the two five pound pikes, dangling from their hooks. "What the…"

"Whatcha think?" Roger grinned.

"Well, you sure the heck didn't get them on your own."

"Nope, got me some help!"

"Help? Who?" he asked, knowing how no one but his and Cory's family were allowed to fish down at that spot.

"I'll tell you all about it, but first give me a hand cleaning these, won't you?"

"Sure!" Sitting his cup down, Max took the fish from Todd's hands so that he could get back to the store.

Meanwhile, telling Max all about his adventure, he left out the part about their conversation.

"Are we talking about the same girl who beat the tar out of me at pool, a couple of night ago?"

"The very one!" Roger smiled.

"You have got to be kidding. First she wipes me off the table, and now this!" Standing there, Max shook his head, as their laughter filled the room.

"Yep, and she sure is something, isn't she?"

Still unable to believe what he had just heard, Max continued shaking his head as the two went on with their cleaning.

Afterwards, getting himself another cup of coffee, Max went out onto the back deck to get some fresh air, while Roger went about cleaning up after themselves.

❧ *Chapter Seven* ❧

"Well," Roger walked out, drying off his hands, once the kitchen was back to normal, "now that, that's done, I think I'll just relax a bit before calling it a night."

"What about the store?" he asked, turning away from the rail, after having been looking off toward the old fishing hole, while unable to see it because of all the trees.

"Todd's got it covered."

"Good."

Knowing that look on Max's face, Roger went up to put a hand to his shoulder. "You know, it's going to take some time to get past what you are feeling here. Bob Hall was a friend to all us. It was a shame, God forbid, his time was cut short."

"Yeah, but Cory...! What about her...? Damn it, Roger, she needs her father."

"Yes, and Rose needs her husband. But it can't be that way for them now. And if you keep at it like you are, you are just going to be putting yourself into a heck of a mess. Not to mention, your mother is plenty worried about you, as it is!"

"Yeah, I know," he groaned, turning back to look out over the area.

"Great," Roger grumbled just then, when looking up

at the growing storm clouds, "those don't look so good," he complained, thinking about Cory at that moment. Whereas, back over at the fishing hole, she was still pondering over thoughts of her father, while not noticing the drastic change in the weather coming her way.

At that very moment, as it all came flooding back to her, she cried out angrily, "Why…, Daddy…? Why did you have to go and die when you did, and just when I really needed you the most…? Why_____?" she cried even harder, when for the first time she was really able to let out her anger and bitterness over his death.

In doing so, her cries had carried across the way, while barely reaching Max, when he suddenly turned, catching the last of it. "Did you hear that?"

"What?" Roger asked, when about to go inside.

"That cry? It sounded like…" He shook his head.

"Like what?"

"Nothing. It must have been my imagination. Here lately I have been thinking a lot about Cory, both back in town, at the park, the other night when bringing Ms. Spencer home, and now, hearing that cry. It's like she's haunting my memories. And God help me, Roger, it's really beginning to drive me nuts."

"Well, you know what they say, when two people are thinking of each other."

"They can sometimes hear the other person? Is that what you're telling me?"

"Or sense them thinking about you. Like there is some sort of connection that can't be helped. And when it comes to Bob's little angel, you have always been a protector for her.

"Yeah, but what good am I now, when I don't even know what's going on with her, while she is clear over in New York."

"Well she's over somewhere, but not where you think she is,"

he laughed under his breath, while gazing off toward the old cabin, hoping at the same time she is watching the weather.

Meanwhile, just as he feared, unaware how late it was getting, as the air began to get cooler, she was going to have to head in earlier than she would have liked. The fact is, a storm was getting ready to blow in, and she was terrified of them.

Looking up at the sky, she saw how dark and stormy the clouds were getting, when jumping to her feet as fast as she could. "Great," she cried sarcastically, while grabbing the fishing gear she had promised Roger to take along the way.

Once she had everything she needed, hurrying back to the cabin as fast as she could go, once inside, she dropped everything and locked the back door.

"Okay, girl, think, what would they do?"

Looking down at the mess, on the floor, at her feet, she smiled, and began picking it up. After getting it all put away, she went into the living room to get a fire going in the fireplace to keep it warm inside.

"Good. Now maybe a warm shower to help me relax before it all really hits," she groaned, looking out the window.

Getting the shower out of the way, she slipped into a nightshirt, before going back out into the living room to switch on the TV, when having decided then to watch a movie.

"Huh, and what better way to enjoy it," she laughed nervously, when hearing the first hint of thunder ring out overhead, while heading into the kitchen to fix herself a mug of hot chocolate to help settle her nerves.

Meanwhile, back in town, worried about her daughter, Rose called Mary, after discovering the phone up at the cabin had gone dead.

"Mary, I'm really worried about her!" she cried.

"Hang in there, Rose, I'll try giving Max a call, and have him go over and check on her."

"Call me back!"

"Sure will."

"Thanks!"

Just as Mary went to hang up, she caught the last of the weather report, "Oh, my Lord…" she gasped, when hurrying through the numbers on her phone to call her son, since he was staying over at Roger's place, while the cabin was being rented out. Reaching him, she cried out, not waiting for him to respond, "Max, I am so glad I reached you."

"What's up, Mom?" he asked, while having just finished pouring himself another cup of coffee, before sitting down to watch TV.

"Rose just tried calling the cabin, but the phone was dead. Could you run right over and check on our girl?"

"Mom…" he grumbled, "she's a big girl…! She can handle a small storm! And just why would Rose be worried about this particular girl anyway?"

"Oh… honey," she cried, not wanting to go into it with him just yet.

"Mom…?" He sat up, when picking up genuine concern in her voice.

"Max…!"

"Mom, what are you not telling me?"

"Oh, honey, this girl…" Mary stopped to think, "has been through a rather bad trauma in the past that you're not aware of. So please, just go over and check on her for us, will you?"

"All right, I'm on my way," he returned, thinking back to the dream Cory had had in the truck. Suddenly, it came to him, and with Roger already having turned in earlier, Max put down his cup and ran for the door, grabbing his keys on the way. *'It's the storm…!'* he realized, while going on out to his truck. "She is terrified of the storm! But why can't I think of who else it was that was so afraid of them?" he continued out loud, hoping it jog his memory.

Meanwhile, back at the cabin, Cory was getting increasingly frightened, as the wind picked up considerably, and with it, caused the lights to go out. "Great!" she cried, while grabbing a blanket off the back of the couch, when suddenly a strong gust of wind blew the front door open, scaring her even more. However, though, if that weren't bad enough, going over to shut it, a large streak of lightning hit a tree out front, causing one of its large branches to come crashing down on the front porch roof, while breaking out a window on its way. In doing so, glass had scattered all over the place, when a piece flew up, grazing her across the cheek, which caused her to cry out.

Feeling the heat of her own blood begin to trickle down her cheek, taking the blanket with her, she gave up on the door and ran for the corner, behind the sofa, where she curled up in a ball, when hearing the next loud clap of thunder shake the whole cabin.

"No...!" she screamed loudly, while hugging the corner a little more tightly. "Please..., Daddy... make it go away...!" she cried, covering her ears, as another loud clap pierced the air around her.

Not hearing Max pull up out front, she went on shivering with fright. Though, out in the pouring rain and an occasional flash of lightning, he couldn't help but notice how much damage the storm had already caused, when he saw the front porch roof pinned under a large branch.

"Oh, dear, God..." he cried, seeing the mess. Right away he became worried about the woman inside who had succeeded in mystifying him from the very start. But then, just as he got out of his truck, wiping away the rain from his face, he heard it. Coming from inside the cabin, was what sounded like a little girl's cry, or was she a woman now, crying for help. "No_____" he cried again, hearing that voice from out of the past. "Cory_____?" he yelled out, running around to the back door, as it was plain to see the front was out of the question. Upon finding it locked, he threw himself into it several times, before the door finally gave way.

Meanwhile, in the corner, upon turning to see a tall, dark, figure standing in the kitchen doorway, she screamed

even louder, "No_____! Max_____! Daddy_____!
Please_____ help me_____!" But then, when the dark,
mysterious, figure ran toward her, grabbing her arms, she cried
even more hysterically, while lashing out at him. "P…please
go away_____! D…don't hurt me, p…please_____!"
she sobbed, not knowing who had grabbed her, through all
the noise.

Just then, she heard a familiar voice calling out to her.

"Cory…! Cory, it's me…! It's Max…! I'm right here,
Cory! It's going to be all right now. You're safe! You hear me?
You're safe now," he yelled out over the loud crashing thunder,
until she finally realized she was really safe.

Looking up at him, she asked, "Max, is it really you…?"

"Yes, you mean, little, brat, it's me!"

"Oh, Max…" she continued to cry, while wrapping her
arms around his neck, "I'm so scared…! Make it go away…!
Please make it go away…!"

"Oh, God, Cory…" he pulled away to look at her more
intensely now, "look at me!" Doing so, he saw the frightened
look on her face, along with the gash at the side of her cheek,
as he shook his head, holding her. "It really is you, and you're
hurt! I've got to get you into the bathroom and stop that
bleeding."

Just as he was about to pick her up, she cried out again,
"Max…?"

"Yes?"

"I've really missed you."

"Same here, meanness," he replied, laughing, while
bracing himself up against the wall to pick her up.

While carrying her into the bathroom, he recalled, when
laughing even more, "I feel as though I've done this before."

"You have!" she smiled up at him.

"Damn!"

"What…?"

"I can't believe it. It's really you!" he went on laughing.

"That little eight year old brat, who used to drive me crazy. And don't you think I have forgotten what you did to my car either."

"Oh, Maxine…!" she went on laughing, too.

"And that laugh!"

"What about it?"

"You laugh like your dad!" he grinned, while sitting her down on a chair, before lighting a candle that he had found, sitting on a corner table, next to the stool.

"Oh? I never really noticed it," she returned, while looking up to see a smile in his eyes that were looking back down at her.

"Well, you do," he continued, while remembering other things, as well.

After seeing to her injury, taking the lit candle with them, they went back into the living room to survey the damage done by the storm.

Upon walking in to see the broken window, she cried, and turned to throw her arms around his shoulders.

"It's all right," he explained, looking down at her. "The branch knocked the porch roof down. That's when it must have broken out the window! What I want to know is where were you when it all happened?"

"I was attempting to close the door, when the wind blew it open."

"Oh? Well, as for this mess, don't worry about it. I'll clean it up in the morning. Right now you look tired."

"No…!" she cried, looking even more frightened at the thought of him leaving her alone.

"Hey, it's going to be okay! I not going to leave you alone tonight," he said reassuring her, while taking her over to the sofa to lay her down.

"Promise…?" she asked, while looking up at him.

"I promise. Now lay your head down and try to get some

sleep. I'm just going back into the kitchen to try and fix the back door."

Doing so, she curled up on the sofa, while he went to secure the door the best he could, before coming back in to stoke the fire a little.

"Max?"

"Yes?" he asked, turning to see her sleepy eyes looking so vulnerable.

"Will you come, sit with me?"

"Sure."

Coming back over to the sofa, she laid her head down on his lap, while he went to prop his foot up on the coffee table.

In the meantime, while resting an arm across her waist, he too, laid his head back to get some rest.

"Cory?" he spoke up tiredly.

"Yes?"

"The barn," he began, smiling, "was that you out at the barn the other day?"

Smiling too, she looked up at him. "What do you think?"

He shook his head. "And the park?"

"Uh huh!"

"I should have known. Your dad taught you how to fix cars. And then that next night when I saw you leaving the park, your voice before you left, I heard it both at the hospital, and then again that night at the park."

"Max?"

"Yes?"

"What I said before. I really did miss you...!"

Rolling his head to one side, he looked down on her sleepy face. "I missed you, too, brat," he laughed, while bringing his hand up to smooth her long, thick brown hair, while loving the feel of it under his touch. "I missed you, too..."

Wrapping her arm around the knee of his artificial leg, she

drifted off to sleep; thinking about the fun the two of them had had in the past, before he had left for college.

Meanwhile, forgetting all about his mother, he too, slipped off to sleep, listening to the rain carrying on outside.

❧ *Chapter Eight* ❧

Some time had passed after the two had fallen off to sleep, when the sound of Max's cell phone woke him.

"Hello…!" he grumbled into the receiver.

"Max! It's your mother! Is she all right?"

"Is who all right?" he grinned, looking down on Cory, while she remained sleeping peacefully with her head still on his lap.

"You know who I'm talking about."

"No, Mom, I don't, since you two never really called her by her real name!"

"Max, don't give me a hard time here."

"Why, is Rose worried?"

"Well, of course she is."

"Is she there with you now?"

"Yes. Why?"

"Put her on the phone," he ordered, sitting up carefully so as not to wake Cory.

"Max, what's going on?" she asked her son.

"Mom, just put her on the phone."

It wasn't long before Rose was on the other end. "Max?" she answered.

"Hello, Rose," he sounded mischievous at that moment.

"Hello, dear! How is she? Is she all right?"

"She's fine now!" he said, with a hint of anger in his voice.

"Is she there with you now?"

"Yes, she's asleep here on the sofa. However, if I had known earlier that it was that little brat, I would have been here sooner to keep her from going through the hell she went through."

"What happened?"

"When the wind blew open the door, she went to close it. At that time, lightning had hit the tree out front, knocking it down through the porch roof, while breaking out a window along the way."

"Oh… no…. is she all right?"

"No… she was hit by a piece of glass, cutting her cheek. By the time I got here I had to break down the back door to get to her. It was like it was sixteen years ago, all over again."

"What do you mean?"

"Hearing her cry out, I heard those words before, when I knew then it was Cory," he explained, gripping the phone heatedly. "Why didn't you just tell me the truth? Why the big secret?"

"Max, Bob wanted you to recognize her on your own. After all these years, he had hoped you would come to care for her, as she does for you."

"I remember," he spoke sadly, while trying to keep his tears in check. "It was one of the last things he said to me, along with asking me to take care of her when I saw her again. Something tells me, Rose, she has already been hurt pretty bad."

"More than you will ever know," she replied sadly. "More than you will ever… know."

"Rose, who is this guy back in New York?"

"Oh, Max…" she cried, "he is bad news, real bad. And worse yet…" She broke off, unable to go on.

"Rose… what is it?" he asked with concern etched in his voice, when hearing her crying over the other end. "Rose…?"

At that moment the line was quiet, before hearing his mother's voice come on the line.

"Max, it's me, honey."

"Mom, what's going on? What's wrong?"

"Its Cory's ex-boyfriend, he's being released in the next two to three weeks from prison, and he has been threatening to kill her when he finds her."

"What the hell…?" he nearly shouted in fierce anger over the news. Getting up, he had to continue the conversation out in the other room, so that his rage wouldn't wake Cory for sure.

"Max…" Rose got back on the phone.

"Hold up there a moment, I have to take this out to the kitchen," he returned, while carefully placing a pillow under Cory's head, before leaving the room.

Getting far enough away, though still able to keep an eye on her, he lowered his angered voice to continue, "Okay, Rose, spill it. What the hell is going on?"

"Oh, Max, I am so… scared for my baby girl. Please, you have got to protect her. Don't let Ted get to her. He has already been calling here. That's why we sent her up there to stay."

"Did he do something to her to be thrown in prison? And if so, what the hell did he do to her?"

"I'm sorry, but I promised not to repeat it. Cory will have to be the one to tell you herself when she is ready."

"When she's ready…?" he questioned, when walking quietly back into the living room to look upon her sweet little girl-like face, as she continued to lay peacefully where he had left her. With a warm grin on his tired, but handsome face, he agreed, "All right, I'll wait. Until then, don't worry about her, I'll take care of her the best way I can. Besides…" he smiled, while still looking down on her fondly, when thinking back to their kiss.

"Max... What is it?" Rose cut into his thoughts, worriedly.

"Rose?"

"Yes?"

"I think my little brat has already done goin and stolen my heart," he replied, warmly. "Oh, and Rose..." he began, while walking around the sofa to work on the dying fire.

"Yes, Max?"

"Who is this older man she has been saving herself for all of these years?"

Smiling to herself, she just shook her head amusingly, "Oh, come on, Max, are you that blind?"

Just then, it hit him. Stopping with what he was doing, he turned to look back at her. *'The age she was when she had fallen in love with him! And to think that all that time she had been trying to tell me...'* "Oh... my... God...! She said, ever since she was eight."

"Yes, Max!"

"Then what you're saying..." He swallowed hard at the realization. "It's me...? I'm the man she had been carrying a torch for all these years?"

"Yes, Max, it's always been you she has loved and adored all these years. She has even had to fight real hard to save herself, hoping someday the two of you would be together."

"But, Ted?"

"No, Max..." she hesitated.

"Rose..." he pleaded, while sitting on the coffee table, sensing more to it than she was letting on, "talk to me. Please tell me what happened, or at least tell me something!"

Knowing she had to say something, she agreed. "All right, I'll tell you what I can, as for the rest..."

"Yes, yes, tell me, please. What all took place in New York, while she was there?"

"Ted," she began, "he couldn't win her heart over. And when he found out why..." She broke off once again to choke back her emotions.

"Rose... Please...!"

"H...he had nearly beaten her to death...!"

"He...what...?" he nearly yelled, while getting back up to walk out to the kitchen, when seeing how his reaction had gotten a stir from Cory, just then.

"Yes," she went on, "he had heard her cry out your name, one evening, in her sleep, just after getting back from her father's funeral. But not before having gone to see you first, that is."

"What? She was there?" he sounded surprised.

"Yes!" she smiled. "Remember that night you thought you saw an angel in your hospital room?"

"Oh, no, that was her...? She was there all along, holding my hand and telling me that I'm not alone?" he groaned, when leaning his forehead against the door frame, while recalling the whole scene in his hospital room. "God, I was out of it most of the time."

"You sure were."

"And now..." He stopped to close his eyes to fight back his own tears. "And now she just had to go and grow up on me. No longer that annoying little brat I used to love to torment," he smiled broadly, while turning around to look up at the sealing, while thinking just how beautiful Cory had become.

"What are you going to do now, Max?" she asked, while going over to the couch to sit next to Mary, who had just offered her friend a warm arm around her shoulder.

"Follow my heart," he began, when going back into the living room to take a seat on the coffee table in front of Cory. "And right at this moment," he smiled, "she seems to have it all tied up in knots."

"Whatever you do, Max, just don't hurt her."

"Trust me, Rose, I would rather die than hurt her. And right now she is sleeping peacefully."

"Good, she needs her rest badly, and so do you. So I'll just let you go to get your sleep."

"All right. Tell mom goodnight for me," he returned, when hanging up the phone to carry Cory into her room.

"Mmmm..." she moaned, feeling his arms going around her.

"Shhh..." he whispered softly, lifting her up into his arms.

Taking in his familiar scent of cologne, she nuzzled her head right back down onto his shoulder, as he carried her off into the bedroom.

After laying her down softly on the bed, he stayed with her for the rest of the night on a nearby chair, where he too, fell off to sleep.

Awakening to the sound of Roger's chain saw the next morning, Max jolted up right, knocking off a blanket that had obviously been put over him by none other than Cory, when she woke to find him slouched down on a chair, with his legs out stretched out in front of him. "Mmmm..." he grumbled, while stretching out the rest of his long frame, before getting up to check on the noise out front.

Seeing Cory still cuddled down in her warm blankets, he stopped long enough to check on his handiwork with the bandage he had put on her cut the night before.

Seeing how it was holding up all right, he leaned down to give her a soft kiss on that very cheek, "Good," he whispered, feeling proud of his work, "now to see what is going on outside," he grinned, while walking out of the room.

"Good morning, sleepyhead," Roger greeted, when he looked up from the fallen branch to see Max coming up from around the side of the cabin.

"How is it looking out here?" he asked, seeing what the storm had done to the place.

"Well, from what all I've seen, we have a lot of downed trees, but this is the worst of the damages."

"That's for sure. Here, let me help," he offered, giving him a hand with the wood he had already cut up.

"Thanks! Oh, and Rose called me this morning to fill me in on what happened here last night, and about Cory as well."

"Yeah, and about Cory," Max groaned, "I was really blown away to find out that she was that little brat I used to torment years ago. Damn, and now look at her," he went on shaking his head, while still thrown by Cory's success and beauty.

"Yes, it sure as heck looks as though she has," Roger smiled.

"Yeah," he gave a short laugh, while looking up at the porch roof, "now why would she have to go and do a thing like that for?"

"Well, maybe it's just because she wanted to impress you when she came back home," a female voice replied, as she walked out from beside the cabin to greet her two favorite men.

"Well, if it isn't our other sleepy head. Good morning, little lady," Roger greeted warmly.

"Good morning, Roger," she smiled.

"And how are you feeling this morning?" he asked, when she went up to give him a warm hug.

"Better, now that I have my two favorite men here!" she exclaimed, when turning to Max with a sweet smile on her face.

"What...?" he growled, not able to believe what he had just seen. "Why do I have a feeling you have known all along! You did, didn't you?"

"Well, yeah, I did!" Roger grumbled sheepishly.

"When?"

"Ever since Rose and Mary called to let me know she was coming up!"

"Damn it, why am I the only one here that didn't know?"

"Because, it was meant to be a surprise," Roger explained, smiling down at her.

"Surprise…? Try upset! She could have been hurt badly last night. Darn it, Roger, when I got here, I found that the roof," he pointed, "had already been knocked down, and Cory huddled in a corner, screaming. Surprised…? You're darn right I was surprised. Hearing her crying out for her father and I, she sounded so much like that little girl, who had gotten lost out in the woods that day we had a real bad storm moving in. So, yes, I'm upset!"

Still looking down at Cory, Roger continued to smile, "I see Max has fixed you right up!"

"Yes, he did!" she continued to smile. But then turning to see his disappointed look, she turned away, while unable to face him.

But that didn't stop him from going after her. "And you," he asked, when turning her around to face him, "were you a part of this too?"

"No, Max," Roger stepped between them. "She had nothing to do with it."

"Max," Cory finally spoke up in her own defense, while coming back around Roger to face him herself, "the first time I saw you was at the restaurant. At first, I wasn't sure."

"What changed your mind?" he asked suspiciously.

"It was your voice and…" She looked away.

"And, what?" he thundered, when turning her back to face him. But then, looking down at his leg, he wondered. "My leg?" he asked heatedly. "Is that it…?"

"No… Well, yes. Yes, it was your leg, and the way mom kept watching the restrooms, like she was afraid I would see you too soon."

"Cory, I have to ask."

"What is it?" she sounded worried.

"The hospital?"

"Yes...?"

"You were there in my room, weren't you?"

"Yes!" she smiled.

"Why didn't you stay?"

"I had to get back to New York!"

"Your book?"

"Yes!"

"And the movie?" He realized even more now that it was her.

"You know? But how?" She looked surprised.

"No, he doesn't, but your father did just before he had..." Roger broke off, recalling the day sadly. "If you two youngins will excuse me, I'm just going to clean things up around here, before Mary and Rose gets here."

"What? Mom is coming up?" she cried, excitedly.

"Yes, she has something she needs to talk to Max and I about. So why don't the two of you go on now, and take a nice walk. You both have a lot of catching up to do. I'll be fine here."

But fine, he wasn't. Roger's expression had looked sad then.

"Well, how about it?" Max turned to Cory and smiled.

"Sure! Oh, but give me a minute," she returned, when seizing an alternative reason for their walk, by running back inside to get something from the refrigerator. Before going, though, she whispered something to him, and pointed to Roger. "Hey, you know, he really looks sad. And as for knowing what all was going on..."

"You're right. I'll talk to him, while you go and get what it is you have to get," he smiled, unknowing what she was up to, when heading back inside. "Hey, Roger," he turned, feeling bad for coming down so hard on him, "I'm sorry I got so upset. It's just that," he turned to look back in Cory's direction, "finding her in the shape she was in last night, I was so upset, when realizing it was her all along. You can't possibly imagine the effect it had on me," he added, when looking back at his friend. "It was more than I could have imagined possible."

"If you think you were surprised. You should have seen the look on my face!" he laughed, just as she returned, smiling.

"What? Don't let me stop you. Go on with what you were going to say!" she insisted.

"Well," he continued, when turning back to Max, "I was even warned about her coming, and still seeing her," he turn back to Cory and smiled, "after all those years, little lady, it was quite a shock to this old goat. Let alone the fact that he bumped right into you at Tony's!"

"Yeah, well, sorry, my mind was somewhere else," he offered sheepishly, when looking down into her beautiful eyes. "Shall we go for that walk now?"

"Oh, but don't you want to get washed up first, before we go?"

"No, I can do that where we're going."

"Oh? And where might that be?" she asked teasingly, while running her fingers over an egg she now had in her jacket pocket.

"It's not far," he replied, putting his arm around her shoulder to head back around the cabin toward her father's old fishing hole.

Getting there, she walked over to sit on her favorite boulder.

While watching her, he laughed, shaking his head. "Now, how did I know you were going to do that?" he asked, while joining her.

"It's my favorite rock!" she exclaimed, happily, while looking off over the pond.

"It's mine, too!"

Laughing, she bumped playfully into his shoulder. "It's so nice down here, don't you think?"

"Yes, it is. In fact, I even found the tree you had carved on!" he teased, while pointing it out. "It says..."

"C. H. + M. B., I know! I even remember the day I put it there. It was some time later after you had just gotten your acceptance letter from M S U! I was so unhappy about your leaving us, and yet so soon!"

"That's also the day you ran off and got lost. Your father was so scared out of his mind that he wouldn't find you, before it got dark. Not to mention, the storm that was brewing up. So I told him I would go out and find you for him."

"I wouldn't have run off if you hadn't thrown that worm on me, you big jerk! And then when that storm hit!" She stopped. "God, I was so scared."

"I know. I felt really bad for doing that to you. All I could think about then was finding you, and bring you back safely. That's when I heard you crying out for your dad and I. Lord, Cory." He shivered, while looking out over the woods, at the thought of her being out there lost and so frightened.

Turning to see his expression, she took his hand in hers. "Hey, I was so glad when you had!" she tried smiling up at him, thinking it would help to ease the moment.

"And now," he turned sadly to face her, "time seems to have repeated itself. Only this time you just had to go and grow up on me."

"Oh, Max..." she cooed, feeling the warmth of his eyes looking into hers, when even he could feel the heat rise within him, so much so he just wanted to take her back into his arms to kiss her, like he had the other night. However, he wasn't sure he should. Instead, getting up, he walked over to the water to think.

Just then, seeing her opportunity, she pulled the egg from her pocket, thinking back to that day, sixteen years ago, when she had first thrown one at him, instead, hitting his car by mistake. Now she aimed this one with much more precise, when hitting right at the base of his left boot, while splattering it up onto his pant leg.

"What…?" he turned, looking down as it ran off the edge of his pant leg. With a large grin on his face, he slowly looked back at her, only to see an innocent smile come over that beautiful face of hers. "You… little… brat," he growled playfully. "You've had it now. I let the first one go, but this one means war," he warned, turning to come after her.

"Max…!" she cried out, getting up off the boulder to run for the cabin.

Not making it though, he tackled her to the ground, pinning her wrists up next to her head so she couldn't get away. "You're not getting away this time, you mean little brat," he growled, laughing at her, while moving himself around to get a better hold on her.

"Well, then, just what are you going to do about it, Maxine…?" she laughed. But then, when their eyes met, he was no longer able to contain the heat he felt building up inside for her.

Looking down at those inviting lips of hers, he lowered his slowly to claim them. "This," he whispered, while taking her lips desperately.

As he did, letting go of one of her wrists, he brought his hand down to place it under the small of her back, to bring her up even more in his arms, as their kiss grew even deeper.

Wanting it to last forever, she pulled her other wrist free to run her fingers through his sandy blond hair lovingly, as she let out a small uncontrollable moan.

Stopping to look down into her sensuous green eyes, he groaned, "Cory, I want you so much," he fought to control his breathing, while running a hand through her hair as well, "but not this way."

"Max…" she cried, afraid she had done something wrong.

"No, Cory." He placed a finger to her quivering lips. "Knowing you're still innocent, I want your first time to be special," he went on hungeringly. "And I want to be the one who makes it that way for you."

"Oh, Max…" she went on with great relief, "I only wish that were true since I have wanted so much to hear you say that, but…"

"But nothing, I mean every word of it. I want you, Cory Hall, in every sense of the word. And knowing I'm the one you have been saving yourself for means a great deal to me."

"I had nearly lost it though, because of…"

"This guy back in New York?"

"Yes," she replied grimly, while shifting herself beneath his weight.

"Am I hurting you?" he asked, seeing her discomfort.

"No, it's just the memory of what he did to me, that hurts so much," she tried to explain, while looking away to hide the hurt in her eyes.

"Cory, please tell me what happened to you! Rose said you had to fight real hard to keep from losing your innocence. What the hell did that maniac do to you?"

"He had overheard me call out to you in my sleep one night right after coming back home from daddy's funeral. So he decided then, that after dating me for four years it had earned him the right to take what I have been saving myself for. He never got it, though," she returned, looking back at him. "*Never!*"

"So I've been told! Not to mention, you had almost died, because of him!"

"I just about did, until mom brought in a picture of you for me to focus on! It gave me a reason to live!"

"I'll try my best not to let anything like that happen to you again," he swore, claiming her lips again, when his hand had lightly brushed passed her breast.

"Oh, Max," she pulled away, "we've got to stop, before we lose ourselves in each other!"

"You're right," he groaned, while getting up to help her to her feet, "if we're to do this right, we're going to have to get married first."

"What...?" She sounded surprised. Though wanting to marry Max, she didn't want it to be this way. And certainly not without a courtship to build on.

"You heard me," he returned. "I won't take you unless we are man and wife."

"I...I know what I heard, but..."

"But nothing," he growled, "I want you to have the kind of life you deserve. It's what your father wanted for you."

"But Max, it isn't that that I'm confused about."

"What is it, then?" he asked, feeling confused.

"I can't just marry you!" she exclaimed, turning away to think things through.

"Why?"

Turning back to see his puzzled expression, she smiled. "Oh, Max, I love you. I have for years, but you..."

"Oh, I see," he replied, thoughtfully. "It's because I haven't had time to love you, is that it?"

"Yes!"

Pulling her back into his arms, he smiled even more. "Then I will just have to learn, won't I?"

"Oh... Max, do you really mean that?" she cried, while allowing her tears of happiness to flow freely.

"Yes," he returned. "I won't take you unless we're married, and I won't marry you until you feel I have learned to love you. But I should warn you, those feelings aren't so far off. You have already stolen my heart, and I can't stand the thought of something happening to you that will take you away from me."

"Really?" she asked mischievously, while changing the subject.

"Yes, really," he smiled, seeing what she was doing to him. "So don't give me such a hard time with your charm and beauty. I can only take so much pressure, before I totally cave in."

"You mean, don't walk up and do this?" she nuzzled her lips along the base of his neck, while running her fingertips along his stomach, while causing him to become acutely aroused.

"That's exactly what I mean, you little brat," he laughed, while holding her back away from him. "Now behave yourself, you have caused enough torment for one day."

"Ah, honey!" she smiled up at him.

"I mean it! So stop it, before I..."

"Before you what?" she continued tormenting him, until he swept her up off her feet to carry her over to the pond.

"Now, you were saying?" he threatened, while giving her that look of contempt.

"It won't work, Maxine..." she laughed. "You won't throw me in."

"How do you know that?"

"Because of my cut!"

"You're lucky this time. However, don't count on it for long. I will throw you in when you get better."

"No... you... won't...!"

"Oh, yeah, and now what makes you so sure?"

"Because, I won't let go."

"We'll just see about that," he replied, letting her down slowly to walk back over to their boulder.

Just then, the look in his eyes registered something she wasn't sure of. "Max, what is it?" she asked, while gently touching his shoulder, when walking up behind him. "Did I say or do something wrong?"

"No, you didn't," he replied, when turning back to pull her into his arms, "I just never thought I would ever let another woman get this close to me again. But then you are so different from anyone else."

"Max, what are you trying to say?"

"I think what I am trying to say, is that..." He stopped, then, and pulled away to silently walk back over to the water.

"Is it that hard to say?" she asked puzzledly.

"I'm afraid so. You see, Karen did a number on me. I just don't know if I have ever gotten passed it or not."

"Because of the accident that took your leg, you mean?"

"That, too! And because of that, what woman would ever want me?"

"How about the one who has always loved you?"

Looking back at her, he asked, "Are you so sure that when we get ready to make love you wouldn't get sick at the mere sight of my stump?"

"Max, the man inside you is still there, that's who I fell in love with! As for your physical being, it's merely just a shell to carry that warm, gentle spirit of yours around in. And it's that spirit of yours that I love. As for your stump..." She stopped to look down at his left leg, before returning to look up at him, "I have already seen it."

"When?"

"While you were in the hospital, the nurse had gotten sick, while helping the doctor. So I grabbed a gown, and some gloves, and took over for her. It was a breeze! The doctor had even thought I was your wife. So he told me how to care for you. After that, he just let me take over, while telling me I was a natural at it. I had rather thought so, myself," she bragged, acting as though she were polishing her nails, and laughed.

"You did all that for me?" he asked, while his eyes glowed with admiration for how she had stuck by him through it all. "Why weren't you there then, when I woke up?"

"I had to get back to New York, for my book!"

"Ah, yes, the book that is about to go into a movie."

"Yes...! I have never been so excited when the producer called to set up a time to meet and discuss a possible contract.

I just wish daddy could have been here to see it all happen. He would have been so proud of me."

"I think from what Roger was saying earlier, your dad had already known about the possibility of the movie, remember?"

"Yes, you're right! But how?"

"I would imagine your mother would have told him, before he had died. And hearing this, he would have been very proud to know that his little girl had done so well for herself."

"Oh, Max," she cried, going up to put her arms around him, "I needed so much to hear that, but how did you know?"

"Come to think of it, Mom told me. Only she didn't tell me it was you. She just said that it was this big writer coming from New York. I should have guessed it was you. And Cory, as for your dad, he had always loved you, and was so proud of you."

"Oh, Max... I'm so glad that he knew!"

Not saying anything more, he just held her.

"Max?"

"Yes?"

"What time is it getting to be?"

"It's getting late, we should be getting back up to the cabin, before our mothers get there."

"Why?" she looked up, smiling once again, mischievously. "Are you afraid that I might get you into trouble?"

"Yes!" he laughed, giving her a swat on the rear.

"Ouch...!"

❧ *Chapter Nine* ❧

"Hey, you two…!" Roger called out. "Food is on the grill. Anyone hungry?"

"Count me in!" Max called back, while taking Cory's hand, when Roger came down to join them.

Needing a moment alone with him, Roger put up a hand, "Max, I need to talk to you first. Would you mind, little lady?" he asked, while trying to hide his real concern.

"No, I don't mind! I'll see the two of you later," she returned, while giving Max another one of her sweet smiles, before walking away.

Smiling back, he called out stopping her.

"Yes?" she turned back just as he walked up to her.

"Thanks for being there for me. At the hospital, I mean."

"You're welcome," she replied, while turning back to head on up to the cabin to see their mothers.

"Okay, Roger," Max turned back to see the expression come over his friend's face, after Cory was far enough away not to hear what he had to say, "what's going on?"

"You aren't going to like what I have to tell you."

"Is it about Cory?"

He didn't answer.

"Come on, Roger," he asked, taking his arm, "what is it?"

"It's not good, my friend," he groaned. "You had best sit down first, before reading this," he suggested, when handing Max a note that had been sent to Rose, concerning her daughter.

Looking down at it after taking it from Roger's shaky hands, he looked up slowly, as a feeling of deep regret came over him. "No…" he groaned, shaking his head.

"Yes, Max, it's from Cory's ex-boyfriend. It's from…"

"Roger, I thought he wasn't getting out yet!"

"He isn't! Well, at least not yet!"

Looking back at the typewritten note, Max's own hands began to shake, as he went to open it.

> *Cory*, the note began.
>
> *Your days are numbered. And when I get out I'm going to do exactly what I said I was going to do. Remember?*
>
> *When I find you, you're going to die for what you did to me. Do you hear me, Cory? And if your precious Max or anyone else gets in my way, I'll kill them too.*
>
> *I'm coming for you, Cory, I'm coming real soon.*
>
> T. H.

"Like hell he will!" Max swore, while crumpling up the letter. "What kind of monster would want to do that to her?"

"A very sick one, obviously," Roger cried, as the tears began streaming down his rugged face.

"Damn it, Roger, I can't lose her to that lunatic, not now, not ever. Do you know what I'm saying?" He asked, taking a hold of both his arms.

"I know what you're saying. I figured it out at the Corral

Bowl, and then again this morning when I saw the two of you in the cabin."

"Roger, nothing happened. When I found her the other night she was terrified. So I stayed with her so she would feel safe."

"I know," he smiled. "And when it comes to Bob's little girl, you have always been protective of her. Now, you're going to be put to the test. Even your own life may be at stake here."

"Yeah, I know. We've got to get some of the guys together, and call Mike to see what he can offer in the way of protection now that he's a part of the State Police."

"Since when?"

"Just the other day!" Max grinned broadly at the look on his friend's face.

"Well, I'll be…!"

"Yes. Now what do you say, we get back up to the cabin?"

"Yes, and I'll call the guys right away."

"Great, I'll do the same, and call Mike. Oh, and Roger," Max stopped on the pathway back to the cabin. "Not a word of this to Cory," he told him, while putting an arm around his friends' shoulder. "She's had enough pain to deal with."

"I understand, but we need to let the others know that we're going to do everything we can to protect her."

"Which reminds me, when is he getting out?"

"In two to three weeks. Or so we've been told."

"All right, but just for safety sake, I'll put in a call to the prison and find out if he will be on any sort of probation. Also to see if they have an exact date when he'll be released, so we can be ready for any kind of trouble, if he were to show up here."

"Sounds like a good plan to me! For now let's just try to enjoy what time we do have."

"You're right, I have better things to do with my time than worry about Ted Harden," he growled.

"And a very special lady to do them with, too," he teased, while the two headed on back.

Upon their arrival, Mary teased, seeing them walking up from the pathway, while trying to look as though nothing was ever wrong, "Well, it's about time...! We thought we were going to have to send out the National Guard to find you two! Supper is just about ready. Oh, and Max, why don't you and Cory run on down to the store and get a few more things for the cookout?"

"Like what?"

"Oh, you'll think of something."

"Well, shall we?" he asked, while taking her hand to leave.

On their way over to his truck, sensing something was wrong, she asked, once getting in, "Max, what's going on?"

"What do you mean?" he asked, while acting oblivious to what she was wanting to know.

"Down at the pond, you and Roger seemed so serious when I left."

"Oh, just talking! Nothing too serious!"

"Max...?"

"All right, I won't lie to you, Cory, but I don't want you to be afraid anymore, either."

"Then tell me!"

"I will! I promise! Just not right now, we have to get some things ironed out first," he explained, while holding her hand.

He knew she would sense something was wrong, but for now he had to keep it to himself, or so he had thought when they arrived at the store.

Getting out, she couldn't hold back the thought any longer. "Max?"

"Yes?"

"Ted is going to try to kill me when he gets out of prison. That, I already know, but you and Roger know something else, don't you?"

"Yes, we do," he replied, quietly, while turning to place an arm around her shoulder, while looking into her frightened eyes.

"He's coming soon, isn't he?"

"Cory..."

"Max?"

"Yes, he is. I'm sorry that you have to know this so soon. But know also, that we are working on a plan to keep you safe. Besides, I promised your dad I would take care of you. And now it looks as though I am going to have to protect you from this monster, who seems to hate you so much."

"He hates me because I wouldn't give him what I have been saving myself for. And now he wants to kill me so that you won't get it either!"

"What makes him think I don't already have it? Or that I don't just marry you right here and now so that I can get it, before he gets out?"

"Because, he knows you're not that way."

"Cory, would you consider marrying me, before he gets out?"

"Oh... Max, I can only marry you for love. Can you honestly say that you love me and mean it?"

"Cory, I do love you. Oh, God, how I love you. But I'm also scared for you. I would literally die if he took you away from me now. I really mean that."

"Oh, Max... how could you love me so soon?"

"A part of it has to do with your dad, and another part was learning how you stuck by me in the hospital. You could have given up on me, but you didn't. That's the sort of love I'd been wishing for. I don't want to lose it, not now. So Cory, please believe me, you are the woman that I have been waiting for. I was wrong about Karen. Please, give me a chance to prove it to you. We both know how much your father wanted this for us. Damn it, Cory, marry me."

"Oh, Max... I don't know what to say. I do love you. I have always loved you. It's just that I had never thought it would happen quite so quickly! Please..." she cried, "I need some time to think about this. It's all happening so sudden!"

"I know, but..." he began, when seeing how she looked as though she could pass out at any time. Pulling her into his arms for support, he went on, "Think about it, and let me know as soon as possible! We can even have the ceremony down at the fishing hole if you would like. It's beautiful down there at this time of the year."

"Oh, but that does sound wonderful," she agreed, while choking back on the overwhelming emotions. "I'll think about it. I promise."

Later that day after they finished eating, while still sitting out back enjoying the sunshine and fresh air, she got up, interrupting the conversation, to go over and stand next to her man, who at the time was sitting on the tailgate of his truck. "Max," she began, while taking his hand, "I've thought it over, and if you're really sure this is what you want, then I think you need to ask my mother first."

"Are you sure?" he asked with tears of joy welling up in his eyes, and a grin on his handsome face, as he went to stand next to her.

"Oh, yes," she replied, while smiling up at him.

"Then I guess I had better ask!" he went on, while looking over at their mothers.

"Ask me, what?" Rose spoke up, while sitting off to one side of the back porch, looking eager to hear what he had to say.

"Rose, Roger, and... Mommy dearest," he laughed, "I would like to have your blessings to marry Cory," he finished, while looking into her eyes with so much love and compassion in his own. "You see, I have asked Cory to marry me earlier. And yes, I know it seems kind of sudden, but I don't want to lose her. So, to make this more official," he looked to Roger, who handed him the ring he had given him to hold, knowing that he had already planned this out. "Cory Hall," he turned back nervously, "my favorite little brat, who just had to go and grow up into this beautiful, successful woman." He stopped to shake his head. "I thought I would never hear myself say these words again. However, someone very special to us all told me that there is one woman out there who will steal my heart and bring it back to life again. And he was right. You, Cory, have done just that. You took my heart, what was left of it, and brought it back to life."

"And in such a short length of time too, I might add!" Roger laughed, while standing next to his truck.

"Well, come on, already, we're not getting any younger!" Mary laughed along with the others. "Besides, we would like to be around to spoil our grandchildren, too, you know."

"Mom… if I don't do this right, there won't be any grand-children to spoil."

"All right, we'll behave," she said, while stifling a laugh.

Turning back, he laughed happily, "Will you marry me… please…?"

With an ornery grin, she said, laughing gaily, "Oh, yes, I'll marry you, Maxine."

"Cory…" he roared out laughing, "I warned you about that."

"Wooo… I love how you talk dirty to me," she smiled sweetly into his eyes, when he grinned, while going on to kiss her softly, before deepening the kiss, knowing that she would have to behave herself in front of the others.

"I love you, Cory," he whispered. "With all my heart, I love you."

"I love you too," she replied, and then added more coyly into his ear, "And I can't wait to have your babies!"

"Keep it up, girl, and we may not wait to get married," he teased, while tracing a finger along her jaw line, when the muscle along his own started flexing at the mere thought of being with her.

"Well," Mary interrupted, while coming up to give them each a warm hug, "I think this is wonderful."

Rose, however, was still worried about Cory's safety, when Roger turned back to see her still seated.

"Rose, we're going to do everything we can to protect her," he replied, while kneeling down to put an arm around her to comfort her.

"And Rose," Max added, while going over to give her a big hug, "I won't leave her. She will always be loved."

"Oh, Max, it's not that. It's just that her father isn't here to give her away! And well, we have so much that has to be done to get things ready."

"When is all this taking place?" Mary asked.

"In two weeks," he stated. "Out at the old fishing pond where, in a spiritual sort of way," he turned back to Rose, "Bob will be there, himself, to give her away."

"Oh, honey…" she cried, "that sounds wonderful."

"Congratulations, you two," Roger replied. "In fact, I have a wonderful idea. Why don't you ladies stay over at my cabin, while you're making the wedding plans?"

"Where are you going to stay?" Mary asked, before going back into the cabin to fix some hot chocolate, since the air was starting to get a little chilly.

"Max and I can stay here, or at the apartment above the store."

"That sounds good to me!" Max replied, while turning to look down at Cory. "Are you all right with that?" he asked, seeing the disappointment on her face.

"Yeah… it's just that I wanted to stay here for a little

while longer. It's where I spent so much of my childhood with daddy, and I'm not quite ready to leave it yet!"

"Cory, Roger has a point, though," Rose put in, when Mary returned with the tray of hot chocolate, as it had always been one of their favorite pastimes, at the cabin, during chilly weather such as this.

"It would give us more room!" Mary commented, while passing out the mugs to everyone, with Rose's help.

"Mom, I know if Ted did try to come after me, he wouldn't know about Roger's place, but…" she began, when Max jumped in, not hearing Cory's continual apprehension toward the end.

"And if he does come here, he wouldn't find her. In fact, we're planning on having some of our buddies watching for him. Not to mention, a few guys from the Police Department, bout which I'll be calling Mike in a little while, as well, to see what he can do."

"This place will be set up to look as though our buddies are here to do a little hunting and fishing," Roger added thoughtfully.

"But not down at daddy's old fishing hole, will they?" Cory asked.

"No, little lady, they all know they can't use that spot. Only Max and I go there."

"Thanks, Roger," Rose replied.

While gathering up their plates, Max suggested they get the ladies moved over to Roger's place right away.

"You're right," Roger returned, while pulling out his truck keys to leave, "I'll go on over and get the place stocked up for you ladies, now."

"Roger, hold up there a minute," Mary called out. "I'll give you a hand with that."

"Rose," Roger offered comfortingly, "things will be all right."

"I know. I'm all right," she smiled, while getting to her feet. "Hey, how about I tag along with the two of you?"

"Sure, how lucky can a man get?" he smiled, while looking down at the two lovely ladies on either arm.

"Oh, Roger, that's old, really old," Mary laughed, while walking over to their cars.

'Their cars!' Cory cried, while looking at the cars parked out in front. "Wait...!" she cried out, stopping them

"What's wrong?" Max asked, taking her arm.

"Their license plates!" she cried, pointing at her mother's car first. "He'll know by the plates that we're up here!"

"She's right," Roger agreed.

"We have to come up with another idea," Max turned, shaking his head angrily, while running a hand through his hair, trying to think of another plan.

"Wait, I think I have just the one!" Cory smiled.

"We're all ears," Roger replied.

"James owes me a large favor. Let me call him."

"Be careful what you tell him," Max advised, cautiously.

"All right," she nodded, while pulling out her cell phone.

Making her call, the others gathered around to listen.

"Hello! This is James! How can I help you?" her publisher asked on the other end of the line.

"James..." she cried out, happily, "it's Cory!"

"Cory...! When are you coming back?" he asked excitedly. "The producer needs to see you ASAP!"

"He isn't there now, is he...?" she asked, catching a look of concern from the others, when thinking she was referring to Ted.

Holding up a hand to calm them, she leaned in closer to listen to James.

"No, but he'll be here in the morning."

"Oh, no...! James, haven't you heard...? Ted is getting out of prison soon!"

"Oh, no… I haven't heard. Now, what am I supposed to do?" he complained worriedly.

"Send Sid over here to work with me. However, you will need to stay there, so that Ted will think you're talking to me from California on the movie rights. I'll have a suite set up there to throw him off. And James," she continued, "let everyone there think I really am in California, including Sally, in case he calls and she slips up and tells him where I really am."

"That sounds pretty clever," he agreed, laughing on his end. "Now, how are you doing?"

"I'm fine! Working on my next book as usual."

"Hey, you're supposed to be resting!"

"Sorry, I can't help it!" she laughed, while going on, "James, I've got to go now. Are we squared away on our plans?"

"You can count on me, girl. He won't know where you are. In fact, I have a friend who can check on his status and let me know when he'll be getting out."

"Thanks, James, I forgot you had a PI on the payroll."

"Well, we can't have our favorite writer's life being threatened. How am I supposed to pay my bills?" he laughed.

"James…!"

"Sorry, honey, I don't want to see you get hurt anymore either."

"Same here," she replied. "Let us know then what takes place."

"I will. And I'll send Sid right over, before he gets here."

"James?"

"Yeah?"

"Send him to Roger's Camp Store."

"Sure thing," he replied, hanging up.

"Well, that takes care of that," she turned to the others to fill them in on what had just transpired.

"So your publisher is going to have a PI keep an eye on

him there?" Max asked, while going over to grab a beer out of the cooler.

"Yes," she returned, while seeing the look of disappointment on his face. "Max…" she cried, feeling somehow she had hurt him. "Please, try to understand why I did this," she explained, while going over to stand behind him.

Seeing how his back muscles were so taut when she went to touch him, she flinched her hand away. "Oh, Max, don't you see, you and Roger are going to have your hands full here. I just thought…"

"Max, she's right, we can use the extra help," Roger put in.

Taking his arm, she turned him back to face her. "Besides, I feel a lot better after coming up with the idea. It had even taken away some of the fear, if only for a short time."

"Cory, I just want to make sure you're going to be safe, is all."

"With all of you here, I feel darn lucky. And guess what?" Her eyes lit up. "The producer is coming here so we can talk over the script! I won't have to go there where Ted might see me."

"That'll be a load off my mind," Rose replied, while heading out with Roger and Mary to get things set up at his place.

"Same here," Roger agreed, feeing the two needed some time alone. "Hey, while we're out of here, and as soon as I get these two settled in, I'll give Jones and the others a call to have them meet us over at the store. We can fill them in on what's going on there."

"All right," Max returned, when looking back to Cory. "Well, lady, what are you going to do until we leave?"

"I think I'll just go on in and take a shower before we go."

"All right."

At that, she smiled up at him as she went on inside, leaving him to clean up the mess.

Meanwhile, while getting her things ready for a nice hot shower, the phone rang, breaking into her concentration.

"Hello…!" she answered. Not hearing anyone at first, she repeated herself, "Hello…!"

At that time, having heard the phone ring, right away, Max came in, hearing Cory repeating herself. *'Ted,'* he though, picking up on the extension in the living room.

"Well, you are there, aren't you," the man said, "I'm coming for you, Cory," he laughed. "I'm coming to take care of you just like I should have a long time ago."

"Ted…?" she cried.

"Who else?"

"Forget it, Ted. I won't be here. I'm leaving first thing in the morning."

"Oh, yeah… where are you going?"

"As far away from you as I can," she cried, when then seeing Max rounding the corner. Thinking quickly, she went on, "Max doesn't even want me after what you did to me. You ruined my life, Ted! Do you hear me? Now, I don't even have the one man I have been saving myself for all those years."

Looking to Max, he smiled his approval of her tactics.

"Well, then, like I said; where are you going to go?" he asked, as the tone in his voice changing slightly.

"Somewhere only James would know of. Besides, mom and her friend are leaving on some trip of their own. So she won't even know what I'm doing. We have never really been all that close anyhow. It's always been just me and daddy."

"I remember, and now you're all alone. No one to love you," he laughed. "I loved you, but I wasn't good enough for you. You just had to have your farmer, what's his name? Max?"

"Well, thanks to you, he's gone on with his life."

"Too bad, Cory, I guess then he won't miss you when you're dead," he laughed even more sadistically just before hanging up.

"Ted… why are you doing this to me? Ted…" she cried out, as they both heard the phone go dead. "No_____! God… no_____!" she sobbed, dropping the phone.

⊱ *Chapter Ten* ⊰

After dropping the phone to the floor, Max saw the color wash from her face, as she went slowly down to the floor herself. "Cory..." he cried out, while giving his own phone a toss to rush right over and catch her. "It's going to be all right. You tried your best to convince him we weren't involved anymore, but..."

"But he's still coming after me!"

"So I heard," he replied, shaking his head. "We've got to get you out of here, and now!" he exclaimed, grabbing his cell phone.

"Oh, Max..." she cried, pulling herself a little more into his arms.

"Hang in there, girl, I'm going to call Roger."

No sooner had he dialed, Roger's voice came over the other end.

"Hello..." he replied.

"Roger, it's me. Have you called the others yet?"

"Yeah, they'll be here right away, and Mike will be here just as soon as he gets our information on Ted!"

"Roger," Max stopped for a painful moment, "I think Ted's out already."

"What? He had two to three weeks to go yet."

"Well, he just called Cory. He says he's on his way. Damn, him, I'm going to find out what had happened. And Roger," he added, "send a couple of the guys over when they get there."

"I sure will," he replied, hanging up.

Turning back to Cory, he pulled back, "I want you to get everything that belongs to you, and put it at the front door. I'll get it all loaded up in the truck when you're through."

"A...all right," she replied, while still shaking over what had just happened, while he went to help her to her feet.

"We will catch him, Cory. Whatever it takes, we *will* catch him."

"Oh, Max... he won't stop until he..."

"No, Cory, I'll never let you go. You have to believe that."

"But I'm so scared..., scared that you won't be here to stop him!"

"Like hell I won't!" he swore, glaring down into her eyes. "Cory, I'm not about to lose you, not now. Not ever."

"How can you be so sure you can catch him? He is so clever!"

"Cory, what is it you're not telling me?"

"Max..." she started, but then turned away.

"What...?" he asked, turning her back to face him.

"I had a...a...a dream last night that Ted had gotten past you and Roger."

"No...!" He shook his head, seeing the look in her eyes. "No...!"

"Yes, Max, it was too late," she cried. "He had already..."

"No, Cory, stop it!" He swallowed hard at the horror that played through his mind.

"But, Max..."

"No...!" Taking her back into his arms, he had to ask, "Do you remember where you were?"

"Next to the couch, on the floor!" she exclaimed, pulling away. "Only..."

"Only what?"

"Only, it wasn't this cabin!"

While shaking his head in disbelief, she turned to pack her things, while he went out onto the front porch to call his old partner.

"Mike," he spoke quietly into the phone.

"Yeah?"

"It's Max."

"Where are you now?"

"I'm here at mom's old cabin with Cory Hall."

"Good, keep her there. I'm on my way to see you. And Max..."

"Yeah?"

"I have some bad news."

"So do I!"

"What?"

"Ted just called."

"He what...?"

"You heard me."

"He isn't supposed to call, let alone go anywhere near her. That's a part of his probation!" he exclaimed. "And to add to that, he isn't even allowed to leave New York!"

"Is he out?"

"I'm afraid so. They released him this morning."

"Damn, he's already broken his probation twice, with the letter, and now this," Max groaned. "What are they going to do about it?"

"They are already on it. They are supposed to get in touch with me when they've finished talking to him."

"That's if he's still there."

"Hang in there, partner, I'm on my way."

"You got it."

Just as he hung up, he turned to see Cory standing in

the living room. The look on her face told him she overheard their conversation. "Cory…" he called out, just as she went running out the back door.

"No…!" she cried out angrily, heading down the path toward her father's old fishing hole.

Going after her, he caught up with her just as she went over to lie across her favorite boulder to cry.

"Oh, Cory…!"

"When…?" she screamed, turning on him, heatedly. "Just when were you going to tell me about that letter? Darn you, anyway," she went on taking her fists against his chest, "don't you know you can't keep something like this away from me?"

"Oh, Cory, I was going to tell you, but not just yet!"

"Then when, after he had already killed me?"

"Cory…!"

"Max, I'm not that little girl you used to torment anymore, Ted has taken that job away from you. Now he is doing the tormenting, and into an early grave if we don't stop him first."

"Cory, we will!"

"Oh, Max, I don't want to die. I want to marry you and give you a lot of babies, and even more gray hair…" she screamed out her anger at him, just as she turned to walk over to the water. "Why…?" she sobbed, turning back to him. "Why does this have to happen to us? Why won't he just accept that I love you, and not him?"

"Oh, Cory, I love you, too!" he tried to smile. "As for the gray hair, it's too late, you have already done that," he laughed. "And as for the babies, I'd take you right here and now if I thought you would let me."

"Oh, Max, I do want you. So much that it drives me crazy when we kiss. I don't even want it to stop!"

"Oh, girl…" he groaned, taking her back into his arms to claim her lips hungrily, "I want you so bad too, but…" He stopped to kiss her again. "I don't know just how much longer

I can wait," he stated, while looking down into her desirable eyes. But then, having just gotten the words out, he pulled her up into his arms and claimed her lips with such fierce passion that she could now feel the hot ambers of their love pouring out through him.

"Mmmm…" she moaned out her need, as she brought her own arms up around his neck more.

'Oh, Lord, I want her so… much,' he thought, while trailing his lips down along her neck, while running his fingers through her hair. But then, coming back up, he reclaimed her lips.

"Oh… Max…! Max…! We have to stop…!" she moaned, hearing someone calling out.

"Damn it…" he grumbled under his breath, just as he looked up the pathway to see his old partner and two other plain clothed men heading their way. Shaking his head over the interruption, he apologized, "I'm sorry, I nearly forgot he was coming."

"Well, it's probably a good thing," she smiled up at his reddened expression.

"Max…! Are you down here?" Mike called out again.

"Yeah…!" he returned, looking back down at Cory. "One of these days, you little brat," he laughed, loving the way her beautiful smile would light up his heart whenever he saw it.

"Mmmm… and I can hardly wait."

"Oh, but you will," he threatened, just as Mike and his two shadows arrived.

"I thought you were going to wait up in the cabin?"

"Sorry, we needed some air," he winked at her before turning to face his old partner. "What's up?"

"Plenty!" he replied, looking to Cory. "I take it you're the one we're here to protect?"

"Yes, she is," Max returned, introducing her to the tall, dark haired, plain clothed officer, along with the other two men standing behind him.

"Ma'am," he smiled warmly, bowing his head.

Returning his smile, she also bowed.

"Max," he turned, looking over the area, "is there somewhere we can all go to eliminate exposure?"

"Sure, let's go back up to the cabin," he suggested, leading the way with Cory at his side.

Once inside, Mike continued with the information he had on Cory's ex-boyfriend, while closing the back door behind him. "This is what I found out so far, your Ted Harden, Miss Hall, was released this morning."

"Y…you're sure?" she asked fearfully, as Max pulled her up close.

"Oh, yes, and he has already accumulated three counts of violation against his probation. The two you know about, and the third…" He turned to Max, shaking his head.

"What is it?" he asked.

"I'm sorry to have to say this, but…"

"Jones…?" Max asked, full of concern.

"He's not in New York anymore," Mike announced, turning to Cory. "Miss Hall, your publisher just called, before we went looking for the two of you. It seems his PI called in reporting that he had seen Harden cross over the state line an hour ago."

"Where…?" Max asked.

"We assumed Canada, so that we can't touch him."

"Max…!" Cory cried, looking frightened.

"I know," he groaned softly, looking to Mike for more information. "What are we going to do now?"

"I'll get every available officer on it, right away. Roger has already given me an idea on the way over here. I'm going to set up some undercover officers here instead of his buddies to make it look like they're on vacation, while I stay with you and Roger up at the store. I'll even put a female officer with your lady here around the clock."

"Thanks, Mike," he returned. "I promised her father I

would take care of her. Not to mention, she has already stolen my heart," he smiled down at her.

"Yeah, so I've noticed," he smiled as well, before going over to the window to look out. "Come to think of it, I know some men who will even come out of an early retirement to do this, along with your friends walking the woods. Ms. Hall," he turned back, "this guy won't have a chance, I'm sure of it."

"Unless he tricks you into thinking he has been seen somewhere else!" she exclaimed softly.

"We'll be ready for that, and any other tricks he may have up his sleeve," he offered reassuringly. "And if you know of anything else that may help us, please let me know right away. Your mother has already told me some things about this guy. And yours too, Max. It seems he has been calling quite a bit, ever since you have gotten here."

Hearing this, she pulled free of Max, feeling all hopes begin to slip away. Then a thought came to her, "Yes," she turned back, "there is one thing I can think of."

"What is it?"

"He's really good at using disguises."

"Okay! You guys heard her. We'll be watching for that."

"If there is nothing else, we should be going," Max suggested, picking up her things to carry on out to his truck.

"No," Mike returned.

"Sir, what do you want us to do?" Kevin, a somewhat tall, lanky young man asked.

"I want this place cleaned up. In fact, so good that there is no sign of her having ever been here," he ordered in his deep masculine voice to show his authority over the two officers.

"Yes, sir," the other man spoke up, while going off to get the cabin striped of all signs, while Mike walked out to talk to Max.

"Just like old times, huh?" Max commented, sadly.

"Yeah," he agreed, holding back on some crucial information, until he was certain they were alone.

Turning back to see the look on his face, he knew something was up. "Okay, what's up, Mike? I know that look all too well."

"Do you still have your service revolver, don't you?"

"Yeah, why?"

"I didn't want to say this in front of Miss Hall, but..."

"Mike...?"

"He's already leaving behind casualties."

"Who?"

"The PI. He had just gotten the report in when Ted spotted him."

"Oh, my God," he groaned, resting his elbows up on the side of his truck, while feeling sick to his stomach. "What am I going to do, Mike?" he asked, shaking his head.

"We're working on it. For now, keep a close eye on your lady. Oh, and Max...?"

"Yeah?"

"You have been reinstated."

"I've been what...?" He looked back at his friend.

"Yep!" he smiled, handing Max his shield.

Seeing the inscription on it, he just shook his head. "This can't be right!"

"Oh, but it is. You are now Captain Maxwell Brummet, working right along with Roger and I."

"Roger, too?" he laughed, at the thought of him having to tote his revolver around again, now that he had already planned his retirement by putting in more time at the store, and to spend more time fishing, and now this. "Does he know yet?"

"Oh, yeah, and boy was he..."

"Let me guess, he cussed up a mean streak over it?"

"Oh... yeah. And Max..."

"What?" he asked, while unable to take his eyes off his new shield.

"I had to work real hard to get that for you. The chief

wasn't all that sure it was a good idea, until I convinced him that you wouldn't just sit back and let us do all of the work."

"Damn straight, I won't," he shook his head, while going around to reach in and pull his truck seat forward to get out his service revolver and shoulder holster. While strapping it on, he continued to shake off the sickening feeling of what was about to go down around them. "Damn it, Mike, I had never thought I would be putting this back on again."

"I know, partner, let's just hope we never have to use them," he groaned, while looking down at Max's service revolver. "Damn, it's just a shame that it's only to be temporary."

"Yeah," he growled, turning to grab his vest.

"Max…?" Cory walked up just in time to see him putting it on.

"Cory…" he turned, seeing her standing there, looking at him strangely.

"You look like a cop," she smiled sweetly.

"He was, once," Mike spoke up, seeing the look on Max's face, "until he lost his leg. In fact, he was one of the best officers on the Department. When he left, it was pretty hard on most of us."

"Daddy never told me!"

"Are you all right with it?" he asked, looking into her eyes lovingly.

"Sure! It even makes you look kind of sexy!"

"I'm glad you seem to think so," he laughed, feeling a little more at ease. "In fact, you have no idea just how much I needed to see that sweet smile of yours right about now."

"Oh… Maxine!" she burst out laughing.

"Maxine…?" Mike cracked up too, while looking at his old partner.

"Yes," he commented, while turning to shoot her a warning look, when taking her into his arms, "it's an old joke."

With that sweet smile of hers, Cory chose to ignore his warning, while lightly brush her lips along his jaw line.

"Stop that, you mean little brat."

"Oh, pooh…" she pouted playfully, "you sure know how to take the fun out of a person's day."

"Yeah, well, we have to be going now anyway, or have you forgotten?"

"O…kay…!" she turned, playfully kicking at a small rock in the driveway. As she did, she sneaked a peek back at him, only to see that he was grinning at her the whole time, while shaking his head.

Arriving back at Roger's place, Mike, Max and Cory walked in just in time to have supper. During the meal, Cory's mind seemed to be elsewhere.

"Cory… where are you, honey?" Rose asked, while walking over to give her daughter a cup of hot chocolate.

"I'm sorry," she jumped up quite suddenly, when nearly knocking the cup out of her mother's hand. "If you'll excuse me, I'm going in to take a shower and get ready for bed."

"Wait!" Mike jumped up, cutting her off, before she could get very far. "Miss Hall, just give me a minute to check things out first, before you go in to take your shower."

"But why?" she began, then seeing Max's expression, she understood. "All right, if you feel you have to."

"I'm afraid so," he replied, turning to Max. "Why don't you come with me?"

With a nod of his head, he got up to accompany his friend into her room, while stopping first to give her a reassuring hug. "It's going to be all right."

"I hope so!" she replied, as he slowly pulled away to walk into her room with his old partner.

"What are you thinking?" Max turned to Mike after leaving.

"From the sound of this guy, we need to check her room

out regularly. He could be here already, we don't know. But just the same…"

"I know, don't let my guard down, not even for a second."

"Yeah, this guy is really dangerous."

"So I'm finding out!" he exclaimed, while going in to check out the bathroom window, while Mike did the same in the bedroom.

Afterwards, the two came back out into the living room.

"Listen," Mike spoke up, heading for the front door, "it's getting late and tomorrow is going to be a very busy day. How about we all get some rest."

"Yeah, but if you two don't mind," Max spoke up, noticing how unhappy Cory was over the whole situation, "I'll see you in the morning. I'm staying here tonight on the couch."

"Sure," Roger nodded.

"Lock up, though, before you call it a night," Mike ordered.

"All right."

Not noticing the change on Cory's face after everyone had gone their own way, looking at the couch, she realized this that it was the same one in her dream.

"No…" she turned quickly and ran into her bedroom, closing the door behind her.

"Cory…?" he called out, seeing her odd departure, and became worried.

"No…" she cried again, while running over to throw herself onto her bed, "it can't be!" she continued, knowing now it was to be in this cabin that she was to meet with her untimely death. "Oh, Daddy, why does this have to be happening to me? Why…?"

❧ *Chapter Eleven* ❧

"Cory…!" Max called out from the other side of the closed door, "are you all right?"

Wiping away her tears, she got up to open it. "Max…!" she tried to hide her tears so as not to worry him.

"Are you all right?"

"Yeah, sure, I'm just tired."

"Are you sure that's all it is?"

"Yes!"

"All right!"

Just as he went to turn away, she cried out stopping him, "No… wait!"

"Yes?"

"Will you wait up for me, I need to talk to you when I get through with my shower? It's about…" She hesitated before going on.

"The dream?" he asked, seeing her nod her response. "All right, when you're ready, come on out."

Closing the door, she went into the bathroom, where once again her thoughts were miles away, when suddenly something hit the bathroom window, bringing her thoughts reeling back to the present. "What…?" she shrieked, while grabbing for her bathrobe. Wrapping it around her securely, she yanked open the bathroom door and proceeded to run back out into the living room, screaming, "Max..." she continued, when bringing him up off the couch in a hurry, while on the phone with Mike.

"Cory..." he called back, while holding the cell phone to the side, when she ran into his arms, crying. "What is it?"

"A...a noise!" she cried, pointing. "Outside the...the bathroom window!"

"Stay in here!" he ordered. "Mike..."

"I heard, and I'm on my way! Wait for me."

After hanging up, he turned back to Cory as their mothers came hurrying out into the living room, hearing all the commotion.

"Max..." Mary cried.

"It's okay, I won't be alone. I was just on the phone with Mike. He's on his way back now."

While Max was reassuring them, Mike showed up at the front door.

"You ready?" he asked, while already having his service revolver out and ready.

"Yeah, let's go," he agreed, heading for the open door, with his revolver drawn.

Stopping, he turned back to Cory.

"Be careful!" she and the others called out after them.

"We will," he grinned, just before turning to head out.

Running into her mother's arms, Cory cried.

"It'll be all right," she returned, holding her close, "they know what they're doing!"

"They sure do!" Mary added, when stopping at Cory's side, before going into the kitchen. "How about if I make us all something warm to drink, while we're waiting?"

Nodding her head, Rose took Cory back over to the couch to have a seat. "It is getting pretty chilly out, don't you think?" she asked, while hoping to take Cory's mind off what was going on outside.

"Chilly, yeah, it's getting chilly," she agreed, sitting down on the couch, while turning to look off into the flames of the fireplace. In the meantime, the expression on her face looked as though Ted was going to succeed, and sooner than she had expected.

Meanwhile, standing in the kitchen doorway, Mary shook her head sadly, when Rose turned back to look at her.

Nearly an hour went by when both Max and Mike returned.

"What happened?" Mary spoke up first, upon seeing them walking in.

"We found a mud ball beneath the bathroom window," Mike explained, shaking his head.

"Oh…?" Cory cried, just as Max came over to join her.

"Yes, but it wasn't anything to worry about."

"No…" she pulled away, "if it was Ted, I know what he's doing."

"What?" Mike asked, going over to sit across from her.

"He's checking out the security!" she exclaimed, looking to Max.

"That would mean…" he began, while both Rose and Mary were bringing in more mugs of hot cocoa.

"No," Mike jumped in, offering a hand, "it's not likely, unless he flew in. And I don't know if he could have done that."

"Why?" Rose asked.

"Because all the airports between New York and here are being watched."

"Even the private ones?" Mary asked, while handing the guys their mugs.

"Even the private ones," Mike returned.

"Unless…" Max spoke up.

"He has changed his looks!" Cory finished.

"And if he has," Mike agreed, "then what we're dealing with is one very sick individual, who won't stop at anything to get what he wants."

"Well, what we need now is some sleep," Mary suggested.

"Yeah, mom's right," Max agreed. "I'll call Roger and let him know that you're on your way."

"Good idea," Mike said, turning to Cory, while Max went on to make the call. "We are going to do everything in our power to keep you safe, Miss Hall. Try and hold onto that, okay?"

"Thanks, Mike, but Ted is clever. He will find a weak spot and get through it. And when he does..." she looked away, "he will kill me. I know him, and he will succeed, or die trying."

"All set." Max turned to see the grim look on their faces.

"Tomorrow," Mike spoke up seriously. "We're going to have to iron out some of these wrinkles."

"We will," Max got up to walk him over to the door.

"Well, if you'll excuse us, we're off to bed again," Mary announced, leaving the room with Rose at her side.

"Cory...!" Rose turned back.

"Goodnight, Mom."

"Goodnight, dear."

Just before closing the door though, Rose looked back on her tired daughter's face, and just shook her head.

Meanwhile, out on the front porch, Mike turned to Max, "Stay close to her Max, she knows something."

"Yeah, and I have a feeling it has something to do with a dream she had recently."

"Oh?" he asked. "Find out what it was. It may help!"

"Yeah, it just might!" He shook his head, while looking back in at Cory, who at the time was curled up on the couch, waiting for him, while still wearing her terrycloth bathrobe.

"Max," Mike spoke up, interrupting his thoughts.

"Yeah?"

"I'm not much into these kinds of things, but I'll take whatever we can get."

"I'll do what I can," he returned, patting his friend on the back. "See ya in the morning, all right?"

"Yeah," Mike agreed, while turning to head back up to Roger's store.

Going back inside, Max went right over to cuddle up next to Cory, after locking the front door. "You know you really should go in and try and get some sleep."

"I can't!" she cried, when turning even more into his arms, while wrapping her own arms up around his neck.

"Cory, it's going to be all right."

"No…" she cried out again, "it isn't!"

"Cory…"

"Max… I'm scared! I'm scared that if I close my eyes the dreams will just keep coming back again and again!"

"Speaking of which, do you remember anything more about these dreams of yours?"

"Only the lights."

"What about them?"

"They went out just before…" she cried, looking up into his eyes.

"Cory, no…!" he cried, as well.

"Oh… Max…!"

Changing the subject, he got up, taking her hands, "Come on," he suggested, while pulling her up with him, "how about if I stay with you until you fall asleep?"

"Will you?"

"Sure, just let me make certain that everything is locked up first."

"All right."

Going back into her room, she quickly changed, while waiting on Max.

"Oh… Max…!" she cried sadly, looking into the mirror on the dressing table.

Noticing how she looked in her gown, she wondered if they would ever be together once Ted was stopped.

It wasn't long after that Max walked back into the bedroom to see her dressed in a long white nightgown. "You look so beautiful standing there," he groaned, admiring how much she had grown into a beautiful woman.

"Oh?" she asked, while pulling back her long brown hair, as his eyes strayed down over her.

"Oh… yes," he replied, pulling his thoughts back to the present, while going over to the bed to pull off his boots.

That night he held her until she was finally able to fall asleep. When she did, her dreams continued to return, with Ted standing off in the shadows of the cabin, sneering at her.

"What are you up to?" he asked.

"N…nothing!" she cried, looking for a way to get away from him.

"Then why do I find that so hard to believe?" he snarled, while going up to pull her into his arms, with one very sick look on his face.

In the meantime, tossing and turning in her sleep, she continued to cry out, while struggling to pull away from him. *"No… I don't love you! Why can't you just accept that I love someone else?"*

Looking into her eyes with that same sadistic laugh, he growled, *"Because you're mine, and if I can't have you, no one will. Not even your precious Max. You're mine, Cory! Mine!"* he repeated over and over in her dream.

"No…! No…!" she cried out in her sleep, while waking Max. Though, with no success, her dream just kept going, with Ted chasing her out of the cabin, and through the woods, as she continued to cry out. *"Max…help me! Please… help me…!"* she screamed over and over again.

Seeing her continuous struggle, Max tried shaking her.

"Cory, wake up…" he called out, "You're having a bad dream! Come on, snap out of it, girl!" he spoke softly, while trying not to wake the others, while he continued shaking her.

"*No! No! Let me go! I don't love you. I love Max! I have always loved Max! There could never be anyone else for me, but him! Please…*"

"*Where is your Max now,*" he laughed. "*And why isn't he here to protect you?*"

"*He is here! He is…*" she cried. "Oh, Max, where are you…? I need you…!"

This time he heard her. "I'm here, Cory! I'm here! You have got to fight him. You can do it," he called out to her through her dream. "Come back to me, Cory! Follow my voice."

"Oh, Max, I can't see you! I'm scared, Max! Tell me what to do…!"

"Run, Cory. Run as fast as you can."

Doing just that, in her dream she ran as fast as she could. Reaching the front of the cabin, she ran inside, closing it behind her. While trying to lock it, Ted showed up, knocking her down as he burst through the door.

"*You thought you were going to get away from me so easily? Not this time, Cory. You're going to pay for dumping me. You're going to pay with your life,*" he growled, while reaching out for her.

"No…!" she screamed, scrambling to get away, as she ran toward the kitchen doorway, only to get stopped once again, as he grabbed for her arm to throw her back into the living room.

Just then, she found herself falling over the couch, the same couch as before, while hitting her head on the coffee table, before ending up on the floor.

Just then, the old dream repeated itself, with Ted on top of her, while holding a stiletto that he had pulled from his boot, when preparing to stab her.

"No…!" she screamed, struggling even harder in her sleep now as the knife began slowly coming down at her. "Oh, God, no_____!"

"Cory…" Max had to shout this time, while pulling her into his arms, "God, please… you have got to help her. Please_____ wake her up_____!"

Suddenly, she jolted back in his arms a couple of times, when making him wonder if she were having a seizure.

"Cory…" he continued to hold her steadily, while watching for her eyes to flutter, as her body slowed itself down some. "Cory!" he called out again.

"M…Max…?" she moaned, waking to the scent of his cologne. "Oh, Max…" she cried, opening her eyes to see the look of concern written all over his face in the semi darkened room.

"Cory, talk to me. What was it? Was it Ted?"

"Oh, Max… I know where I'm going to die…!"

"What? Where?"

"It's here. Here in this cabin."

"What…? Are you sure?" he asked, pulling away to look into her eyes.

"Yes! Oh, God, yes! It's that couch out there. It's the same one in my dreams!"

"Oh, God," he held her close, "what the hell have I done?" he swore. "I have to get you out of here!"

"And just where would you take me? Ted will only follow!"

"I don't know!" he shook with building emotions. "God help me, I don't know!"

"Oh, Max, whatever happened to our normal life?" she cried on his shoulder.

"I wish I knew," he turned to sit more on the edge of the bed, while running his hands through his hair. "Damn… I wish I knew."

Getting up to get her a cool washcloth, he soon came back

to offer it to her, while she cried, curling up next to him, when he went to join her once again. "Max, I'm so scared…!"

"I know you are," he held her close, "I am too. God, I am too."

"Please… don't ever let me go…! Just hold me…!"

Doing so, after getting them settled back into bed, he covered them both, before wrapping his own arms around her waist and shoulders. "Cory?" he whispered softly in her hair.

"Mmmm…?"

"I want you to know, you will never be alone while you're here. We will get married," he told her, "and we will have those babies, believe that."

"I want so much to believe that, but…"

"But, nothing. You have to, Cory. I love you. Hold on to that, and never forget it. *Never.*"

"Mmmm… Max…" she whispered wistfully, "I love you, too!"

Kissing her forehead tenderly, she was finally able to slip off to sleep without any more bad dreams.

While holding her in his arms, he slipped the wet washcloth from her hand, while listening, as she laughed lightly in her sleep, when dreaming this time of him at the old fishing hole, holding a little fair-haired boy, while teaching him the techniques of being a good fisherman.

By morning, Max woke before she did, to go into the bathroom and wash off the effects of what the night before did to him. "Damn," he grumbled, seeing the face looking back at him from the mirror.

Finishing, he returned to see that she hadn't moved much. Smiling tiredly, he tucked the blanket up around her shoulders, before going out to see what the others were doing.

"Good morning, dear," his mother greeted, as he walked into the kitchen. "Are you feeling all right?"

"Cory…" Rose began.

"She's sleeping still. Do we have any coffee on? I feel as though I could drink a whole pot."

"Sure! Just let me get it poured for you," his mother offered.

"The dream again?" Rose asked.

"We heard her cry out," Mary explained. "When we came out to see what was going on, we saw that you were in with her. It sounded pretty bad."

"It was," he shuddered at the thought of what had happened once it was over. "Rose, we need to get her in to see a doctor. Last night…" he began, "she nearly went into a seizure."

"Oh, my Lord!" She jumped up to head for her daughter's room, when Max held out an arm to stop her.

"She's all right now," he explained, when a soft smile came to his lips.

"Max…" they both asked, seeing it, "what?"

"When she fell off to sleep again," he laughed, "I think she began having another dream." Seeing their alarm, he held up a reassuring hand. "No, I have a feeling it was a rather good one, this time."

"Oh?" they asked.

"Yeah, it was about us!" he smiled richly. "And now, if you don't mind, how about that coffee?" he returned, when going over to the counter to get it himself, just about the time Cory walked in.

Looking up to see the lines under her eyes, Mary shook her head. "Are you okay, dear?"

"I am now," she replied, taking a cup offered her from Max, before going over to have a seat at the table.

"The dream didn't come back, did it?" he asked, while joining her for breakfast.

"No," she whispered, when her mother walked up to hand

them each a plate of food. Looking at it, she tried to smile, "This looks pretty good, Mom!"

"Thanks, dear," she replied, hearing the front door open, and then close.

"What do I smell coming from the kitchen?" Roger asked, while walking in.

"Hey!" Max greeted. "What's going on with the security?"

"Mike's up working on getting his crew together right now," he announced, while going over to get a plate of food Rose was offering him. Smiling, he turned back to go over to the table before continuing. "We're to meet with him in about an hour at the store."

"Good, let's just hope that we will have enough coverage."

"Me too," he replied, while looking over at Cory. "Now, don't you worry none, things will work out, you'll see," he offered, while patting her on the hand.

"Thanks, Roger," she smiled, while getting up with Max to take their dishes to the sink.

"Anything for my little lady!" he laughed.

"Oh, Roger…" she cried, coming back over to give him a surprising hug from behind.

Blushing, he shook his head, and continued to eat his meal, while she and Max walked out onto the back porch for some fresh air.

"It's even beautiful here too, don't you think?" she asked, while taking in the breeze, as it lifted a few strands of her rich brown hair.

"Sure is!" he agreed, but not about the scenery out over the valley, but what was standing right in front of him.

Turning, she saw his admiring smile, as he went to lean back against the rail. "What are you thinking?" she asked warmly.

"About that little brat I used to torment years ago," he grinned.

"Oh… and do you think she's thinking about you?" she asked, while leaning in beside him.

"I don't know, is she?"

"Always," she turned to look back out over the valley.

Pushing away from the rail, he took her into his arms. "Oh… and what is she thinking?" he asked lovingly, while bringing her up even closer to him.

"This," she replied, while going up on tiptoes to claim what she'd been waiting for since last night.

As they kissed, feeling the heat building between them yet again, he tightened his hold on her, until he felt her fingertips going up through his hair, and her body molding to his. "Oh God, girl, I want you…" he groaned, while running his hand up through her long soft hair, to pull her head back to look up at him, while his breath was so hot against her face.

"Mmmm… Max…" she groaned as well, through smoldering eyes, when at that very moment, he bent back down to reclaim her lips.

Soon their moment was about to be interrupted, when finishing his breakfast Roger walked out onto the back porch, not meaning to interrupt them. "Ah…" he cleared his throat, looking slightly off to one side, smiling, "are we about ready to go?"

"Sure!" Max returned, while pulling away to catch his breath. "How about you?" he asked, while looking fondly into her smiling eyes.

"Just give me a minute," she replied, heading back inside.

"Take your time…!" he called out.

After seeing her off, joining him at the back rail, Roger offered, "Sorry, my friend."

"No, don't be. I needed the interruption," he grinned sheepishly.

"Oh…?" he questioned, seeing Max's flushed expression.

"God, Roger, I want her so bad," he groaned, shaking his head. "Even just looking at her, I can feel the two of us making love. God, it's so intense just being close to her."

"You really got it bad for her, don't you?" he burst out laughing, when Max turned to rest his elbows on the rail.

"Yeah, and then some. Damn it, Roger…"

"What…?"

"He knew…! He knew she loved me."

"Who are we talking about? Who knew? Ted?"

"No. Bob! He was just about to tell me, when…"

"His heart was about to give out?"

Shaking his head miserably, he stood, turning back to face his old friend, while looking even more miserable, "We had no business out there, damn it anyway!"

"No, but you know how he was. If it had to be done, he'd be out doing it."

"Yeah, but I should have said something to him. God, we both knew it was going to rain that day," he groaned, running his fingers through his hair.

"Yes, and if I recall, we were expecting a cold snap to come through. He didn't want to get you out in that with your job and all. He knew you were too vital of a cop to be missing work."

"Damn the work. What good did it do me when I lost my leg?" he growled, taking in a shaky breath, before going back in to join Cory.

"Hey, there!" Mary stopped short of the back door, when Max walked in, passing her by in a huff. Turning to Roger, who remained on the back deck, she asked, "What's going on?"

"Our boy there is finding it growing more difficult to wait until the honeymoon to have the woman he loves, not to mention Bob's death."

"Oh…?" Rose spoke up, joining them.

Meanwhile, hearing the laughter out back, Max stopped

for a moment, thinking what might have caused it. Smiling, he went on into Cory's room to get her bed made up, before heading up to the store for their meeting.

"Max?" she called out, hearing him.

"Yeah?"

"What is this?" she asked, opening the bathroom door to show him a little crystal horse.

"Well, it seems you have a reminder of my undying love for you," he smiled.

"Oh...?" she smiled too, while walking out past him.

"What?" he asked, turning back to see what she was doing, when she turned back to hand him a small red velvety box.

Opening it, she stood, smiling up at him.

"What?" he nearly fell back on the bed laughing, when he saw the delicate wood carved egg. "When did you get this?" he asked, holding it out in front of him.

"Before I got here!" she continued, while running a few fingers over its soft surface.

"Damn, I remember when you threw that God forsaken egg at me."

"Yes, and I hit your car instead!" she laughed.

"And to think you were in love with me then."

"Yes."

"Wow, waiting all those years for me, not knowing what I'd be doing, either."

"Daddy told me not to give up, just before he died."

Feeling the sting of those words, he forced back the tears of that horrible day in the field to try and put a smile on his face. "And," he began, having to work hard to keep his words from giving away the pain he was feeling, "I have a feeling he was trying to tell me that, too!"

"Oh?" she asked, while looking deep within his eyes, as the pain had barely stayed at bay.

"Yes, but he didn't, and you never did, did you?" he asked, turned away, when feeling her puzzlement.

"No, I knew somehow you were one."

"And don't you ever forget it, either," Roger replied, while walking in on them. "Well, shall we get the show on the road?"

"Yeah," Max agreed, heading out to the living room with the little wooden egg in hand.

Looking back to see Cory's apprehension, Roger offered her a warm friendly hug on their way out. "It'll all work out, just you wait and see."

"Sure it will!" she grumbled quietly, while grabbing her jacket, on their way out. Though, it wasn't so much the meeting that had her bothered, but something in Max's eyes.

❧ *Chapter Twelve* ❧

Arriving at the back door of Roger's store, Mike greeted Max, Cory, and Roger, when they walked in, closing the door behind them. "All right, now that we are all here, let's get started, shall we?" Mike instructed, while going over to a table to pick up a stack of fliers with Ted's picture on. "Kevin, pass these out. Make sure everyone gets one," he instructed.

"Yes, sir," he returned, while giving one to each person in the back room.

"First, let me start by introducing my crew," Mike went on. "Frank and Lois Miller," he pointed in their general direction, "will be staying at the old cabin. Tom and Bill are to be your watchdogs. They'll be staying close by at all times."

"You don't have fleas, do you?" Cory laughed, while trying hard to make light of the situation, after the dream she'd had the night before. "Sorry, but I wish I really did have a dog."

"Don't worry, we know you must be feeling pretty uncomfortable about having to live like this," Tom, a husky built man in his late forties, offered thoughtfully, "and especially, with a wedding to plan for, we hear."

"Yes, and yes I am, but I know it has to be this way until he's caught."

"Hopefully, Miss Hall," Mike spoke up, "this young lady standing next to you will be able to help make you feel more comfortable," he went on, when pointing to a young officer not much older than Cory, with brown hair and eyes. "Miss Hall," Mike cleared his throat, "your companion, Kate Martin. She'll be your secretary, friend and sounding board."

"Oh…?" Cory smiled. "Do you like music, Miss Kate?"

"I love music! What kind?"

"The oldies, easy listening, you know the kind you can sing to!"

"Captain Jones, I am going to love this assignment."

"Good, but we have to drop our official names. This Ted Harden is bad news. He has already killed one man that we know of, so let's watch ourselves out there. Try to blend in as much as you can. And now it's Roger's turn to introduce his crew," he announced, turning the floor over to the storekeeper.

"All right," he began, "if Ted is out there hiding, Leo, Paul and Marcus, here, will spot him. They know every inch of these woods, and will get with one of us if they see him. Not only that, Leo is one of the best tree climbers around. He will work most of the time up high. So don't you worry none, little lady, we will find him, and we will… stop him."

"All right," Mike took over, seeing that he was finished, "memorize everyone's faces. Ted may even try to pass himself off as a plain old Joe. So stay on your toes, and trust no one. Max, as everyone here should already know, is Miss Hall's fiancé. He was also one of our finest on the force back in Cedar Rapids, and my old partner, and friend," he turned to Max, proudly, and smiled. "If you can't find me, go to him for help."

"I'll be nearby at all times," Max announced, looking down on Cory.

"Yes, he will, and to add to all of this," Mike went on, holding up one of Ted's fliers, "Max has also been threatened by this man. So I want everyone here to carry one of these, and remember what this man looks like, and watch for him. If you see him, don't play the hero. He would just as soon kill you, as to look at you. Man or woman," he put in morbidly, "he doesn't care. He is on a mission here, to kill Miss Hall, so that he can keep these two a part."

"If there isn't anything else," Max spoke up, seeing Cory's expression turn grave at what was being said.

"All right then," Mike finished, "let's start by getting acquainted with each other, and then go on to our appointed areas."

"Miss Hall," Kate started up, looking puzzled, "Captain... I mean Mike, told me that I am to look as though we're working on your book...?"

"She's a writer," Roger replied, walking up with a huge grin on his face, while giving her a warm fatherly hug, seeing how she looked as though she could use one. "And to add, a darn good one at that."

"Oh, wow, now I know who you are...! You're that ghost story writer, Ms. Spencer!"

"Yes, I am. But here, I'm known as Cory Hall."

After giving them all a few more minutes, Mike interrupted, "All right, now that we have that covered, let's move on now to our areas."

"Shall we go?" Max asked, taking her hand in his, while putting an arm around her shoulder to leave.

Heading out the back door, everyone went off to their own assigned areas.

"Captain... I'm sorry, I... mean Mike?" Kate spoke up, while Max took Cory off for a walk, before she went up to get started on a book she had been working on.

"Yes?" He turned to see her questioning expression.

"Shall I follow along, just in case they run into trouble?"

"No, Max is quite capable of handling things if they run into any kind of trouble along the way. Besides, I have our other men out walking the woods now to keep an eye on them. They'll be fine out there."

"What shall I be doing while they're out for their walk?"

"Getting settled in. You did bring some things with you, didn't you? Because I'm sure I told everyone to do so in case this could get pretty lengthy."

"Yes, sir, I did."

"Good. In that case go on back to the cabin and get yourself familiar with your surroundings. Oh, and both their mothers are there now, so you won't be alone for the time being."

"All right." Taking her leave, she went out to her car to get what things she had brought with her, while Mike slipped out back to watch his old friend walk down a path that was sure to take them over by her father's fishing hole.

"Watch yourself out there, buddy," he spoke just above a whisper.

Sensing Mike's concern, Max turned back and offered a reassuring smile, before turning back to the woman on his arm.

"He'll be careful out there," Roger spoke up, when coming out of his store, while leaving his young assistant to watch over things for him.

"Yeah, I'm sure he will, but this Ted Harden…" Mike turned to Roger, "he's hell bent on getting what he wants."

"He'll have to go through the whole lot of us to get to her, too," he swore, gritting his teeth. "I'll play hell before he hurts my little lady."

"Your, little lady?" he laughed. "Just how did you come up with that name?"

"Just look at her," he grinned, seeing the last of Cory, just before they had time to round the bend.

Hearing her feathery light laugh, Mike agreed, heading back down to Roger's place to go over a few more last minute details he and Roger had yet to work on.

Meanwhile, getting closer to the fishing hole, Max went on, "This has to be hard on you, and Lord only knows it's tearing me up inside, as well."

"It is," she agreed, reaching their favorite rock. "I just wish it would all go away."

Going around to stand in behind her, he brought her back to wrap his arms around her waist. There, they stood in silence, while listening to the water running off its small supply that came down from the hillside, which fed off a nearby river.

Breaking the silence, he shifted his weight from his bad leg to his good, "Your new companion, she seems nice enough!"

"She does, doesn't she?" she agreed, while turning in his arms to face him. "What will you be doing now that she's here to watch over me?"

"Work with Mike and Roger. Not to mention, keeping tabs on Ted's location, in case he's ever seen in the area."

"Will I…"

Knowing what was on her mind, he placed a finger to her lips, "Count on it. I wouldn't dare stay away from you now. Not with that lunatic out there running around loose, trying to scare you."

"Oh… Max…!" she cried, reaching up to hug him.

Standing there for what seemed like hours, just holding onto each other, he finally pulled away to study her saddened expression, "You aren't still thinking he'll get to you, are you?"

"I'm trying not to, but…"

"Cory, we'll find him, we will!"

Finding him though, wasn't going to be as easy as they thought. As the next few days were quiet, when the film producer arrived and went over the script with Cory to iron out a few wrinkles.

Afterwards, Kate helped her work on her next book, after she had seen her mother and Mary off.

"This is a lot of fun, isn't it?" Kate asked, sitting cross-legged on the living room floor, while going over a few of the pages, catching errors that Cory was making due to the surrounding circumstances that were keeping her bottled up in Roger's cabin.

"It would be if we were out on the deck where the fresh air is!" she complained, while giving the pencil a toss across the room, where it landed next to the fireplace.

Pushing away from her laptop she got up to go into the kitchen to fix them both some coffee. "Kate," she called back.

"Just a minute!" she returned, going back to Mike, whom she had called, when Cory left the room.

"What's going on?" he asked, sensing a problem.

"It's Cory, she's feeling closed in back here. Can we get her out onto the back deck for some fresh air, if we put some guys back there to cover her?"

Looking over at Max, who was preoccupied with something else, he came back, "Sure, I think we can take care of that!" he grinned.

Looking up at him, Max asked, "Take care of what?"

"You'll see," he smiled. "Kate?"

"Yes?"

"Since there hasn't been any trouble lately, I don't see a problem with that. So tell her to hang in there for just a couple more minutes, to give me time to move the guys around."

Wondering what was going on, Max gave the stack of papers he was working on a toss on the counter, before walking over to see what Mike was up to.

"Thanks, boss," she smiled, when Cory too, was wondering what that was about, when appearing poised in the kitchen doorway, waiting.

"Kate…?"

"Hang in there, Mike's working on something so that we

can get you out on the back deck for some of that fresh air you so deserve."

"Thanks...!" she cried, coming up to give Kate a grateful hug.

"Now," she pulled back, "what were you about to ask, before I had to cut you off?"

"Coffee. Did you want some French Vanilla in it?"

"Sure, that sounds great!" she agreed at the thought of the smooth taste of French Vanilla being put into her coffee. Following Cory back into the kitchen, she went on gaily, "You know I haven't done anything like this in such a long time."

"Anything like what?"

Stopping suddenly in their tracks, both girls spun around, not hearing anyone come in.

As for Cory though, she had nearly dropped her cup at the sudden surprise of seeing Mike standing in the kitchen doorway. "Mike... don't do that!" she screamed.

"I wouldn't have had to if a certain cop had done her job!"

"Sorry, sir," Kate suddenly felt chastised. "I didn't think you would have gotten back here that soon!"

"Take it easy, Kate, I don't mean to come down on you quite so hard, but we do have to be careful."

"Yes, of course, sir, we do!"

"Mike... where's Max?" Cory asked, looking around him.

"I have him working on something," he smiled coyly. "And now, if you're ready for that fresh air, I'm ready too, since we have some men up in the trees and walking the grounds, as far back as the other side of the valley."

"That's pretty far!" Cory thought out loud, while turning to look out over the back deck.

Taking that moment, looking to Kate, he just shook his head.

Without warning, Cory turned back to excuse herself. "I'll just go and get my recorder, before we get started," she replied, heading back into the other room, where she found herself starting to have flashbacks of the dream that was to take her away from the man she loved.

"I feel so bad for her," Kate went on, while pouring her coffee. "Do you want a cup?" she offered.

"Sure, but I can get it," he smiled shyly, when coming around her to pick up a cup from the dish drainer. "And for Max, too, as this is really tearing him up, after promising her father he would watch over her. Though now he feels as if he is about to fail her somehow."

"That is bad," she agreed, while taking a sip of her coffee.

"Yeah, it is."

Walking over to the back door with his cup, Kate asked, sensing more to this then he was letting on. "What is it? What's really going on?"

Turning back, he just shook his head, "None of us really realized just how dangerous this man could really be."

"And Max, where is he now?"

"He'll be here soon," he replied, looking toward the living room doorway.

Sensing something was wrong, he was about to head in and check on her, when she returned, carrying her recorder and a blanket.

"I'm ready!" she announced, shrugging off what had just been going through her mind, while in the other room.

"Are you sure?" he asked, studying her expression.

"Yes. Why?"

"Oh, nothing," he shrugged, noting her apprehension, as she suddenly looked away. "I'll see you two ladies later," he smiled, while going over to open the back door for them.

"But I thought…" Cory began.

"He has something to take care of," Kate smiled, knowing all along what was going on, when Mike went to take his leave.

Out on the back deck, Cory went over to sit on the swing,

when Kate went over to stand by the railing to look out over the woods.

"Can you see any of his men?" Cory asked.

"Not yet, but they're out there!"

"How can you tell?"

"I can feel them," she was saying, when she caught sight of one up in the tree.

Turning so as not to give him away, she went over to take her seat near Cory.

Just about the time they were into her ninth chapter, Max walked up the back steps to see one very sleepy Cory, who was now putting aside her recorder.

"Hi, there," Kate greeted, noticing how Cory was about to curl up in her blanket to fall off to sleep. "I'll just leave the two of you alone now," she smiled.

"Thanks, she'll be all right with me," he grinned, while going over to join Cory on the swing.

Leaving the two to spend some time alone with each other, Kate went back in to get herself another cup of coffee.

"Are things going all right out there?" Mike asked, when walking back in to join her.

"Sure looks like it," she replied, while going over to the back door with him to look out at the couple, when seeing how Max so lovingly wrapped the blanket up around her more. "Wow, he really loves her, doesn't he?"

"Yes," he grinned, seeing his friend in a whole new light.

"Mike," she spoke up, interrupting his thoughts, "I'm going to need some more clothes to finish out the week. Can I possibly go and get them, since we have plenty of people here to cover things?"

"I don't see why not. It's been pretty quiet around here."

"I won't be gone very long."

"See to it that you're not," he ordered, when turning to look back at her.

Meanwhile, out on the back porch, Cory turned into Max's arms, yawning. "I…I'm so… glad you'…re here…!"

"Me too…!" he smiled down at her, as she was now slipping off to sleep in his arms. "Me too," he repeated, while he went to rest his leg up on the chair across from them. "Oh, Cory…" he went on thinking out loud to himself, while listening to her soft wisps of breaths, "if only I had the insight on our future that you have, I could have saved myself the headaches Karen had caused me. And then again maybe that God awful day out in the field would have never happened, and your father…" He stopped, when feeling the pain of Bob's loss return, *'God, why…?'* he cried silently.

Later that day, after letting Kate go to get some clothes, Cory had just finished her book.

"Well this one was sure easy!" she thought out loud, while packaging it up to get it ready to mail.

Stopping for a moment, she went over to look out the front door, not knowing Mike had a man nearby. Seeing the smoke coming from the chimney up at Roger's store, she wondered what the guys were doing.

"Miss Hall," Kevin spoke up, not meaning to scare her.

"Kevin…!" she cried, when then recalling him from the old cabin, and again the other day from Roger's store.

"Yes, ma'am. Were you wanting to go somewhere? I can take you, if you did!"

"No, just thinking what the others were doing, is all. Kevin?" she stopped, when just about to close the door.

"Yes, ma'am?"

"Has anyone heard from Kate, yet? I thought she would have been back by now."

"Not that I'm aware of, no."

"Okay, thanks!" she smiled, while turning to close the door.

Meanwhile, up at the store, they were discussing what Mike was going to do with the extra men, since it had been so quiet.

"I'm thinking about pulling some of them off for a while, just to see if that might bring Ted out of hiding," he was saying, while pouring himself another cup of Roger's powerful brew, which Roger fondly refers to as coffee.

"Are you sure you want to do that?" Max asked, sounding worried.

"What, pull some of the guys off, or drink some of Roger's coffee?" he laughed.

Seeing what his friend was trying to do to ease some of the tension, Max just grinned, and shook his head.

"I sure hope so. Besides we have a storm front moving in, and I don't want any sick people on my hands."

"Hey, Mike," Kevin called out, when coming in through the back door, after being relieved from his post to tell Mike about a call he had gotten from the man who had relieved him, "we just got a call from Tony. It seems that his car broke down on his way back from town. Do you want me to take a guy and go and get him?"

"No, damn it!" he growled, tossing some papers down on the counter, before turning to Max. "Why don't you come with me? We could sure use some fresh air."

"Yeah, but what about Cory?"

"She should be all right with Kevin watching over her, as well as Roger's guys walking the woods. Not to mention, Roger here. Right Roger?"

"Yeah."

"Besides, I haven't called the others off just yet, so that'll keep things around here pretty safe, until we get back."

"Sure, all right. Just as long as we're back before dark," he agreed regretfully. "But if we're going, I'd better go back and talk to Cory first."

After he had left, not seeing the look of confusion on Kevin's face, Mike turned to the two of them, "While we're gone, I want the two of you to keep a close eye on her. We shouldn't be gone that long."

"That reminds me, just when will Kate be back?" Roger asked, from the open doorway of the storeroom, while holding his own cup of coffee in hand.

"Shortly, but still we don't want to take any unnecessary risks when it comes to Ted."

"No doubt," Roger grumbled.

"Kevin," Mike turned to study him, "is there something on your mind?"

"No. Well maybe."

"Which is it?"

"The man, who told me about the call, said he would keep an eye on her."

"One of your men?" he turned looking to Roger.

"Could be. What did he look like?"

"Tall, lean…"

"Mike, that sounds like our tree man, but he wouldn't have left his spot, unless to relieve himself!"

"Let's go check it out. Kevin, come with us. Terry," he turned to a fresh faced officer he knew, "Stay and keep an eye on things here."

With a nod of his head, they were out the back door.

Meanwhile, not seeing anyone out front of the cabin, when walking in, Max found Cory finishing up with what she was doing. "Another masterpiece ready to go out?" he teased, seeing it on the coffee table all stamped and ready to go.

"Sure is!" she announced, when turning to see the look he was trying so hard to keep from her. "Max… what is it? What's going on?"

"Mike asked me to tag along with him. It seems that

Tony's car broke down, while on his way back from town. Will you be all right until I get back? It shouldn't be very long, and I told Mike I wanted to be back before dark. It seems we have another storm front moving in."

"S…sure, I'll be all right!" she replied, while putting on a brave front so that he wouldn't feel bad. "Besides, you need to get out once in awhile."

"Are you sure?"

"Yes, now go!"

"I'll be back before dark," he repeated, while leaning down to give her a kiss, before turning to head out the door. "Oh, that reminds me, our wedding is just around the corner. How are the plans going?"

"Fine, not a thing to worry about," she teased, hoping to take some of the fear out of her, which she was now feeling about being left alone.

"Good," he grinned, as he was about to turn to leave.

"Max…" she cried out, running up to give him another kiss, only this one wasn't just any ordinary kiss. She put even more feeling into it when he had to push her away.

"Oh, God, woman…" he groaned, shaking his head, smiling.

"What is it?"

"Our wedding!"

"Oh… are you worried that you might be getting cold feet?" she went on teasing him.

"No, that's not what has me worried!"

"Then, what is it?" she began, suddenly getting worried.

Seeing her grave expression, he quickly kissed her lips softly, and whispered, "I just hope my heart can handle what comes afterwards!" he laughed.

"Max…!" she laughed gaily along with him.

"What did you think I was talking about?"

"Well… not our honeymoon. But still that's funny!"

"Oh…?"

"Yes, you poor thing," she laughed, "can't handle a little thing like me?"

"Handle you? You'll be the death of me if you keep kissing me the way you do!"

Turning away, she literally shook at the thought of the word death.

"Hey," he took her back into his arms, "I didn't quite mean for it to come out that way. But for the last few days, all I have been able to think about is the day when we say I do."

"Me, too," she turned back to hold him, before Mike and Roger walked in, when not finding their mystery man.

"Ready?" Mike asked, standing in the open doorway.

"Cory…?" Max looked back down into her questioning eyes for some sort of sign to ask him to stay.

"Go," she smiled, "but just make sure you're back soon."

"I'll hurry," he returned, kissing her once again. "Roger…" he turned to his old friend.

"She'll be fine. Now get going, this storm isn't going to wait much longer."

"All right, see ya in a little while."

"I'll be waiting," she returned, while holding back her tears, until after Max had gone.

Seeing the growing sadness within those beautiful eyes of hers, Roger offered her a shoulder to cry on.

"I'll be a…all right!"

"Sure, you will. Besides, we still have the guys out walking the woods, and Kevin nearby if you need anything. Plus Kate ought to be back soon."

"I guess I have just gotten so used to having Max here all the time!"

"Well, if you feel scared of being back here alone, you can always come up to the store and keep me company! That and I still have some paperwork to do yet, if I am to get in a fresh supply of goods for the upcoming campers this season."

"Oh, yes, this is the time of the year you start to get busy.

No, I should be all right. I'm just going to pop in an old movie and fix up some hot cocoa with the weather changing, and all."

"All right, sweetie, I shouldn't be too awful long. Call me if you start to get scared if Max isn't back yet."

"I will. And Roger! Thanks."

Smiling, he walked out, running into Kevin on his way. "Any sign of our mystery man?" he asked, looking around.

"No, but I swear, he had to have been one of your friends. He talked just like them."

"Yeah, well I'm still waiting to see what comes back, after putting out a call to them. So far, nothing yet."

"You think it was this Harden, guy?" he asked quietly.

"I sure as hell hope not. Not with our best guys out picking up Tony, and Kate still out, God knows where. That girl should have already been back by now. What in tarnation is keeping her?"

The answer was waiting back in town, when traffic was tied up over some accident that should have been taken care of long ago. That and it was just too odd that her cell phone battery should be drained so soon, having been on the charger all night.

Chapter Thirteen

With the guys seeming like been gone for an eternity, Roger was still busy at the store doing his paperwork, while all alone in the cabin, watching TV, Cory felt a sudden chill going down her spine.

Without any warning, the power went out, leaving her in near darkness.

"That's odd!" she thought out loud, while getting up to go over to the door. "It shouldn't be getting this dark yet, it's still early!"

As the wind was beginning to pick up, she figured the storm was closer than she thought, while turning to go back inside, when not realizing Kevin was not at his post.

"Okay, Roger, where do you keep your candles?" she asked herself, while looking around for them. Just then, the front door blew open, scaring her half to death. "Gosh darn it! I've got to stop getting so scared!" she was saying, when the phone started ringing, adding to her list of fears. "Hello!" she answered.

"Cory…! It's Roger. Are you all right back there? If not, I can stop what I'm doing and come back and keep you company, until Max gets back, if you think you need me."

"No. I'll be fine. He shouldn't be very much longer. Oh, and Roger, any word on Kate yet?"

"No, nothing. Though, I called the number, Mike gave me, and got a recording."

"Yes, but shouldn't she have been back long before now, or do you think she had trouble, too, along the way?"

"It's too hard to say, but Mike said he will look into it when he gets back, which shouldn't be much longer now. They have Tony, and everything is fine."

Good. Oh, and Roger?"

"Yes?

"The lights just went out. Do you have any candles?"

"Oh, goodness, you'll find some in the kitchen drawer, just on the other side of the sink."

"Thanks, I'll just sit the phone down and go and have a look."

As she did so, Roger stood by hearing her rummaging through the kitchen drawers, until she came across them.

"Found them!" she called out, while unaware the back door wasn't completely closed, when heading back into the living room to pick the phone back up.

Just then she heard a noise coming from her bedroom.

"Now what?" she asked, knowing Roger could hear her.

"Cory…" he called out over his end, as she went to check out the noise. "Cory…!" he called out again worriedly. "Come on girl, come back to the phone."

Not knowing whether he should hang up and go back to check on her, he continued to wait, hoping he wasn't making a grave mistake.

Meanwhile, finding the room in total darkness, she wasn't able to see well, and decided to return to the living room, while feeling a little uneasy at that moment. But then suddenly, as she was about to turn and leave, a pair of hands came out of the darkness, and grabbed her from behind.

"Gotcha!" he laughed in her ear, as she tried futilely to get free of him.

"Mmmm…! Mmmm…!" she uttered a muffled out a cry for help, as he attempted to drag her over toward her bed.

Feeling his grip over her mouth and around her waist grow tighter, she had to find a way to break free, if only long enough to get out an audible cry, hoping Roger would hear her. When somehow she was able to do just that, while letting out a horrifying scream.

Hearing it, Roger cried out from his end, "Cory…! Cory…!" he repeated, when suddenly hearing the sound of a lamp being knocked off a table, shattering its bulb.

"Roger…" she cried out again, while trying to get away from her attacker, "help me…! Please…!"

"Oh, God, Cory… hang in there, little lady, I'm coming…!" he shouted. And just as he did, both Max and Mike walked in, seeing the look of horror on his face.

"Roger…" Max asked worriedly.

"It's Cory…" he cried, shaking with fear, "I think Ted has gotten to her!"

"What…?" he yelled, grabbing the phone out of his hand, only to hear her horrifying screams off in the distance. "Cory_____!" he cried out, throwing the phone, before running out the door, shouting on his way, "Mike, we have got to get to her! He's going to killer her if we don't stop him first. Oh, God, Cory_____!" he continued, while pushing himself harder down the path to Roger's cabin, than he had ever had to before, to get to her, before Ted could really do any serious damage to her.

"Roger," Mike called back, while going after him, "call for back up and an ambulance. We may need them, as well," he yelled, clearing the back door in no time.

Meanwhile, back at the cabin, Ted had grabbed her once again, while pinning her down on the couch, as she fought back with all her strength.

"P…please, Ted_____ don't do this to me_____!"
she cried even harder.

"Keep begging me, girl, when I'm through with you, you
won't be worth saving. You'll be dead_____!" he laughed,
while trying once again to take her.

But then, getting one of her hands free, she went to scratch
at his face, which only served to infuriate him even more.

"Why you little…" he growled, while repeatedly hitting
her, until she fell off the couch, and onto the floor.

At that time, he reached back with his right hand, and
pulled a stiletto out of his black leather boot, and began
cursing her even more, "You shouldn't have done that," he
yelled, taking the knife to the left side of her face, as she tried
unsuccessfully to avert his attack, but only too late.

Again, bringing the knife up, she let out a bloodcurdling
scream that filtered in with the storm that was still building
outside.

Hearing this, sent chills down everyone's spine, while
inside, Ted succeeded in driving the knife down into her chest,
at a downward angle, barely missing her heart. However, it
had pierced her lung, without a doubt.

"N…o…!" she gasped, feeling the pain reaching into her
very soul, as he was about to do it again.

At that moment, Max came bursting in through the front
door, while breaking its glass along the way. At that moment,
seeing the flicker of the blade in the air, he threw himself at
Ted, tackling him up over the couch, and onto the floor on
the other side, while knocking the knife out of his hand.

As the two continued to fight, Ted had somehow broken
free, while making a mad dash for the back door, when getting
away just as Mike and several others ran in to join them.

"Max_____!" Mike called out in the darkness, and an
occasional flash of lightning.

"Don't let him get away_____!" he yelled back, while

getting to his feet, when his old partner took the others, and ran passed him in the kitchen doorway to go after Harden.

Stopping in the same doorway, Max looked back over at Cory. Through the aid of the occasional lightning, he saw her near lifeless body lying there on the floor in the semi darkness of the living room. But then, with the exception of the steady light given off by the fireplace, he cried out, while rushing over to her, "Cory_____! No_____! No_____!" he continued to cry, while knocking the coffee table, with her manuscript on it, out of his way, while going down on bended knees to lift her bloodied body up into his arms. "Oh, God… Cory_____!" he carried on, while looking around the room, until he saw it. *'Oh, God, no…! She said it would be here,'* he thought to himself, while looking back down at her. "God, no_____! Please_____, not my Cory…!" he cried out painfully. "No…! No…! Please, God, don't take her from me too! Cory_____!" he continued to cry, "I love you, Cory! Please don't leave me_____!"

"M…ax_____!" she cried softly, coming to, but only to tell him that she loves him.

"I'm right here, Cory," he cried, looking into her eyes, as they fluttered slowly open.

"Oh, M…Max… I…I love you_____ I'll… a… always… l…love you_____" she whispered faintly just before her body succumbed to the darkness around her.

"Cory…? Cory, no_____! Come on, you little brat, don't do this to me. Don't leave me! Please_____" he kept calling out to her, when Mike came running back in.

"Max…?" he called out, coming around to join him, while seeing the look on Max's face, when he looked up, "Is she…"

"No, but we have to hurry, with what little light we have left, I think she's lost a lot of blood," he returned, while looking back down at her, and wishing he had stayed behind. "I should have realized what she was feeling."

"How could you have known?" he asked, just as the doctor came rushing in with Roger at his side.

"Cory...?" Roger cried out, brokenheartedly, while going over to kneel down next to Max. At which time, the tears began streaming down his old rugged face, when he took her hand in his.

"What happened here?" the doctor asked, while trying to get in to check her out.

"Ted got to her, before we could stop him," Max explained, while choking back on his emotions.

"Where is this Ted now?" he asked, making certain the area was safe enough to get a good look at what happened to her.

"I'm afraid we couldn't catch him," Mike offered sadly.

"Oh, Cory," Max began, "how could I have let this happen to you? And after making a promise to your father to take care of you, now look at what I've done. Not to mention, your mother, when she finds out what has happened. God_____!" he cried out angrily into her hair, "Why her? Why, Cory?"

"Max. Max." Mike took his arm to pull him away. "Come on, let's give the doctor some room here."

"Mike..." Max groaned miserably.

"I know, buddy. I know."

Moving right on in, the doctor called out, "I need some lights here...! Where are the lights?"

"I'll check on them," Roger offered, while getting to his feet.

After getting the lights back on, the doctor just shook his head, seeing the bruises all over her face, as well as the cut along her cheek. "Oh, my God, what madman would do something like this to her?"

"A very sick one," Mike spoke up, standing next to Max.

Then suddenly, there it was. "Oh, dear sweet Jesus," he cried out, seeing the stab wound to the chest.

"What is it?" Max asked, while pulling away from Mike to go right over and offer the doctor a hand.

"We have a bleeder here!" he announced, applying pressure to the wound, while the blood kept right on coming.

"Where the hell is that ambulance?" Max yelled.

"It's on its way!" Roger announced.

"Well, it had best be hurrying," the doctor groaned. "We have to get her to the hospital right away, she's bleeding badly, and I can't keep holding it back forever. From the looks of it, she has lost quite a bit already, and she can't afford to lose much more!"

"Here, let me help," Max offered, while tearing off his shirt to use to apply pressure with.

Just then, they heard footsteps coming down the path, toward Roger's place, followed by the sound of equipment rattling on its way, as well.

Going over to the door to look out, Mike called back, "They're here now!"

"Well it's about time!" Max groaned, while fighting back more tears, as he went to move out of the way, when the EMT's rushed in.

After assisting the doctor in every way they could, they got her lifted and placed gently onto the stretcher.

"We're ready anytime you are," they announced.

"Let's get her out of here, then," the doctor ordered, while turning to Max. "Are you riding with me?"

"Yes," he replied, turning to Roger. "Call Rose for me. Tell her…"

"I know."

"Roger, she's going to be pretty upset, so help her through it until you get to the hospital. I'll talk to her there. Oh, God, I just hope she will find it in her heart to forgive me for what has happened here."

"Don't be so hard on yourself, she's still alive."

"Yeah, alive," he shook his head, and walked on out the door.

"Roger," Mike spoke up, "if you need me to…"

"No, I'll call her," he returned, while going about locking up the cabin, when Mike went on out to gather up some of his men.

"What's this…?" Roger asked, when coming upon Cory's tape recorder.

Hearing him, Mike came back in to see what he was referring to.

"It's nothing," he replied, when going over to pick it up. Seeing how it was still on, he scratched his head puzzledly. "She must have been working on another book, while watching TV!" he thought out loud, after Mike had walked out again, while leaving him to lock up, before calling Rose and Mary. "Huh, just maybe, it will have something on there to do with her attack tonight?" As he questioned the idea further, he shut and locked the door behind him, while taking the recorder with him. "Mike…?" he called out, heading for his truck, when seeing him with a group of officers. "See if you can have some guy keep an eye on the front door of mine, until I can get it fixed."

"No problem, I'll take care of it for you. Just go and see to our girl."

"What about Kate? Any word on her yet?"

"She's going to meet up with me later, at the hospital."

"Mike?" Roger, being angry that she wasn't there to do her job, walked up to ask him more privately. "What the hell kept her?"

"A suspicious accident that should have been easy to clear up. And too, it looks as though our friend out there has been having some fun on our behalf."

"Meaning?"

"Tony's break down was no ordinary break down, and the call we got. Or I should say was given to us by our mysterious officer, was given by none other than Ted himself, while in disguise. As for Kate's phone, I think Ted got in to switch out her good battery with a bad one. And though he could have done them both in while they slept, I think he just wanted to prove to us he could slip in and out without notice."

"Damn," Roger growled, shaking his head.

"Hey," Mike spoke, "You should know, he spared one other person's life here."

"Who?" He looked up angrily.

"Kevin's."

"What?" He looked around, not noticing the young officer having been missing, until spotting him with a technician that came with an extra ambulance. "Ted did that to him?"

"Yes, by knocking him out, and put him under some brush, before killing the lights."

"Who found him?"

"Your tree climber," he laughed. "Oh, and Ted had been busying himself down at the old cabin too!"

"Don't tell me."

"They're fine, just mad that he gave them the slip, but not before boarding them up inside."

"Anything else, before I go? I still have to call Rose and Mary still."

"As the reports come in, I'll you guys know. Just get going, and I'll see you soon."

Heading out, after giving Rose and Mary a call, he proceeded on off to the hospital.

✑ *Chapter Fourteen* ✑

An hour later, Rose and Mary walked in, spotting Roger right away, coming down the hall.

"Roger?" Rose called out, going up to him with Mary hot on her heels.

"Rose!"

Meeting them halfway, he took them to where they still have Cory in surgery.

By the time they reached the surgical waiting room, Rose turned back to ask, "Are you telling me everything?"

"I'm telling you what I know at this time. She *is* alive, and they are doing everything humanly possible to save her," he explained, while unable to get his mind off her recorder, while continuing to look at it.

"Why did you bring that thing with you?" Mary asked, seeing it.

"It's just a hunch, but I think Ted just might be on it."

"Oh, my God…" Rose cried, "that'll prove he did this to her!"

"What more proof do they want? They already have all the evidence they'll ever need!" he exclaimed, while seeing

Max walking up, all bloody and broken up from where he had been holding Cory in his arms.

"Max!" both Rose and Mary cried, seeing the look on his face.

"What's going on? Is she going to be all right?" Rose asked, when joining up with him.

"They're still with her," he explained, while unable to look her in the eye.

"Max… Max, look at me," she ordered painfully.

"I can't."

"Honey, I'm not blaming you for what happened to her."

"I wouldn't blame you if you did," he struggled to say, as his emotions began to build back up inside, "I handled everything all wrong."

"Max," Roger spoke up, "before you get too carried away, you should listen to this tape recording of hers. It was still running when I stuck around to lock up the cabin. Well at least for the most part. Mike is going to take care of the front door."

"Oh…?" he asked, looking down at the recorder.

"Which part? The front door or the recorder?" he tried adding in a little humor.

"Roger!"

"Okay." Handing him the recorder, he suggested, "We should have Mike listen to it, too, in case there is something on it that will come of use. He's in the main waiting room now with Kate, while filling her in on everything that has happened. In fact, I'll just get him for you now."

"Yeah, tell him to come to the Chapel," Max called back, when Roger got ready to leave.

"Okay."

At that time, Max and the others went off to the chapel to hear what was on the recorder, while Roger went to get Mike.

Meanwhile, during surgery, the doctors were rushing

around trying to plug a punctured lung, when one Doctor cried out, "Damn it…! Nurse!"

The woman in scrubs knew right away what he wanted, while wiping away the sweat from his brow, while the other continued applying gauze to the area.

"Yes, I think I have it!" he called out, dropping one suture onto the tray, before grabbing up another, prepared by the technician to close with.

"Doctor," the nurse attending the surgery spoke up, "what are her chances?"

"We will know in twenty-four hours. Until then, if anyone here is a praying person, I suggest you start," he replied solemnly.

"And for her fiancé, as well," she added, when recalling seeing him, when they brought her in.

Back at the chapel, Roger and the others walked in fifteen minutes later, when Max and both their mothers had just enough time to hear most of the tape.

Taking the tape out to flip it over, they all got to hear Max's voice just then, telling Cory that he loved her.

"When was that put on there?" Roger asked, as everyone gathered around to hear it.

"I don't have to look to see when it was taped, I already know," he smiled for the first time, since getting to the hospital. "It was earlier today, on the back deck, after she fell off to sleep. I didn't even know she had it on."

"Max, take it to her. Let her hear it," Rose suggested.

"But she'll still be unconscious!"

"Max," Roger spoke up, "she may be unconscious, but she can still hear what's going on around her."

"Take it to her anyway, Max," Rose cried, just as he stood to walk over to the altar, "That way when she gets out of surgery, she'll hear your voice and know that you are nearby."

"All right, I'll let the doctor know too, that you're here in case he needs to see you," he said, giving the tape to Mike. "I want it back as soon as you're done with it."

"I'll have a copy made right away," he replied, as Max turned to leave the chapel to go and see if there was anything new on her condition.

Arriving back at the nurse's station, he was told she was being taken up to the ICU unit.

"Thanks," he replied, when turning to go up to her room. Stopping, he turned back to the nurse. "Will you let the others know?"

"Of course," she smiled. "Now go on up, we'll take care of things here."

"Thanks, just give me a head start first before you do."

With a nod of her head, the nurse turned to another, while Max hurried off to see Cory. "Now that's a man in love," she shook her head sadly.

"Yes, and I just pray that everything goes well for the two of them," she returned, seeing Max walk onto the elevator, just as the door began to close behind him.

"Me too," the other agreed, wistfully.

Arriving at the nurse's station, when seeing the doctor, Max went right up to ask, "What's happening with Cory Hall? Is she…"

"Are you Max?" he asked.

"Yes."

"Well, she seems to be holding her own right now, but she isn't out of the woods yet. As we were able to patch the hole the knife had left in one of her lungs, so far it seems to be holding its own."

"Can I go in and see her?"

"Sure! She's been calling for you in her sleep."

"Really?" he asked, while filled with so much hope.

"Yes. Now come with me. I have to check on her anyway."

Following the doctor in, he explained some of the things Rose and Roger had recently told him.

"Now talk to her, Max," he suggested. "Let her know you're here."

Doing so, he walked up to her bed, while looking down at her bandaged face from where Ted had beat her, and cut her with the knife. At that moment, all the strength he had in him to hold back his emotions seemed to have left. "Oh, Cory... you have got to fight this, you little brat. We've come so far, don't give up on me now, I need you."

"Oh, Max, I couldn't fight him off..., he was too strong for me!" she cried, unaware of what she was doing, when the monitors suddenly picked up.

Concerned, Max looked up at the doctor. "What just happened? Is she..."

"No, no. Whatever you just said caused a reaction from her. Say something else. Keep the conversation going. She needs to hear your voice. It's all we can do for her, from this side."

Looking back down at her, he took her hand in his, before going on, "So, you can hear me, can't you? You little brat. So please, show us another sign that you're with us. Please. Anything. Squeeze my hand. Call me a lousy good for nothing jerk even. Damn it, Cory Hall, I love you. Please...!"

Hearing this, Roger and the others walked in to add their support.

"What's going on?" Rose asked.

"She's showing signs of awareness," the doctor replied, while sounding hopeful.

"Oh, my!" she cried, going over to her daughter's bedside.

"You're not alone, girl," Max was saying, when Rose took her other hand, "we're all here."

"Max..." Rose spoke up, reaching out to him.

"I'm not giving up on her, Rose. She has to pull through. I can't bear the thought of being without her now."

"Yes, I know that, but…"

"Rose, you both were right all along, if I'd just met and have gotten reacquainted with her on my own I would have fallen in love with her. Well I did, and I am in love with her," he was saying, when all of a sudden, Cory squeezed his hand. "Doc…!"

"What is it? What happened?" Rose asked.

"She just squeezed my hand!"

"I'm… trying, Max. I'm… trying real hard, just for you and mom."

"Max… look at that!" Roger too, cried, seeing her eyes flutter, but then stopping.

"Looks like she's trying to come around!" the doctor exclaimed, while checking the monitors. "Just give her time, and most of all," he turned to face them, "let these wounds of hers heal. We can't rush things here."

"Yes, of course," they all agreed, as he went back to check on the other monitors.

Still, there was nothing, while they all stood back silently waiting for word, while he went on to check her pulse.

"Doc?" Max spoke up, seeing his apprehension.

"Sorry, Max, Mrs. Hall, she's just not strong enough to pull out of this, yet."

Feeling his heart bottoming out, he pulled up a nearby chair and plopped himself down on it, while looking lost. "Cory, I know it's early yet, but please…! Come back to us!" he cried, while bringing her fingers up to his lips to kiss each one lovingly, before bringing her hand up to his cheek.

Later that night, as her condition was slowly got better, Ted's whereabouts were still unknown.

"Mike?" Max spoke up tiredly, seeing his friend in the door way of Cory's room.

"Yes?"

"She has to pull through."

"She will. The monitors show that."

"Yes, but why hasn't she come to yet?"

"Give it time, she's taken a pretty bad beating!"

"I should've never left her. She was trying to be brave, but she was just kidding herself. I should have known that."

"Well, it's too late now for speculation, as we have more pressing matters at hand here."

"Ted?"

"Yes. Kate is on her way up now to give you a break."

"I don't need one. And after what happened…"

"You don't trust me to do my job anymore?" the female officer spoke up, upon her arrival, when seeing his disappointment.

"Kate!" both Max and Mike turned just then to see her standing there.

"I can't blame you, Captain Brummet, I was supposed to have been there for her, but I left to get some more clothes to finish out the week. And then there was that strange accident."

"I know about that. I'm just upset that you had to leave at all."

"Officer Martin," Mike spoke up.

"No, he's right, I shouldn't have gone. I should have arranged to have someone bring me what I needed."

"Perhaps, but you were excused just the same. So don't be blaming yourself for what had happened here. As for what transpired while you were trying to get back, Harden is to blame for that. He had to have slipped in while you were sleeping, and switched out you cell phone battery. You're just lucky he didn't kill you in the process."

"Yes, you're right on that account. I should have stayed awake, and stood guard."

"No, that's what your replacement is for. Your job is primarily during the daytime."

"Wait a minute," Max spoke up puzzledly. "If he had done that, it must have been while I was in with…"

"Cory? Yes, which must have messed up his plan to take her out of the picture then. So he went to Kate's room instead, and saw his chance to miss with her phone, just to toy with us."

"But why my phone, of all things?"

"Start out small, and get more brazen later," Max grumbled.

"Something like that," Mike interjected. "And too, it was his way of telling us we can't catch him," Mike grumbled. "As in, he was able to successfully get in, and successfully get out without so much as a detection."

"Damn," Max growled.

"Yes, well there's more," Mike went on regretfully. "Max… I'm sorry for not telling you, when I thought we had it taken care of, but he even had Kevin fooled, when acting as an undercover officer, passing on the information that Tony's car had broken down. Thus, by getting Kevin to leave his post to come and tell me, he thought he would be able to get to Cory then, and do what he came to do, until you showed up and messed up his plan a second time. As for Tony, I didn't learn about his car from him, until I called him right after you went to talk to Cory about going."

"He was without a doubt there then, and you didn't say anything?"

"Like I said, I thought we had it taken care of. The guys were all alerted of the situation, and at the time, with everyone we had, I thought it was safe enough to go and see about Tony. But then it occurred to me, when Kate ran into trouble, it was Ted's way of getting her out of the way, as well."

"By eliminating the playing field," she guessed.

"Yes, then relieving Kevin, when knocking him out. This would be Ted's third attempt to move in on Cory, do what he came to do, then get back out, before any of us got back."

"But then I showed up once again and messed up his plans," Max announced, looking to Cory regretfully.

"You mean you saved her life!" Mike corrected, when feeling bad for not telling him when he should of.

"Which reminds me," Max interrupted his thoughts, "Everything you told Roger, before he got here?"

"You already know?"

"Yes, we talked briefly in the waiting room, while everyone was getting them something to drink."

"Good, that saves me from having to repeat myself. Still I'm sorry I didn't tell you about Ted earlier. I really thought I could take care of it myself."

"And Captain Brummet," Kate spoke up apologetically, "I'm truly sorry for leaving her at all. Please let me show you I can be here for her now."

Looking at Cory, Max swallowed hard on his anger. "I am, too." Getting to his feet, he turned back to her, "If you promise to stay right by her side, never leave her, I could use a small break, but not for long." He looked hard at his old partner. "I mean that, I want to be back in case she were to come to."

"Not a problem," he noted, while reaching out an arm to his friend. "Shall we go, then?"

"Sure." Stopping, Max went back over to whisper something in Cory's ear, "I'll be back soon, and when I do, you had better be ready to wake up. Y…you hear me, you l… little brat?" he broke down, as a tear made its way down his handsome face to her cheek.

"*Oh… yes, Max, I hear you!*" she cried lovingly, as his tear then slipped down to her ear.

Turning to go, Cory felt an unexplainable urge to reach up and touch the tear. Sadly, no one saw it.

"Well, now," Kate spoke up, taking a seat next to her bed, after the men had left. "I just so happen to have brought my recorder with me, thinking if perhaps you were to hear some of your favorite music, you might come to a little sooner," she suggested, hopefully, while placing the small recorder on the bedside table, before putting in a tape the two had been singing to. "Remember this song?" she asked, as a soft melody began to play. Listening to it, she began to sing softly, unaware that sometime into the song, Cory had uttered a few words as well, although not as audible as Kate's sweet voice, but just as loving.

Meanwhile, down in the waiting room, Max was pouring himself another cup of coffee, hoping to wake himself up more. "Any word yet on Ted's whereabouts?"

"No, it's as if he had just vanished."

"Damn, where the hell is he?"

"I wish I knew," he sounded frustrated, while joining Max with his own coffee. "Heck, even Tony and Kevin are both out combing the woods along with Roger's men, as we speak."

"Oh?" Suddenly, Max jumped back, spilling his coffee. "Damn…"

"What is it?" Mike asked, sounding alarmed.

"Why didn't I think of it?" he groaned, heading for the door to go back to Cory's room.

"What?" Mike asked once again, while following after him.

"Ted…!" he called out over his shoulder, when Roger showed up out of nowhere.

"What's going on?" he asked, joining the line back to Cory's room.

"If Cory is here," Max stopped suddenly to face his two friends, "where would Ted be about now? Think about it! He wants her dead!"

"So you think he would be nearby?" Mike asked.

"Well, of course!" Roger agreed, looking worried. "Who's with her now?"

"Kate," Mike offered, picking up their pace, back to Cory's room.

Meanwhile, another song began to play, while Kate went on singing.

Sometime into it, while unaware the men had returned, though, hearing it, Mike was taken aback, as if thinking an angel was singing to the woman lying silently in bed.

"Mike?" Max spoke softly.

"She's..." he began, then shook off the thought, not wanting anything to cloud his judgment, when trying to do his job. "Officer Kate?"

"Captain...!" she jumped up, feeling embarrassed by being overheard. "I...I'm sorry, I didn't hear you come in!"

"I can see why!" Roger smiled thoughtfully. "You sounded beautiful just then."

"Well, it's just that I thought it would help!"

"Oh? Any trouble, then? Aside from that of course," he asked, when taking her aside.

"Well, no. I..." She stopped.

"You were too busy singing?" he asked sternly.

Going over to Cory's bed, Max thought he had heard something.

While listening closely, with the music still playing, her voice was coming out faintly. "Cory?" he cried. "Hey!" he called out, bringing everyone in the room to a standstill. By then he really heard her. "Oh... my God...!" he cried, taking her into his arms. "You are coming back to me. You really are!"

"Max?" Mike broke away from Kate to go to his friend. "What is it?"

"She's singing!" he cried. "She's..." Max looked to Kate, "singing the same song you were when we walked in!"

"When we were working on her book, that very song came on, and, well, we…" She broke off, while turning away sadly.

"Kate," Mike spoke up apologetically, "you may have just brought Cory back to us. But, with the music, how could you have known?"

"She loves it!" she returned, while looking on at Max and Cory.

Feeling Cory's breathing change, Max looked down at her. "Cory?" he called. "Cory, can you hear me?"

"Max?" Roger spoke up just as he went to lay her back down.

"She's starting to come to!" he cried, smiling down at her. Just as he did, her eyes began to flutter open.

"You're right, Max!" he cried, seeing Cory's beautiful green eyes, clouded as they may be, but still, she was coming to, all the same.

Hearing all the commotion going on, one of the nurses came running in to check on her. "Mr. Brummet?" she asked, while seeing everyone looking so overwhelmed.

"Get the doctor!" he ordered.

"Of course!"

Before she could reach the door though, the doctor walked in. "I heard the news. Has she regained consciousness yet?"

"Yes, she's just now coming around!" he returned excitedly.

"Good!" he answered, going over to check on her. "Cory…" he called out, "do you hear me? It's Doc Tanner. Remember me? I'm the doctor who took care of your young man here!"

"Mmmm…" she began moaning, when the pain in her shoulder became apparent, as the medication started to wear off. "Oh… God, it hurts…!"

"Take it easy, young lady. We'll get you something for your pain. Now, do you know where you are?" he asked.

"Where… I'm at?" she asked, just as her mother came walking in. "M...Mom?" she cried weakly at first.

"I'm right here, honey!" Rose cried, going over to stand next to her daughter's bed. "I'm right here."

"Ro…ger…?"

"Right here, as well!" he smiled warmly.

When finally looking at Max, she just stared up at him.

At that moment, feeling as though she would never forgive him, he turned sadly to walk away.

❧ *Chapter Fifteen* ❧

Reaching the door, he heard that small voice of hers, as she called out.

"Max...ine!"

At that moment, everyone in the room busted out laughing, when he turned to laugh along with them.

"You little brat," he continued, while coming back over to take her hand, before giving it a gentle kiss.

"Welcome back, young lady!" Doctor Tanner smiled. "You had us all pretty worried!"

"She sure has...!" said a familiar voice from the open doorway.

"Angela? Jenny?" Cory cried, when sounding surprised to see them.

"I called the girls when you were first brought in," Rose explained, while smiling down at her daughter.

"And Ted, what of him? Have they caught him?" she asked.

"I'm sorry, Cory, but Ted got away," Roger replied, looking to Max.

"We will get him, Cory," he told her, while still holding

her hand with tears in his eyes. "Somehow, I swear, we'll get him."

Seeing her expression change, Doc Tanner interjected, "Miss Hall, take it easy now. I don't want you getting all upset. You're still not out of the woods yet."

"She will be all right," Max put in, while looking into her pain-filled eyes, with so much pain in his own. "I'll be here with her, until she's ready to go home."

While looking over at what was once a soft and gentle face, only to see it half covered with bandages, he was unaware of Cory's close observation of the attention he was giving her.

"Mom?"

"Yes, dear?"

"Will you give me a mirror? I have to see myself. I have to know..." she asked, while swallowing back the tears, "I have to know what he did to me!"

"Oh, honey, it's too soon! Why don't you just wait a few days to give it time to heal?"

"Mom, what aren't you telling me?" she cried, looking from her mother to the others, and then back again.

Coming to Max, who tried to look strong, he just shook his head. "Cory, your mom is right. Give it time to heal, then look at it."

"How bad is it?" she cried out again, while at the same time trying to get up. "Please, somebody, tell me! What did he do to me?"

"Miss Hall, you have to lay back," the doctor ordered, while waving to the nurse, who hadn't said a word the whole time she'd been in there. "Get me two cc's of Demerol," he told her, when she nodded and left the room to get it. "Now, Miss Hall, it's going to be all right. I'm going to give you something to help you relax. It may even cause you to get drowsy. Don't fight it, though."

"No... Please... I can't stand not knowing what he did to me. Is it that bad?"

"Well…" Max grinned. "Remember that one Halloween night, twelve years ago, when you tried to wear your mom's clothes?"

"How did you know about that? You were…"

"Gone? No, I wasn't! I came back that weekend."

"You're the one…?"

"Who, me?" he laughed.

"Oh, you…" she laughed lightly, feeling the pain shooting through her injuries. "Don't you dare try and deny it now, you're the one who was following me that night."

"Yep!" he conceded. "As if I didn't have anything better to do with my time, then to babysit you, you little brat!"

"Cory," her mother spoke up, "your father was worried about your going out alone that night. So he called over to see if Max had come home yet for the weekend!"

"Oh, great, send a woman out to do a man's job," she teased, as the pain at the side of her face and chest grew more intense.

"Cory, are you all right?" Max asked, while moving around to comfort her.

"It hurts to laugh!" she exclaimed, while trying to smile up at him, when he offered to wipe away her tears.

"Yeah, but it was good to hear you laugh again," he smiled down on her.

"As soon as she gets better, you should be hearing even more of it," Doc. Tanner spoke up, while about to administer Cory's shot, before going around to remove some of the monitors.

Leaving her hooked up to the IV for the time being, he was just about to leave when Mary spoke up, while offering to get Cory something from the cantina.

"I'm sorry, but she's not to have anything now. It'll be a day or so before she'll be ready for solid foods," he explained.

"Thanks, Aunt Mary," she smiled faintly.

"Max," his mother asked, "what about you?"

"I'll pass this time, Mom," he returned, looking really tired then.

"All right, dear."

"Hey," Roger spoke up, seeing how Cory was just about to slip back off to sleep, "why don't I take the ladies out to eat, before dropping them at a hotel for the night? This way we all can get some rest."

"Sure," Max agreed, tiredly.

"See you in the morning then, dear," Rose tried to smile, when she gave her daughter a hug. "And you," she turned to Max. "You tried, so don't be punishing yourself anymore for what Ted did."

"Thanks, Rose, but I still can't help but feel I have failed her, as well as her father."

"Max, you'll get him. I know you will," Mary spoke up firmly. "Now get some rest."

"Yeah, I will."

After everyone left to give the two some time alone, it was only a matter of minutes, after Max had settled back down on a nearby chair that he rested his arm up on her bed, while still holding her hand, he too fell off to sleep.

"Captain Jones," Kate spoke up just outside Cory's room, "what now?"

"We're staying here," he returned, grabbing a few chairs a nurse brought out earlier.

"All right," she returned, seeing a selection of books and magazines setting out on a table, as well as a fresh pot of coffee and doughnuts. "You thought of everything, didn't you?"

"Well, it's going to be a long night, and I don't want any of us to fall asleep."

"Us?"

"Yes, I have a few men here, as well, walking the hallways."

"Do you think he'll show up here?"

"Max said something awhile ago to that extent. I tend to wonder that myself!"

Taking her seat, she sighed heavily, while picking up one of the magazines. To her surprise, under it was a wedding magazine, as well as a music digest. Smiling, she picked them both up and looked over at Mike, who tried to look as though he were busy looking at something else. "Did you have these brought up too?"

"Me? No…, of course not. A nurse heard about their wedding. As for the music digest," he had to think, "well, I play a guitar once in awhile and like to see if they ever put in a music sheet."

"Oh…?" she thought, not knowing a whole lot about her superior officer.

By the next morning, Mary had already been in and left, after placing a blanket over her son, when the nurse came in to give Cory her medicine. At that time he had awakened to the aroma of coffee, eggs, bacon and toast coming into the room.

"Mmmm… something smells good!" he commented, when stretching his leg out in front of him, while getting up to give Cory a light peck on the cheek. "I'm going in to brush my teeth. Can I get anything for you?"

"No, thanks!"

"Okay."

After going into the bathroom and turning on the cold water, he called out, "Where is everyone?"

"They went down to the cafeteria thinking you would want to eat up here with me. Nurse…!" Cory suddenly let out a small cry of pain, when she moved her arm.

"Give it time," the nurse replied, when coming back in to give her something for it. "Here, this will help you to relax so your injuries will heal better. You may even find yourself wanting to sleep a little throughout the day."

"Sleep…?" she questioned fearfully, though the previous night went undisturbed.

Hearing the tone in her voice, Max came back into the room to offer his reassurance that she wouldn't be left alone. "I'll be here to keep you company if those dreams start coming back," he smiled, seeing her body begin to relax.

As the day went on, the others went back to the cabin to get some cleaning done, after the police did what needed to be done. As for Max, he stayed behind like he promised.

"Hi there," he greeted later that evening, while walking back into the room with the nurse and some flowers to give her.

"Oh, Max… these are beautiful!" she cried, while taking them to smell.

"I saw them down in the gift shop. They told me, they wanted to be up here with you," he laughed, when seeing her wrinkle up her nose at his joke. "No…?" he teased.

"Not even," she laughed back at him, while he went to place the beautiful mix of roses, daisies and lilacs in a vase of water provided by the hospital.

"Do you think you could handle something to eat or drink now?" the nurse asked, while going over to fluff her pillows.

"I could use some tea!" she exclaimed, while shifting herself in bed.

"All right, one hot tea, and a very large hot cup of coffee coming up," she smiled cheerfully.

"Thanks," Cory returned, while waiting for the nurse to leave the room. "Max, will you go and get the other nurse for me?"

"Sure!"

As soon as he was gone, she got up slowly to go over and look in the mirror nearest to the bathroom.

Meanwhile, out at the nurse's station Max was just about

to say something to one of the other nurses when all of a sudden he heard it.

"No_____!" Cory's scream as the room began spinning around her.

"Cory_____?"

"We had best be getting back in there to see what happened," the doctor suggested, while following right behind Max.

Just as they arrived, she had already fallen to the cold hard hospital floor, before Max could reach her.

"Oh, God, Cory!" he called out, rushing over to grab her up into his arms and carry her back over to her bed. Afterwards, the doctor moved right in to check her over.

"Doc?" Max sounded worried.

"I can't say just yet."

Standing back, Max looked on impatiently, while the doctor went on with his exam.

Coming to, she had only seen the doctor, and the two nurses at first.

"Cory…? Cory…? Can you hear me? It's Doc Tanner."

"No...! No...! Not my face!" she cried over and over again.

"Cory, give it time! It's going to be all right! You'll see, in a few days the bruising will start to fade away."

"But what about the scar…? Will it just fade away, or will I be permanently marked for life?" she cried. "And how will I ever be able to face Max now with a face like mine?"

Moving off to one side, Cory saw him standing behind one of the nurses.

"Oh, God… no_____!" she cried, closing her eyes.

"Cory…" Max moved in to take her hand.

"No… I'm so... ugly! How could you ever want me after what he did to me? He was right! He said he would fix it so that no one would ever want me again…" she went on crying, until the doctor gave her a shot to help her sleep. "No_____"

Staying with her throughout the night, Max sat listening to her cry out in her sleep from time to time.

While laying his head on the pillow next to hers, he rested his arm lightly across her tummy, carefully trying not to disturb her IV, while trying to comfort her the best way he could. One way was to tell her how much she had come to mean to him, since she had returned. "Oh, God, Cory," he cried, "I'm here for you, and I am never going to leave you," he went on. "So please, don't push me away now."

By the following evening, a new security guard came in to introduce himself to Max. "Captain Brummet," he spoke up, "I'm Officer Costess, and I am here to guard Miss Hall for you."

Getting up slowly, while Cory continued to sleep, he took the new guard just outside her door. "You know what all you're to do?" he instructed firmly, when looking back in at Cory.

"Yes, sir."

"Good, make sure no one comes in here unless they are on the visitors list. And I mean, no one. Do you understand?"

"Yes, sir," the guard replied just as Rose walked up.

"Max…?" she looked puzzled.

"I'll be right out here, if you need anything."

"Thank you," Max returned.

Walking back into the room, Rose looked up at Max, "Have you gotten any sleep yet?"

"I will, once this is over," he grumbled.

"Max, you can't wait until then. What good will you be to her if you're all run down?"

"What good was I to her when all of this happened?"

"Max, you can't keep punishing yourself! What happened, happened."

"I should have been there, Rose! She wouldn't have been in this shape if I had stayed behind."

"Well, you weren't there," Mary interrupted, when joining them. "And she is, but she at least, is alive because of you. Now, will you get some rest?"

"I suppose. Besides, she'll be sleeping throughout the night, and the new guard is just outside the door. If Ted were to show up," he replied, leaning over to give her a kiss. "I won't be very far away this time. So sleep peacefully now," he whispered softly.

That night Max caught a few hours of sleep out in the waiting room, along with the others. However, Cory's sleep was interrupted, when the guard had to take a break.

Asking an orderly to stand by, he left to use the bathroom.

Waiting until the guard was out of sight, the so-called orderly slipped into her room to tamper with her IV.

Opening her eyes, she saw a man's figure standing over her, as she whispered Max's name.

"No, it isn't your long lost lover. It's your worst nightmare coming back to get you," he laughed.

"Ted...?" she cried, looking around the room. Not seeing Max, she felt totally helpless.

"What's wrong, you thought you got rid of me?"

"Why are you doing this to me? Haven't you done enough, already?"

"No, I haven't. Not until I think you have gotten all that you deserve, and that will be when they bury you."

"But why?"

"Ever since you came back from the funeral, you had been acting differently. And every time I would try to hold you, you would pull away from me."

"Ted, I had just lost my father!" she cried, trying to shift herself up in bed.

"That worked for awhile, but after I heard you call out his

name in your sleep, I knew it wasn't just your father you were thinking about. It was Max all that time wasn't it?"

"Oh, Ted, Max and I go way back, and he was in the hospital, because of some farming accident!"

"The same farming accident that took your father?" he sneered.

"What are you saying?" she cried out, not wanting to believe anything he had to say. And since no one had ever told her what had happened that day, Ted was trying to make it sound like Max was to blame for her father's death.

"Why, didn't they tell you?" he laughed.

"No...! You're lying. It wasn't because of Max. He would have never done something to cause my father's death. He loved him!"

"Think about it, Cory. It all happened around the same time."

"No! You're lying! You're lying! It wasn't that way!"

"Oh, but he did. He got himself caught under the plow."

"That had to have been an accident. Ted you're just grasping at straws."

"Am I, Cory?" he moved closer to her.

"Ted... what do you want from me?" her voice was shaky, just as she started stiffening up.

Just then, the guard returned. Hearing the sound in her voice brought on concern. "Miss Hall," he called in, "are you all right?"

Ted glared down at her with a warning look in his dark and angry eyes, but she didn't heed to his warning.

"No... I'm not!" she cried, fighting back her fear, while staring back up at him.

At that moment, Max showed up in the doorway. "What's going on in here?" he asked, walking in to turn on the soft light over her bed. Seeing the orderly standing near her, the look on their faces told him something was definitely wrong. "Cory..." he called out, taking another step into the room.

When he did, it was then, seeing the expression in her eyes, this was no orderly.

Nudging the officer in the side, he moved slowly toward the man.

Just then, Ted felt trapped.

Looking one last time at Cory, he sneered, "It isn't over with yet. I will be back, and you will pay."

Swallowing hard, she looked to Max for help, as Ted turned slowly to face him. "You will never have her. I'll kill her first before you even get the first button undone."

"What makes you think I haven't already had her?" he growled.

"Because she wants the traditional love," he returned angrily.

"Well, for your information, I've already been to bed with her more than once. But then you would already know that, having been in our room when you snuck into the cabin that night." Max was grasping at straws, when not knowing what night that was.

But then seeing Ted's reaction, Max knew he was playing with fire.

Turning, Ted gave Cory one of the most hideous looks ever. "You little whore…" he growled

"Ted," Max broke in, "I said I've been to bed with her. We still haven't made love yet. But soon we will, and I'm sure it will be the most beautiful experience you will never have with her," he grinned broadly, before taking another step toward him.

"She'll never live that long, Brummet."

Suddenly, without warning, Ted bolted past Max, while plowing right into the guard, when knocking them both off balance, while making a beeline out of the room.

Quickly recovering his footing, Max took after him, when tackling him to the floor, out in the hallway, with the aid of the guard, and a few of Mike's men, who came running, when they heard all the commotion.

"Max…" Mike called out, as he and Kate ran up the hallway, when realizing what was going down in front of them.

"It's Ted," he yelled, ramming his good knee into the center of his back, while jerking his right arm up behind him, "You're not getting away this time, you sick son of a…," He broke off, growling, while taking a set of handcuffs from Kevin, who stood ready in case Ted were to try to make another attempt to get away.

"Don't count on it," he sneered, "I'll find a way to escape, and when I do, I'll be back. You hear me, Cory…? I'll be back…!" he yelled over and over again, as Mike and the others hauled him away. "I'll be back, Cory…! You hear me…? I'll be back…!"

Covering her face, she began shaking her head from the fear and confusion she felt, when Ted first arrived, telling her what he had about her father.

"Cory…" her mother and the others cried out, when running into the room, "we were called to come back in. Are you all right?"

"Y…yes," she cried, when turning to stare up at Max, when he walked back in to check on her.

"Cory, what is it? Why are you looking at me that way?"

"Mom, was daddy alone when he had his heart attack?"

"What…?" Mary cried, knowing Rose hadn't told her yet.

"Mom, tell me…! Was daddy alone…?"

"No…" she cried, "he wasn't!"

"Then…" she swallowed, "it's true? Max was with him?"

"Yes, he was," she returned.

"How did you know?" Max asked, worriedly.

"Ted, he told me. He said," she hesitated, "that you caused it!"

"Cory…!" her mother cried, scoldingly.

"No, Rose," he put up his hand, looking so brokenhearted, "she's right. I did cause his death. If I hadn't been so bullheaded that day, we wouldn't have gone out there when we did. The weatherman was calling for rain later that afternoon. And like a jerk, I wanted to get the field done, before it started raining. However, we were caught in a downpour, and the plow had gotten clogged. I thought I could take care of it myself, but I fell under one of the blades, while I was trying to remove the caked on mud."

"And then what happened?" she asked, while fighting back the tears.

"Bob saw what had happened, when he got out of his truck to help. Having set the safety switch myself, somehow it had failed, and the blade fell on my leg, nearly severing it. While trying to dig the dirt out from beneath my leg, he tried pulling me out, which brought on his attack."

"How did you both get out of it?"

"He got to the radio and called for help. Cory," Max began, looking deep into her tear filled eyes, "he fought real hard to hang in there until help could arrive." Stopping, he looked down at his hands. "I'll never forget the look in his eyes, or the last words he spoke to me that day. You see, Cory," he looked back at her with a sad smile on his own pain filled face, "I've known for some time how you've felt about me."

"But how?"

"Bob, he wanted to make sure I knew, though, he didn't tell me it was my little brat. Things just started adding up."

"The egg?"

"Oh… yeah," he smiled. "But then, Karen," Max's expression turned angry, "he wanted me to know that she had already planned on leaving me."

"Max… What?"

"Now, it's because of me, your father isn't here for you."

Shaking his head, he turned quietly and headed for the door to leave, while passing Roger on his way.

"Hey!" he called out, seeing his expression. Not getting a reply, he turned to Rose puzzledly once he had walked into the room.

"He's still blaming himself for what happened to Bob!" she cried, when turning back to Cory. "Honey, it's time that you know the whole truth about your father."

"Mom?"

"Yes, dear, Max has been blaming himself for so long, and it's been for something that he couldn't have changed."

"I…I don't understand! What couldn't have changed?"

"Honey, your father knew," She broke down, as both Mary and Roger came to her side. "He…he was dying a long time before the accident had happened."

"What…? No…!" she cried tearfully.

"Yes, little lady," Roger offered, while taking her hand in his. "We weren't sure how to tell you. So we thought perhaps it would be best to let you remember him the way he was, happy and proud of his little angel."

"So," Mary added sadly for all of them, "don't blame Max for what happened. He would have died alone out there if Max hadn't been with him. And then again, it could have been Max out there alone!"

The thought of Max being out there all alone made her wince. "Oh, Mary, I don't blame him. I know that he wouldn't have put daddy's life in danger on purpose. He loved daddy, as much as daddy loved him!"

"Like a son," she added painfully.

"Cory, they were only doing what they have always loved to do, and that was farming," Angela spoke up from the doorway, when she and Jenny walked in.

"I know that, I'm just mad because no one bothered to tell me what really happened!"

"Then tell him that," Rose cried, shaking her head.

"Roger?" Cory turned.

"Don't worry, little lady, I'll find him," he smiled down on her, before turning to leave the room.

"Thanks," she smiled back. "Oh, and Roger…!"

"Yes?"

"Please, tell him I'm sorry!" she added, calling out softly to him.

With a nod of his head, he left the room to go and find one very upset Max.

"He'll find him, dear, don't you worry," Mary replied.

Closing her eyes, Cory cried deeply, "Why didn't anyone tell me that Max and daddy were working together? Why…?"

"At the time," Rose looked away sadly, "we never thought of it!"

"How are you feeling now?" Angela asked, while standing at the side of her bed.

"Like I could use a bath," she replied.

"Well, we can arrange that first thing in the morning," Doc. Tanner offered, when coming in to check her IV. "But first, let's get this contraption off. You won't be needing it anymore."

"Thanks," she sighed, as the needle was being removed from her arm. "Mom," she turned, "do you have a brush with you?"

"I'm sure I do somewhere in this purse," she replied, while looking for one. "Here it is! Would you like for me to brush your hair for you?" she asked, while putting her purse back down on the floor.

"Sure!"

After giving her daughter a quick once over, the others joined in to help give her a light bath, before the guys returned.

In the meantime, Roger had located Max sitting in the hospital chapel. "Well, I should have guessed you'd be here!"

"Yeah, I missed out on Bob's funeral, because of that accident," he groaned, when lowering his head. "And now his daughter is in here because of me."

"Well, Max, she isn't dead, but she is in a lot of emotional pain. Now the way I see it," he went on, while going around to take a seat next to him, "you can be there for her, or you can walk away. Which is it going to be, my friend?"

Looking at him, Max shook his head, sadly. "But she's blaming me for her father's death!"

"No, you're doing that all on your own. She's too much in love with you to be blaming you for what she now knows couldn't have been helped."

"Did she tell you that?"

"No, she didn't have to. She did ask me, though, to go and bring you back."

"Really?" his eyes lit up in a grin, just then.

"Yes, really, you goofball, now let's get you back up there!"

"Well, let's go then," he laughed, getting up to head for the door. Turning back, he saw that Roger was still sitting there, grinning. "Well… what are you waiting for?"

"Not a thing," he chuckled, following Max out of the chapel.

❧ *Chapter Sixteen* ❧

Meanwhile, back up in Cory's room, her friends were giving her one last look of approval, before cleaning up their mess.

"Well… how do I look?" she asked nervously.

"Like a lady waiting for her love to return," Angela tried hard to search for the right words to say. The bandages simply weren't helping matters, when the men came walking back in.

Looking at Max, she felt her heart jump, as he walked over to give her a warm hug.

"I'm sorry, Max! It was just a shock to hear about daddy. I wasn't trying to blame you for what had happened. He saved your life, and I consider him a hero for what he did," she cried, as he continued to hold her.

"For the record," he replied, "I really do love you, no matter what. So don't you ever doubt that for a moment, you little brat!"

"Oh, Max…" she went on to whisper something much more private to him.

"Oh, yeah!" he grinned back broadly. "Mmmm, I just might have to hold you to it, too!"

Seeing how all was better now, Angela walked over to say

her goodnights, "I'll see ya in the morning. I'm going back to the cabin to get some sleep."

"Yes, and that goes for the rest of us," Mary added tiredly.

"Max?" Cory cried, not wanting to be alone.

"I'm not going anywhere," he replied, looking over at Roger.

"I'll take the ladies back."

"Thanks."

"Goodnight, dear," her mother replied, giving Cory a little kiss on her forehead.

"Goodnight!" she smiled in return.

After everyone had gone, Max got in carefully to lay next to her, as she slowly, and with a minimal amount of pain, snuggled up beside him.

"Max?"

"Yeah?"

"What you said to Ted!"

Grinning broadly, he knew she was referring to his announcement of having been to bed with her.

"You had me wondering."

"I just had to burst his bubble. He had it coming to him."

"Oh…" she smiled, while bringing his arm even more around her, "you can be so mean," she laughed lightly, just as she slipped peacefully off to sleep.

By the next day, her friends and family were back to see how she was doing.

"Well, it sure looks as though you slept pretty well last night," Mary teased, seeing the look of contentment on their faces.

"We did," Max smiled down on her, before leaning over

to give her a kiss. And just in time too, when the nurse came walking in with a wheelchair.

"Miss Hall?"

"Yes?"

"Are you ready for your bath now?"

"Yes, I sure am!"

"Good, the doctor says you are to get a whirlpool treatment today. However, I must remind you that your body has been through a rough ordeal. You may even be upset with what you see at first. So I was told to prepare you for the possibility that you may not be able to handle this."

"I think I've already found that out," she announced, while smiling at Max.

Turning to Rose, the nurse just shook her head.

"May I go down with her?" she asked anxiously.

"Yes, that would be a good idea," she replied, while getting everything put together.

"Cory," Max spoke up, taking Roger's arm, "while you're gone, we'll be down in the cafeteria to get something to eat."

"All right."

"And the rest of us will just stay behind and wait on them," Angela added, while standing back out of the way for the nurse to move the wheelchair around for Cory to get in.

"Ready?" she asked, just before helping Cory out of bed.

"Sure!" she tried smiling, though the soreness she was experiencing at the time prevented her from doing so.

Following her out of the room, Max turned quietly to Roger after giving her one last kiss goodbye. "Have you heard from Mike and the others yet?"

"Yeah, he'll be here shortly."

"Good, then let's get the food and come back up here, I don't want to be gone too long."

"Max?" Angela called out, standing just outside Cory's room.

Stopping, he turned back, forgetting about the others. "Damn! I'm sorry, what?"

Laughing, she asked, "Do you want us to tell Officer Jones anything when he gets here?"

Shaking his head at her amused expression, "Have him to wait on us. We'll be right back. We're just going down to order our breakfast to be brought up here."

"All right!" she smiled, while the men turned to catch the elevator, just as the doors began to close.

Meanwhile, back at the whirlpool, Cory, the nurse, and her mother were preparing for her bath. With the lights turned down low, the nurse put some solution into the water to assist with her healing process.

"Are you ready now?" she asked, helping her out of the chair.

"Yes, I'm ready. I think," she replied nervously, at the tub. "Mom?"

"I'm right here, honey." She held out her hand for Cory to hold.

"You might want to turn your head, Mrs. Hall. The first glance won't be easy for you or for your daughter."

"No, I've seen it before. I'll be fine. I want to help her get through this."

"All right then, shall we continue?"

"Yes," she said, closing her eyes as the robe came off.

Getting into the tub, the water felt good on her, as the whirlpool did its job.

Afterwards, Rose and the nurse worked together to comb out Cory's hair, and help her get dressed.

"I'm going to put you into these pajamas. It'll help you stay warm," the nurse offered, while bringing over the pastel flannels her mother had brought along with her.

Looking into the mirror at her total reflection for the first time, since the nurse had replaced some of the old bandages with new ones, she cried out horrified at what she saw staring back at her.

"It's going to be all right, dear," her mother said, while trying to comfort her. "You been through this before, so you know it will look like this until it heals!"

"Yes, but that was then. Max wasn't around to see it when I got home. How am I going to face him now, I look so…"

Cutting her off before Rose could respond, the nurse gave her a stern look. "Now you listen to me, young lady. Stop right there with that negative thinking. Remember, bruises do go away, and so will these bandages. So keep in mind, that you have a handsome fellow up there waiting on you. Who by the way, went through his own horrible accident awhile back, if you recall. And with time, and your friends and family, you will get through this, too."

"That's easy for you to say, you're not the one who was attacked!"

"Cory!" her mother scolded.

"No," the nurse put up a hand in defense. "That's okay! She has every right to be mad. But you are wrong, Miss Hall, I was attacked. Seven years ago, about this time, I wouldn't give in to this man I was seeing. I wanted to save myself for our wedding day. However, he had other plans."

"That sounds a lot like Ted," Cory replied, unaware of the nurse's reaction.

"Ted…?" she cried. "What was his last name?"

"Harden."

"Ted Harden…? The one that was put into prison for almost killing that writer?"

"Yes," Rose replied, looking solemnly at her daughter.

"I am that writer," she told her, while getting into her chair to head back up to her room.

"I had no idea! I'm so sorry I brought it up!"

"No, that's all right. He was here last night, trying to finish the job," she explained.

The nurse just shook her head with a shiver, before taking her back. "One more thing, before we get there," she was about to say, when coming around to squat down in front of her, while on the elevator, "This fella of yours, why would he react any different, when he's been right here by your side all this time? In fact," she went to touch her had, "after the bath you had, you look even better than before you got one." She smiled brightly, before the doors opened to her floor.

Cory knew she was right. *'I... I guess I do...!'*

Arriving just outside her room, she heard Mike and Kate's voices coming from inside, while talking about Ted's arrest.

"Nurse, wait!" she cried, holding up a hand to hear more.

Stopping just short of the door, the three listened in more on the conversation, until the right time came to go on into the room.

"He didn't go quietly," Mike was saying with a grin in his voice, she could tell.

"Why?" Max asked, when she suddenly heard his voice. "What happened?"

"He swore to get even with you for jerking his chain, so to speak," he laughed, seeing Max's broad grin. "What the hell did you say to him, anyway?"

"I told him..." he began, when turning in time to see Cory standing in the doorway. Smiling, he went on, "I told him we had already been to bed with each other. In fact, several times!"

"You what..." his mother cried.

"Mom...!" he laughed.

"Well, Mr. Brummet," Cory teased, "I guess you will have to marry me now!"

"Mary," Rose laughed at seeing her friend's expression, "they didn't do what you are thinking. Cory told me what all had happened, while down at the whirlpool."

"That made Ted pretty mad," Max went on laughing.

"Yeah, just mad enough that he may try that much harder to break out and come after you again," Mike grinned, shaking his head.

"He won't be able too, will he?" Cory cried, when feeling faint after having been on her feet too long.

"No," Max answered, while coming over, just as the nurse was about to offer her the wheelchair.

Motioning for her to take it away, he lifted her up in his arms and carried her over to her freshly made bed.

"Miss Hall," Mike offered, seeing how Max had his hands full, and loving it, "your Ted Harden is being placed in a maximum security lock up, back in New York. He won't be able to break away from that anytime soon, I assure you. However, if it will make you feel any better, I am prepared to leave Kate here with you, until the two of you can get married."

"Well, Kate?" Cory smiled.

"I'd like that!" she turned happily, seeing Mike's expression.

"Angela, Jenny," Cory turned to see their faces, "she's an officer, and I would feel better having her around, as well as the two of you."

"Sure!" Jenny laughed, seeing how Cory had felt after seeing her best friend's expression go grim at feeling misplaced. "Come on, Angela," she prodded, "you know it's for the best!"

"I'm not trying to take your place," Kate offered thoughtfully. "You do want her to be safe, don't you?"

"Yes, of course!" Angela conceded with a small smile, and then the smile grew as Cory, too, grinned.

"It'll be fun, you'll see!" she put in.

At that time, a special meal cart came around, bringing everyone's food on it.

After eating their fill, they talked further, until she began to tire from the medication she was still taking.

"Max," Roger spoke up, "how about I take the ladies out of here for awhile and let the two of you get some rest?"

"Sure," he agreed, walking Mike and Kate out into the hallway.

"I'll keep an eye on things with the prison warden," Mike turned quietly to offer, just outside her room.

"And I'll have her room ready for her when she gets released," Kate put in, while still feeling bad for not having been there, when everything went down.

"Thanks," he returned, while looking in at Cory and the others.

"She has a lot of people pulling for her, Max. She will be fine," Mike smiled warmly, before leaving.

"That she does, buddy! That she does."

After everyone had gone to get some rest, Max went back over to join Cory.

"Max?" she whispered.

"Yeah?"

"My face! It's going to be scarred!"

"Cory?"

"Yes…?"

"You didn't turn away from me when you saw my leg missing. Why would I turn away from you now, when I love you so much?"

"Oh, Max, I wish I could believe that, when the bandages come off!"

"When will that be?"

"In a few days!"

"Are you nervous?"

"Very! What if…" she began to say when he claimed her lips to reassure her.

"I'll always love you just the way you are."

"But…"

"But, nothing," he growled. "I'll be here for you, all the way!"

Realizing she had fallen off to sleep with her head resting on his shoulder, he thought sadly. *'Oh, Cory, it wasn't just your beauty that I fell in love with. It was your innocence that captured my heart and soul.'*

Hearing her cry out while clinging to his shirtsleeve, he realized then she was dreaming.

"Mmmm…please, don't leave me…!" she cried out softly in her sleep, feeling as though he were pulling away from her once the bandages were taken off.

"I'm not going anywhere, Cory. I promise…!" he called out to her.

Unaware he wasn't alone, there came a woman's voice just then, breaking the silence, "I hope you can keep that promise!" she exclaimed from the open doorway.

Looking up, not liking the intrusion, he saw the same nurse who had helped give Cory her bath, standing there.

"What do you mean by that?" he asked heatedly.

"Promises are made to be broken. Ted attacked me too, seven years ago, and my new boyfriend made that very same promise. However, he soon left me for a model."

"I'm sorry to hear that, but not everyone is like your boyfriend."

"No, I can see that. The two of you have that special kind of love that only comes around once in a lifetime."

"You will find it again. Just give it time, and put the past behind you."

"I'll do that," she replied, while coming in to take her vital signs. "Do you need anything?"

"No, I'm just going to stay here with her."

"All right."

Leaving them to their privacy, he watched as the nurse, with her long blonde hair, pinned up in a bun at the back of her head, walked out, closing the door behind her.

"Damn you, Ted Harden," he growled, taking note of what he had learned to pass on to his friend later.

The next few days had gone by quietly, when she had gotten some flowers. One group that caught her attention was from Max himself, whereas, the rest came from Roger and the others, as well as her producer and agent.

And now the time had come for her bandages to come off.

"Hello young lady," the doctor called out, walking in with her nurse. "Are we ready for the unveiling?"

"Max!" she cried out across the room to him.

"I'm here!" he assured her, when coming over to stand by her side.

"Well, let's get started then," he announced, as he began first removing the bandage from her face. "Now keep in mind, the stitches will have to stay in for another week so your wound will heal properly."

"Oh, no…" she cried, "I have to be in New York before then, to help on the movie! I can't miss that again!"

"Then you will just have to go with the stitches! We can't take them out too soon, or you will run a risk of scar badly!"

"Will they be out in time for opening night then?"

"When will that be?"

"Two weeks, possibly, if everything goes well!"

"Well then, I see no reason why they shouldn't be able to! In fact, you'll look just fine for your grand finale."

"I wish I had some of your optimism," she grumbled, while feeling the first of the bandages being lifted off.

After a short while, the doctor stood back. "Well now, are you ready to see how it looks?" he asked, getting her a mirror.

Looking to her mother, who was standing off to one side, along with the others, she looked worried.

"Cory, it doesn't look too bad!" she tried to sound reassuring, while taking the mirror from the doctor to give to her.

At first glance she was horrified, while trying to cover her face. "It's awful!"

"Take it easy," he explained, while looking over the stitches closely, "and keep in mind, the light needs time to get to them for a little while, before they will begin to lighten up some."

With a reassuring laugh, Max replied, "I kind of like it that way. It reminds me of that tough little brat I knew," he said with a smile, while lightly tracing her jaw line.

"But Max… I look horrible."

"Give it time. Besides, how do you think I felt for the last several months? I felt like a freak. I lost my leg, and my marriage was going down the toilet! Although, she was leaving me anyway! It wasn't easy to start over."

"Cory, you have it a lot easier here. Max is in love with you, and you have accepted his handicap," both Mary and Rose reminded her.

"You're right. It's just a big shock seeing such an ugly scar." Then it hit her.

"Cory, what?" most of them asked.

"We are supposed to be getting married in a week and a half. How can I go through with that, looking like the bride of Frankenstein?"

"Hey now, slow down some here. Don't be making any rash decisions yet," Doc. Tanner suggested. "Wait until the stitches come out first. From the close examination that I have just done on you, at most, this scar will only look like a scratch."

"I hope so," she replied, looking from Tanner to Max, and then to the others. "I sure hope so!" she thought then more to herself.

"Doc, can we take her home now?" Max asked.

"I don't see why not! I think she'll probably heal just as

well in her own environment, as she will here. I'll just have the nurse come in to help you get ready."

"That won't be necessary," Rose spoke up, "I can do that myself."

"All right then! I'll have the discharge papers waiting for you at the nurse's station, when you're ready."

✥ *Chapter Seventeen* ✥

Later that day, sitting back in the old cabin, on the sofa, Cory was reading over the agenda for the following week, when she was to go to New York.

"I wish you wouldn't go. Or at least take your friends with you," Max was suggesting, while coming over to sit next to her. "I still have to get the cabin roof repaired in time for the wedding. That's unless you're going to cancel it!"

"I don't know! I need some time to think things through! Right now I…"

"Feel that I couldn't love you like you are?"

"Yes."

"Cory…"

"Max, please, just give me some time!"

"Okay! But for now I'll just go over and get your things from Roger's place," he offered, while leaning over to give her a kiss.

As he did, she turned her head unintentionally, while causing him to kiss her cheek.

Pulling back to look at her, he sadly shook his head, "I understand, you're not comfortable with a man getting too close to you right now."

"I know that it isn't you, though. Like I know it's Ted that is to blame for this," she explained, just as he went to get up and walk over to the door.

"Yeah, well I'll see ya later."

"Max…?" She jumped up, and went after him.

Turning back to look at her, the expression etched on his face was one of pain, and yet the look in her eyes were clouded and full of fear.

"I love you…!" she cried.

"I hope you never stop!" he gave her a slight grin, just as he turned, and was about to head out.

Just then, he felt a tug at his arm.

"Yes…?" he turned back to look down into her warm, and yet unhappy eyes, when her bottom lip began to quiver.

Leaning down, he went on to kiss her.

"You know, I'm really going to need your help," she whispered, when he went to kiss her again. Only this time the kiss had gotten deeper, as their lips pressed on even more, while tasting their desire for each other.

"You've got it, and then some," he groaned, pulling away to look down into her eyes. "But let me remind you, you are still so darn beautiful to me. So make sure you behave yourself. We still have over a week before I can make you my own."

"Do you really still want me?"

"Oh, girl…" he gritted his teeth at the thought of just picking her up and making her his, "don't you *ever* think I don't." Turning back to go on out to the truck, he called out over his shoulder, "Hey, when I get back, we're going for a walk!"

"Fine!"

After seeing him off, she was just about to turn and go back inside, when the phone began to ring.

Sitting right next to it, Rose picked it up, before the second ring. "Hello!" she said, answering it.

"Hello! Is Cory Spencer available? This is Sid, the producer of the movie we're doing on her book."

"Oh, yes, I know who you are! This is her mother. She's right here," she replied, looking to her daughter. "Are you ready to talk to anyone?"

"Is that Sid?" she asked, taking the phone.

"Yes."

Sitting herself down near her mother, she cried out, happy to hear from him, "Sid!"

"Yes, and how are you holding up?"

"I'm holding! I guess you're calling about next week?"

"Well, sort of! We really need you, Cory. I know this is a little sudden. However, we are prepared to have security beefed up to prevent any more attacks. We'll even have two men outside your hotel suite, and two people in the room with you. As for the studio…"

"Sid…! Sid…! I'll be there. I just need to talk to my fiancé and the others first."

"Great! Then we'll be seeing you tomorrow?"

"What…? No…!Tomorrow…? That's too soon…!"

"Yes, Cory, tomorrow. Can you be here?"

"Well…" she had to think quickly, while resting her forehead into her free hand. "Yes, sure…!"

"Great! I'll see you then."

After hanging up, she looked lost for a moment.

"Cory… are you sure you're ready for that?" Rose asked.

"No, not really! But I have to do something to keep myself busy! And there is the matter of a lot of time and money put on this project that he has spent on it."

"All right, but tomorrow…? Why so soon?"

"They are wanting to try it out on Broadway first!"

"Well then, why don't you call and ask your friends to go along with you?"

"Yeah, I'm going to do that now! As for Kate though, I

doubt that she would be able to go, since New York would be out of her jurisdiction."

"That's a shame! She has really come to like you."

"I know. I really like her too."

A short time later, while still on the phone with Angela, Max and Roger walked in with their things in hand.

"What's going on?" Max asked, seeing the awkward look on Rose's face.

"I'll let Cory fill you in," she replied, when Max turned to walk back outside after overhearing bits and pieces of her conversation with Angela.

Getting through with her talk, she turned to the others, "Well, that's all taken care of! Angela said she would be right up as soon as she closes the shop!"

"And Jenny?" Rose asked.

"She can't, she has a lot going on right now."

"Oh… well, at least you have Angela to go with you."

"Yes," she agreed, looking around the room.

Feeling helpless, Rose nodded off toward the door. "He's outside. I think waiting for your walk."

"All right!"

Getting up, Cory couldn't help but notice how Roger was looking a little sad at how her mother was taking things. Instead of pondering over it, she walked over to the door to see Max standing near his truck. Not all that sure of what to say, she went on out to join him.

Hearing her approach, he turned slowly to face her, when the look on his face was full of emotions. "So, when do you have to leave?" he asked quietly.

"Tomorrow morning!"

"That doesn't give us much time then, does it?" he asked, while taking her hand to walk down to their favorite spot.

"No, I guess it doesn't!" she stated, when stopping to look up at him. "Max…"

"I'm sorry," he replied, turning away so that she wouldn't see just how much this was really bothering him. "It's just that I don't want you to go back to New York. I want you to stay here with me. Let James handle the darn book!"

"I wish I could, but they want someone that knows the impact of the story. So I have to do this myself! Won't you please come with me?"

"I can't! I have to get the roof fixed!"

"Then won't you at least be there for the opening night? Mom and Roger are coming, along with your mom!"

"I'll definitely try," he replied, while turning to look back into her eyes. "Besides," he smiled, "I want to see this masterpiece of yours."

"You would be really proud of me. The book was a great hit. Now the movie is going to be even better!"

Putting his arms around her, he held her close. "No doubt in my mind! You have always had a good imagination for things like that."

"Uh huh! And as for my going…" she added with her own very special smile.

"You had better call me every day. Which reminds me," they continued walking. "how long will you be gone?"

"Following opening night, next Friday!"

Reaching their spot, they went over to take a seat, while bringing his good foot up to rest the heel of it against the rock, while resting his elbow on his knee.

Taking that time, he looked off in the distance. "You know," he finally spoke up, breaking the silence, "I'm going to miss you like crazy, you know that, don't you?"

"I hope so!"

"Cory?" He turned back to look at her.

"Yes?"

"Before you go," he stopped to push himself back off

the rock, "there's something I want to give you to help you remember how there is a man back here that is truly in love with you."

"Oh...? And what might that be?" she asked, not seeing that he had bought anything with him. But then, no sooner had she said anything, he turned to pull her off the rock, and into his awaiting arms.

"This..." he exclaimed, claiming her lips passionately.

As the kiss grew deeper, his hand went to the small of her back to bring her up even more in his arms.

Moaning her response, "Oh, Max, you aren't going to make this any easier for me, are you?" she breathed heavily, while looking up into his smiling face.

"That's the plan," he laughed, while still holding her.

"Oh..." she too laughed, "and what plan was that?"

"How you'll be so busy thinking of me, and our honeymoon that you won't be able to concentrate on anything else."

"Oh... you are so... mean!"

"You think? In that case, my plan will work. Now," he went to pull away, while taking her hand, "what do you say we get back up to the cabin? You're making me hungry!"

"Mmmm... good, because you're making me crazy!"

That evening, after enjoying another one of Rose's famous pot roasts, both Cory and Max slipped off, back down to the fishing hole, to be alone, while Rose, Mary and Roger started up a friendly game of cards. As for Angela and Kate, the two had each found a book to read, while curling up on each end of the couch to get comfortable.

"Mmmm... this is nice," Cory sighed, while leaning in close to him, as he wrapped his arms around her to help keep the chill off.

"Just think how it's going to look once it's fixed up for the wedding!"

Pulling back, she looked up into his warm loving face. "You know you could always change your mind! We don't have to rush into it now that Ted is behind bars!"

"Who's rushing?" he asked, wondering if she was still having doubts.

"Well…"

"Cory, you aren't going to change your mind, are you?"

"Oh, Max, I just…"

"Hush," he growled, pulling her back into his arms, "I'm not about to change my mind. I want you in my life, little Cory 'Brat' Hall."

"Oh, yeah!" she laughed tearfully.

"God, girl," he too laughed, taking that moment to tilt her head up to claim the softness of her lips to his. Doing so, he found them trembling. "Are you cold?"

"A little!"

"Damn," he swore, taking her by the hand, "I have got to get you back up to the cabin, before you go and get sick."

"Max, I'm not going to get sick!" she laughed, while going along with him. "Really…!"

"Sure. And I'm not going to be standing in front of a firing squad if you do. Your mom would have my hide if you were to get sick now. Not to mention, all those people depending on you for this movie coming up. That's all I need."

"And our wedding!" she reminded lovingly.

Stopping along the trail, he turned back to see her sweet smiling face, and knew she was serious. "And… our wedding," he smiled broadly.

"Uh huh," she returned, seeing how he was worried that she would call it off. "I'm trying, Max."

"I know you are, and I love you for it."

"You know it's still kind of hard not to see what all Ted had done to me, but…"

"Cory, it's going to take time, no doubt! However, don't forget that you're not alone here, I care and so do the others!"

"I know, and I'm really glad that you and the others are here for me. If not for that, I would have just let him…"

"No…!" he stopped and spun her around, before taking her back into his arms.

Nearly crying at the horror of what he would have found if Roger hadn't had spoken to her on the phone that night. He didn't want to think about the nightmare anymore, he just wanted her, Cory Hall, in his life, and safe where she belonged.

"Oh, Max…! Mmmm… it feels so right being here in your arms!"

"Mmmm… and holding you," he pulled back slightly, as she gazed up at him, "Lord, woman, it's almost eerie."

"Eerie?" she asked, wrinkling her nose up at him.

With a small laugh, he explained, "You and me, standing here, sixteen years later."

"Ah… who would have figured? Your little brat all…"

"Hush," he laughed, covering her mouth. "Don't remind me, it's taking all that I have not to have you right now."

"Max?"

"Yes?"

"Thank you!"

"For?" he looked deep into her eyes, as the sun was about to disappear behind the hills.

"Loving me," she replied, bringing her face up alongside his to whisper into his ear, "I love you so… much."

"Same here, meanness. Mmmm… same here," he groaned into her soft sweet smelling hair.

After breakfast the next morning, Cory and Angela got their things loaded up to leave for the airport. Turning back to Max, she could see that he was trying to put on a happy front.

"I guess this is it?" he asked, while putting the last of her things into the trunk of her car.

"Yes, and I wish you would change your mind and let someone else fix the roof."

"I wish it were all that easy," he replied, while holding her for a few more minutes, before they had to leave, "but until I can get away, take care of yourself over there. Even though Ted is back in prison, he still poses a threat to you."

"I know."

"Cory?"

"Yes?"

"Call me when the two of you get in!"

"I will!" She kissed him goodbye. "I love you!"

"I love you, too!"

Fighting back the sudden urge to cry, she placed two fingers to her lips, as she backed away to get into her car.

Starting it up, Max's cell phone began to ring.

"See ya!" the others waved goodbye, as she and Angela pulled away.

"She's going to be fine!" Mary announced, seeing Rose's worried expression.

"I hope so!" she returned, while she and Mary went back inside.

"Roger...?" Max called out, getting off his cell phone.

"Yeah?"

"I've got to go! Can you get some of the boys to give you a hand on the roof, until I get back?"

"Yeah, sure! What's going on?"

"Mike! He wants to see me!"

"Don't worry about a thing, just go."

Having a sneaking suspicion what Mike wanted; Roger waved goodbye.

Meanwhile, the drive to the airport was long, but sad for Cory, having to leave her loved ones behind.

"Cory," Angela spoke up, sensing her friend's sorrow,

"you'll be seeing Max, before too awful long! With all that you have to do to get this project off the ground, the time will simply fly by."

"I know it will. I just wish I didn't have to go back quite so soon!"

"Because of Ted?"

"Yes. I can't bear to be in the same state he is. What if he makes good on his threat, and breaks out?"

"They will catch him."

"Catch him? He nearly killed me back there! How are they going to be able to stop him again?"

Sitting in the seat next to her, Angela didn't have an answer, and yet for the first time she could feel what Cory was going through. *'God, please help us all if he were to get out again,'* she thought quietly.

Arriving at the airport, Mike met Cory and Angela after she had parked her car in one of their security parking lots. "Cory!" he called out in the crowded terminal, as he made his way toward her.

"Mike? What are you doing here?"

"Just doing my job!" he smiled. "I have a young lady here that will be going with the two of you."

"Oh? Who?" as if she had to ask, when he pointed her out over at the exit ramp, "Kate…" Cory cried, as she went up to hug her.

"Hello!" she greeted happily, while looking over her shoulder at Mike.

Seeing another one of Mike's plans walking up, she pulled back smiling.

"What?" Cory asked, sensing something was up.

"Hello, Mike, I see she has met her extra companion."

"Max…?" Cory cried again, when hearing his familiar voice coming up behind her.

Turning to see him standing there with a big grin on his face, she wanted to smack him.

"Hi, beautiful," he grinned, seeing her surprised expression.

"*You* set this up?"

"Well, sort of!"

"Mike…?" she turned questioningly.

Smiling even more, he conceded, "Max told me that he had a lot to do back here, and since he couldn't be with you, the least I could do is send Kate with the two of you."

"When Captain Jones called last night, while the two of you were out, I was hoping he would be able to find a way for me to go with you to New York."

"Thanks, Mike," she replied, turning then to Max. "And you…" she teased, as Max tried looking like an innocent bystander, "thanks for making me feel so safe."

"I wouldn't have it any other…" Max began.

When over the intercom, a woman's voice announced, "Delta flight 239 to New York City, gate 7. Delta flight 239 to New York City gate 7."

"Well, I guess this is it," he announced sadly, while taking her into his arms once again. "Remember to call me the minute you get there."

"I…I will," she replied, as their tears began to find their way out.

"God, Cory…" he cried, "I wish this didn't have to be so hard for me to just let you go!"

"Max," Mike interrupted, "you've got to let her get on her flight! You'll be with her soon enough! It's just going to be a couple of days or so, that's all!" he explained, while taking Max's arm after he and Cory kissed one last time.

"I'll call you!" she called out, as she and the others turned down the ramp to board the plane.

Smiling, both Max and Mike watched as the plane taxied down the runway. "Hey, how about we go and get some coffee," he offered, "I want to hear more about these wedding plans the two of you are working on."

"Sounds good to me! I could sure use a cup right about now."

"Yes, I can only imagine how hard it must be to watch someone you love get on a plane and fly away."

"More than I had ever known possible," he groaned, while looking out the large plate glass window one last time. "I just never thought we would be falling in love. Not to mention, getting married. Man, Mike, I have known her ever since she was just a little brat. And now look at her," he went on shaking his head. "She has really stolen my heart, man…! Big time!"

"Yes, I can see that," he agreed, turning away from the window, once again. "Now, what do you say we go and get that coffee?"

"Sure!" he agreed, walking off toward the airport coffee shop.

Meanwhile on the plane, Cory and the others were going over her wedding plans that she had brought with her.

"Oh, Cory… this dress looks beautiful!" Kate cried, looking over at a long white, flowing gown in one of New York's finest catalogs.

"They told me that it would hold up better for an outside wedding," she was saying, while admiring its delicate lace, and off the shoulder style.

"And just to think that Max is going to be fixing up the pond for the ceremony," Angela stated warmly.

"I wish I could help," Kate cried, when Cory turned just then, remembering how sweet her lily-like voice was, when they sang together back at the cabin.

"Oh, but you can!"

"How?"

"By singing at our wedding!"

"Oh, no, I don't know about that. My voice isn't all that good!"

"Yes, it is! And you won't be singing alone either!"

"I won't?" she asked, looking from Cory to Angela.

"Don't look at me!" Angela laughed. "When it comes to singing, I'm a frog!"

"No…" Cory cracked up laughing, "Mike will be singing too, while playing his guitar."

"Really?" she asked excitedly.

"Yes."

"All right, then, I'll do it!"

"I hope you mean that!"

"Yes, I do!"

"Ladies and Gentlemen…" the attendant announced, "Please place your tray tables in the upright position and fasten your seatbelts. We are now approaching JFK. And as usual, thank you for flying with us."

Doing just that, the plane was now getting ready to land.

"Wow, New York," both Kate and Angela cried, wide-eyed at all the high-rise buildings and skyscrapers, unlike anything they had back home.

"Yes, wow," Cory, though groaned, feeling a slight shiver of panic racing up her spine.

After getting off at the plane, they were greeted by a couple of officers to take them into a private office.

"Ms. Spencer?" a somewhat tall, yet rugged, sandy blonde haired man, spoke deeply.

"Yes?"

"I'm Captain Samuel Broady, with NYPD. I'm here to make sure your stay is a safe one."

"Oh…?"

Seeing her apprehension, he went on, "Captain Jones and I were partners for a while after we got out of West Point Academy."

"I see," she returned, feeling a little more at ease.

Turning then to the others, he looked at Kate, "You must be the one called Martin! Mike told me you would be watching Ms. Spencer and her friend here."

"Yes, sir," she stood at attention.

"Relax, Officer Martin," he ordered. "As for what you were sent here for. In order for you to do that, we had to have you temporarily assigned to my unit. As for your qualifications, Mike says you're one of his best female officers. With that said, let's get you ladies over to your hotel so that a certain bride-to-be can call her fiancé," he smiled.

"Thank you, Captain," Cory replied, smiling back.

"Ladies," Broady stopped at the door, "what do you say we stick to a first name basis, while you're here, starting with calling me Sam."

"All right!" they all agreed, while filing out to an awaiting limo.

"When we arrive," he stopped to turn back, "you will be meeting your personal guards, Sandy, Gregg, David and Cord. They'll be there at the hotel and studio at all times. Cord and Gregg," he continued on out to the car, "will be staying by your side at all times. As for Sandy and Kate, they will be with you as well. Kate, you're Cory's companion and secretary as you were in Minnesota. And Sandy, when you meet her, will be your maid."

"What does David do?" Cory asked once they reached the limo.

"He and another undercover officer will be staying at your door."

Just as the limo came within reach of the hotel, Sam went to pull out his walkie-talkie to call the undercover officer that was waiting on him. "Gregg?"

"Here," he replied over the radio.

"We're just about to pull up out front."

"We're on our way now."

"And Cord, did he make it in all right?" he asked, while looking over at Cory with a half-baked smile on his handsome face.

"He sure did!" Gregg returned with a hint of humor in his voice.

Looking puzzled, Cory asked, "Sam... why does that sound so much like Mike Jones on the other end?"

"Because it is!"

Turning to Gregg, who was now opening their door, once the limo had stopped, Sam introduced the women to both undercover officers. "Gentlemen, this is Cory Spencer and her companions. Treat them well, and you both just might get a nice tip," he said, hiding a grin.

"Yes, sir," they both bowed their heads.

Turning to Cory, while dressed up as two bellhops, Gregg spoke up first, while taking her hand to kiss, "Ma'am, we are glad to be of service to you and your companions, here."

"Oh, Gregg is it?" she teased.

"Yes, ma'am."

"If you so much as drop my things, I will have you fired," she returned, while fighting to keep a straight face.

"Yes, ma'am," he smiled, seeing Sam's expression turn serious.

Looking at the other undercover officer with dark brown hair, mustache, and a pair of glasses, she added, "And Cord!"

"Ma'am," he replied with a deeper voice, while looking from Cory to Gregg, hoping that she hadn't realized who he was, when Sam stepped in to interject.

"Gentlemen, we should be getting these ladies things taken up to their suite now."

"Yes, of course, sir!" they both replied, while quickly getting their things loaded up on the roller rack, before taking them up to their suite.

Standing back for a brief moment though, Cory studied their disguises, before Sam spoke up again, breaking into her thoughts, "Ms. Spencer, shall we?"

"Yes, yes of course."

❧ *Chapter Eighteen* ❧

Arriving at their luxurious suite, done up in the early twentieth century style, Cory was greeted by a medium built woman with graying hair and glasses, looking to be in her early fifties, *'That had to be a disguise.'* "Sandy...?" she cried out excitedly, while going up to give her a hug. "Oh, my, gosh! This is incredible! You look so much like your mother standing there!"

"Hi yourself, Aunt Cory!" she chuckled.

"This isn't good," Sam shook his head.

"Sir?" Sandy spoke up, standing more at attention, when she looked over to see his apprehension.

"You two know each other?" he asked, looking serious.

"Yes," Cory explained. "Her mother took me in when I first came to New York. Later, I knew Sandy wanted to be a police officer, I just didn't know she became one, yet!"

"Sandy..." he began.

"Sir!"

"With this bit of information, are you sure you are going to be able to do your work effectively?"

"Oh, yes, sir, I can!"

"Sam," Mike cut in, looking at the two women, "we just might have something here."

"What's that?"

"They already know each other. That'll take the edge off things!"

"And I can still be protective of her!" Sandy put in. "She's been more like an aunt to me then my own aunt has."

"All right, but there is no room for screw ups," he ordered, when turning to the others. "I want everyone's attention here. Sorry, Ms. Spencer."

"Please, Cory."

"I'll try to remember that," he smiled, but only briefly, before going on. "Now, we need to keep our eyes open at all times, in case Harden succeeds with his threat to break out of prison. He may be in there now, but he is hell-bent on getting out to hurt Ms. Spencer here. Sorry, Cory. If by chance he does break out, the prison warden will contact me right away. Any questions?"

Looking around the room, everyone looked amongst themselves, wondering why the seriousness.

"Sam," Mike spoke up, "are you positive he has been trying to break out?"

Looking at Cory, he didn't answer, instead he went on to discuss other matters. "All right, you know what your duties are. Let's also remember, if you have to relieve yourself, do not ask a stranger to fill in for you. Don't trust anyone, not even an employee of this hotel. Ted has already posed as an orderly. He can just as well pose as a bellboy, too."

"Excuse me, Sam!" Cory interrupted, while feeling ill at ease.

"Cory?"

"He wouldn't hesitate posing as a housekeeper, female or not."

"You heard her! So let's be on our guard, at all times."

"You sound as though he were already out," Officer David Brice commented.

"Sam... is he?" Cord/Max asked, while not being careful to hide his voice, when Cory looked at him questioningly.

"No, but he has been trying," he replied, looking to Cory. "Sorry."

Seeing the expression on her face, along with Max's, as he started to reach out to her, Mike stopped him so that Kate and Sandy could comfort her. "What are they going to do about it?" Mike asked.

"They're placing him back in maximum security now."

"But they were supposed to have had him there already!" Cory cried.

"They did."

"And they don't now?" Cord growled.

"He had them fooled, but not anymore. While you're here in New York," Sam turned to Cory, "they'll keep him there under lock and key."

"Good," Mike replied sharply, while looking to Cord. Noticing how much this was getting to him, he took his arm. "Come on, let's go get things set up."

"One more thing," Sam interrupted. "If I'm not here, you are to answer to Mike. He'll be in charge."

"Yes, sir," both female officers returned, while gathering up their suitcases to take into their appropriate rooms to unpack.

Turning as well to go into one of the two bedrooms the suite had to offer, Cory passed Cord on the way. Catching the scent of his aftershave, she quickly spun around to look up at him. Doing so, she stumbled, when losing her balance. At that moment, he automatically reached out to catch her.

"Are you all right?" he asked, while helping her up.

"I'm fine!" she smiled, while trying to hide her excitement at realizing Max got to come after all.

"Are you sure?"

"Yes, it was just that aftershave lotion of yours," she continued coyly. "I wish my boyfriend could smell so nice."

"Thanks," he grumbled miserably. "If you're sure you're all right, I'll just be going now."

Sounding disappointed, he turned to walk over to the door to leave with the others.

But then Cory cleared her throat. "No, I'm sure! Thank you!" she called out, fighting back a sly grin.

At that time, he looked back with his all knowing smile.

"Cory," Sam added, "I'll be needing an itinerary of what your week will be like."

"All right, I'll have one ready for you by dinner."

"That'll be fine. Shall we go, gentlemen, and let the ladies do their thing then, before dinner?"

"Ladies," Mike turned to nod his head along with Max, who gazed over at Cory for a moment longer, before walking out.

"Cory... was that Max?" Angela asked, surprisingly.

"Sure was!" she grinned. "Hmmm, and I wonder if he had this planned out, too?"

"No," Kate put in, "Mike planned that out, knowing that Max would want to be here with you."

"But what about the porch roof?"

"Mike went to Roger, behind Max's back, and asked him to handle it, along with some of the other guys."

Feeling relieved at having him so close, she went in to call James to get their itinerary.

Meanwhile, back at the prison, it wasn't Ted they had back in maximum lockup, but a look-alike he had exchanged shirts with that had their numbers on. There for, the guards had no idea they had the wrong man, while he snuck out through his usual escape route, a fence out in back, near an old shack.

Finding his hidden duffle bag of clothes, he quickly changed into his black faded jeans, tennis shoes, and an old plaid work shirt, before bending down to search for yet a smaller bag. One which held a small bottle of chloroform and a rag, meant to be used on Cory. "Soon, Cory," he sneered, looking down at the bottle in his hand. "Soon I will have what was rightfully mine, and life as you know it, will be over for you and your sweet farm boy shortly. Just to think, I will have taken your innocence, before he knows what hit him, when they go to bury your cold, dead corpse in the ground. Oh, yeah, I'll have my way with you! To think, you; laid out after having been chloroformed and carried off to take what I have waited for, for such a long time." With that said, he laughed quietly, while shoving the bottle back down in the bag, before making his final getaway.

Later that evening, Cory gave Max the cold shoulder, acting as though she were still oblivious to who he was, while giving Sam the list he was asking for.

"Good, I'll have this copied and given out to the others," he returned, when arriving just outside their suite. "As for now, ladies, it's getting late."

"Yes, it is," they agreed, saying their goodnights, when Mike turned to Max at that time.

"Are you staying with them tonight, or am I?"

"Why don't you? I'll cover it tomorrow night."

"All right, I'll see you guys in the morning then," he replied, saying his goodnights to both Max and Sam, when at that time, Sam turned to go on into their suite, leaving Max hanging back in the hall.

Turning to the guards outside Cory's room, before the women went inside, Mike asked how things were going.

"Fine, sir!" David replied.

"Good, we'll have coffee on over in the security suite if you guys need any. However, one of you must stay at your post at all times."

"Thank you, we could probably use some later tonight," the other officer admitted gladly.

"Fine," he nodded, looking back at his friend.

"Goodnight," he grumbled, looking slightly to Cory, in hopes she would finally recognize him, before turning to take his leave.

As he did, she tried frantically to think of something clever to say, before he went in, closing the door. Then it came to her, *'The aftershave lotion,'* "Oh, Cord!" she called out, stopping him, just as he started to open the door.

"Yes, ma'am?" he turned to look back at her, while not wanting to look too eager.

"I've been meaning to ask…"

"Yes?"

"Where did you get your aftershave lotion?" she asked, with that ornery grin of her.

"My girlfriend got it for me." he replied with the same ornery grin.

"Gee, I'll have to tell my fiancé about it," she smiled sweetly.

"Yeah, I'm sure he would really like that, you mean little brat!" he laughed, seeing now that she was fully aware of who he was.

Smiling down at her, he turned to go on into his own suite.

"Cord…" she whispered, as he turned back to look into her slightly tear filled eyes, "I love you…!"

"You had better!" he returned, shaking his head with still yet, a warm smile on his face to cheer her up.

"Well, gentlemen," Kate spoke up, smiling, while taking Cory's arm to go inside, "goodnight."

After closing the door, Mike turned back to Max, grinning, "I think she knows!"

"Oh, yeah, she knows!" he laughed, going into her suite.

Once inside, he looked across the room, as she slowly turned to look back at him.

"Oh, yeah, she definitely knows!" he smiled. "Don't you, brat?" he asked, as she ran up throwing her arms around him.

"Oh, yes, I sure do!" she cried, just before he could claim her lips.

"Hey, you two!" Kate and the others laughed. "What would Max think if he knew you were kissing another man?"

"Why tell him!" she exclaimed, looking up into his smiling eyes. "I found my true love, right here!"

"I don't know..." he laughed deeply, "I'm pretty crazy about my girlfriend!"

"All right, Maxi..." she started, when he went to cover her mouth.

"Oh no, you don't," he warned, looking into her eyes warmly.

"Oh, pooh, you sure know how to take the fun out of one's evening," she complained playfully, when they heard a knock at the door.

Going over to answer it, it was Sam, and the look on his face wasn't good. "Sam..." Mike started.

"Mike!"

"What's up?"

"Miss Hall," Sam apologized, "if you will excuse us. We need to leave you for a moment," he explained, while taking Sandy and Kate with him and the others across the hall.

Before leaving Max looked back at Cory, "See ya, squirt!" he laughed.

"Yeah, see ya!" she returned, looking a worried, when he closed the door behind him.

"Wow, he really looked intense!" Angela commented, while going in to unpack the rest of her things.

"Yes, he certainly did!" she agreed, while thinking what to do to get her mind off the look that was on Sam's face, by flipping through the room service pamphlet. "Hey..." Cory called out, walking over to take a seat on the sofa, "I could sure use a snack, how about you?"

"Why, what do they have?" she asked, returning to the living room.

"Ice cream, fresh fruit and veggies," she replied, when looking up from the pamphlet. "How does that sound to you?"

"Sounds good! Can we go ahead and order?"

"I'll just go and ask the two guards outside!" she returned, while getting up to head for the door, when Max walked.

"Where are you going?" he asked, closing the door behind him.

"To let the guards know we were going to order up room service!" she explained, while he went to put an arm around her shoulder.

"I'm all for that! What were you two having?"

"Ice cream, fruit and veggies!" Angela returned, while plopping herself down on the sofa, in a soft light blue pair of sweats.

"Great!" Going over to the phone, he called it in for them, before going out into the hall to let the guards know.

"Just make sure you're on your toes," he whispered.

"Yes, sir. We will."

"Max…" Cory came up behind him, and as usual, she suspected there was something wrong. "Do you want to tell me just what's going on?"

"Cory," he began, not wanting her to be scared, "Sam just wants us on our guard in case Ted succeeds in breaking out."

"Has he?" Angela blurted out, when the door opened and Sandy walked in alone.

Seeing his expression, Cory began wondering the same thing. "Max… is he…?"

"Cory," he groaned, knowing he was trapped into telling her one way or another, "we're not sure yet. For now, we want you to stay here at the hotel. It'll be safer for you here, and Sam is putting on extra undercover officers at every stairway, door, and elevator, even at the front desk and kitchen. As for room service, there will only be two waiters bringing up your food. If they aren't the ones bringing it to you, Sam wants you to use this to call us," he explained, holding out a paging device.

"Max... No..." she cried, throwing her arms up, as he went to try and comfort her.

"Cory... I'm sorry...!"

"No... this can't be h...happening again...!" she continued, when he was finally able to get her settled down enough to pull her into his arms. "This can't be! Not again...! I was hoping this was all finally over with!" she sobbed.

"We were all hoping that very thing," he offered lovingly.

"But then what..."

"We don't know. Sam is over there working on it now. We just have to wait and see what he comes up with."

Just then, they heard another knock at the door.

Pulling away, Max went to check it out, "Who is it?" he asked, while resting his hand under his vest, where he kept his service revolver.

"Room service!"

"He's clean, sir!" Officer Brice called out, when Sam walked out of the security suite just then.

"Sorry," Max replied, while opening the door, "we have to be careful."

"Brice, you did good," Sam spoke up, introducing the new undercover officer. "This is Officer Tate," he went on, walking into their suite, "he will be one of your waiters from now on."

"Your fruit, veggies and ice cream, ma'am!" he offered.

"Thank you."

"Tate!" Max returned, walking him back to the door.

"Yes, sir?"

"Max, tip the poor man!" Angela teased.

"That's not necessary," Tate returned with a smile.

"That's it!" Cory cried out.

"Cory...?" both Max, and Mike spoke up, when Mike entered the room, hear the conversation.

"Sure... that can be our signal! If the waiter was to accept a tip, then he isn't one of Sam's men!"

"She has a point!" Sam commented.

"All right, that's what we'll do then," Mike agreed, while walking Tate out.

Turning to the others, Sam announced, "After you're all finished here, we had better be getting some sleep. Tomorrow will be here soon enough," he concluded, as he turned to head back over to the security suite to check on a few more things.

After spending a little more time together, Max had to go. While walking him to the door, she gave him a warm and loving hug goodnight. "Thanks for being here!"

"I'm glad Mike suggested it," he was saying, just as Mike walked in.

"Hey," he ordered cheerfully, "don't you think it's time for everyone to get some sleep around here?"

"Well, I guess that's my cue," Max laughed, kissing her goodnight. "I'll see you in the morning."

"Yeah, I...I'll see ya!" she returned, watching him walk slowly out the door.

Going back into her room, Sandy followed, offering to brush her hair for her, like she had done before. "You know, I have always loved fixing your hair," she smiled, "it's so long and thick."

"Really, would you like to fix it in the morning for me, then?"

"Sure, I'd love to!"

"Good! Now, if you don't mind."

"I know we've got to get ready for bed."

Giving Cory a warm hug, Sandy jumped up off the bed, and started for the door. Stopping, she turned to look back. "I'm glad you're back. I've missed you."

"Same here," she smiled, while watching Sandy rush off to get some sleep.

By the next morning, Cory and the others were up and dressed, before the guys, when walking into the living room they all stopped, when seeing Mike asleep on the sofa.

"Should we get him up?" Kate asked, looking down at him lying there.

"Perhaps we should, he would be pretty upset if we didn't," Cory suggested in a warning-like tone.

"How do you want to handle him?" Sandy asked. "He sure looks pretty much out of it."

"I have an idea!" Kate grinned.

Kneeling down next to him, she began whispering in his ear.

Suddenly, catching her by surprise, he grabbed her by the arms and flipped her over onto the sofa so fast she barely had time to react.

"Mike…" she cried, "that's not fair!"

"What do you expect?" he returned, looking down into her sparkling brown eyes.

"Well," she began, while feeling his grip loosen. Taking advantage of it, she threw him off balance, and onto the floor, where she now had him pinned, "revenge," she smiled.

Grinning up at her, he then quickly rolled her over onto her back, before kissing her half passionately, though that part of it was not intended.

Taken aback by his sudden action, she felt dazed.

"And now, Miss Kate," he growled lightly, while gazing puzzledly into her soft, gentle brown eyes, yet with his own confused blue ones, "revenge or not, you never ever want to approach a man sleeping on the sofa to whisper sweet nothings into his ear."

"I'll keep that in mind!" she laughed, just about the time Max and Sam walked in.

Seeing the two of them on the floor, Sam cleared his throat, "Well, what do we have here?" he asked, with his hands resting on his hips. "Mike? Kate?"

Looking up over their heads to see Sam and Max standing there grinning, Mike grinned as well, while turning back to look down at Kate's embarrassed expression, "Oh, just a little lesson in what happens when a certain female officer tries to wake her commander, who by the way, was already awake," he explained with a hearty laugh, while helping her up. "I heard you ladies talking, so I thought I'd just teach you a lesson."

"Oh… I see…" she frowned, "because if that's the best you can do at kissing, I'll have to pass on any future lessons."

"All right… Kate…!" the others cheered her on, with the exception of Mike, as he looked at her profoundly.

"Okay, Miss Kate, I'll remember you said that," he laughed. "Now, who's ready for breakfast?" he asked, heading for the door.

"I think we all are," Max replied, holding out his arm for Cory.

As everyone headed down to the hotel restaurant, they all laughed over various subjects which had come up, including her movie, before heading over to the studio to finish up what needed to be done, before Friday night's opening.

Nearing the main floor lobby, Max turned to Cory and asked, "So, how was your night?" he smiled.

"Fine! But…"

"But, what?" he asked, when his smile began to fade, worried that her dreams may have come back to haunt her.

But then, seeing a hint of a smile, he relaxed.

"Lonely," she replied.

"Oh, not for much longer, I hope!"

"Mmmm… I can hardly wait."

Knowing what she was thinking, he smiled, while holding her close.

It wasn't long after having finished eating a hearty breakfast, a limo was sent to take them to the studio, where they were escorted in to find Sid and the others working.

"Well, you made it!" he called out, greeting Cory and her friends warmly. "What do you think?"

"Cool!" she replied, looking over the stage, while the others walked over to observe from a safe distance.

At that point, leaning over, Mike whispered a warning into Kate's ear, "Remember what you're here for."

"Yes, sir."

"Cory!" Max spoke up.

"Yes?"

"We won't be far. We're just going around to check things out, while you're working on the script. While we're doing that, keep Kate and Sandy with you at all times."

"I will, I promise," she smiled, while giving him a hug, before going off to get some work done with Sid and the others.

"Hey, you ready?" Mike asked, walking up.

Smiling, he nodded his head, while watching his lady run off to get started. "Yeah, I'm ready," he agreed, unable to help but feel proud of her, before going around to check things over throughout the studio. Even then, the thought of wishing she hadn't come back to New York with Ted still being a constant threat still bothered him.

"What do you think?" Mike asked, while looking over the stage props.

"I don't know," he returned, while looking at the lighting equipment, "this stuff doesn't look too promising."

"You're right," he agreed, making a note of a few frayed cable wires, "let's have it checked out, before opening night."

"Damn!" Sam groaned just then.

"What is it?" Mike asked.

"This studio, it has all sorts of hiding places Ted could hide in," he growled heatedly.

"You're right about that!" Max agreed, while turning back to Mike with a serious look on his face.

"Have you told her yet?" Mike asked.

"No, I was hoping we would have enough security to watch over her. She has already been through so much."

"Yeah, well," Sam spoke up, "you know for yourself just how dangerous this man is!"

"So I've had the dubious honor of finding out."

Seeing all that they could, the three headed over to stage three to continue with their check.

Meanwhile, the others continued working, until the time had passed to break for lunch.

"Are we ready?" Sid asked, while tossing the main script onto the desk.

"Sure!" they all agreed, except for Cory.

Sensing her hesitation, Sid turned back to study her for a moment. "Cory?"

"Yeah?" she returned, staring down at the last few pages of her script.

"Are you ready?"

"No, not just yet. I'm sorry!" she exclaimed, looking up from the desk. "Why don't you guys go ahead without me. I'm going to stay and finish up on the last few pages, before calling it quits."

"Are you sure? You know you shouldn't overdo it?"

"Yeah, I'm sure!"

"All right, but don't work too long. We're going over to stage three to rehearse the last act."

"All right. And Sid…"

"Yes?"

"Tell Max I'll be fine. There's a security guard here to keep me company."

"I will," he returned, heading out to his car with his crew, as she started back to work on the last two pages of the script.

"Cory..." Kate spoke up.

"Go, I'll be fine!"

"I know, but..."

"Kate, go!"

Seeing her determination, Kate pulled Sandy and Angela aside, "We can't leave her here alone."

"I know," Sandy agreed.

"What do we do?" Angela asked quietly.

"Angela, I want you to go with Sid, while Sandy and I stay off in the shadows just in case..."

"In case, what?" Angela gasped. "He's out, isn't he?"

Looking at each other, Sandy took Angela's arm to move off toward the door where Sid was talking with a few of the cast members. "She doesn't know yet, and Max wants to keep it that way."

"It's just for now," Kate whispered, coming up.

"All right, I'll go. And when I see Max..."

"Let him know what we're doing," Kate finished, just as Sid came walking up.

"Ready?"

"Yes," Angela returned, when shooting the two of them a worried look, before leaving.

✒ Chapter Nineteen ✒

After an hour had gone by, when Cory put the script down to take a stretch, when the security guard came walking in. "Ms. Spencer, I have some coffee here. Would you like some?"

"Sure, I would really love some," she replied gratefully, while taking the cup he was offering her.

"How are things going here?"

"Fine. I just can't seem to get this last page perfected, is all."

"You'll do fine. For now I should be getting back to my post. Oh, and good luck with it."

"All right. Oh, and thanks for the coffee!"

After turning to go back to work on the script, Cory, nor the others hadn't heard the small thud outside in the hall, when the guard was knocked unconscious.

Meanwhile, Kate and Sandy were busy quietly strolling around, thinking that they heard a noise coming from the sound booth, down a hallway, from where Cory was working.

"I'll check it out, cover me, though," Kate told her, before making a move in that direction.

"Kate… don't you think we should call the guys first?" Sandy asked, worriedly.

"No, we should be able to handle this, ourselves!"

"All right…!" she returned, while pulling out her service revolver, along with Kate, who took the lead, while trying to hide the fear that was now eating away at her gut, after hearing more about how ruthless Cory's ex-boyfriend really was.

Unaware they were heading for danger, both girls went in search of the noise coming from up ahead.

"Darn," Ted growled, seeing how his plans were about to change, "I can't let those two get in the way now!"

Finding a rack of clothes that were going to be used for Cory's movie, he ducked in behind it, where he waited with baited breath, when Kate walked by first with her back to him.

"And now for you," he sneered quietly, while waiting for Sandy to pass, as she held her revolver up and away from her.

Coming up quietly behind her with the treated rag of chloroform, he slipped it quickly over her mouth, while taking the revolver out of her hand.

Not knowing what had hit her, she went down without a struggle, as she hit the floor, while bumping her shoulder against the wall, on the way down.

Not wasting any time, he went up carefully to take care of Kate, who was just about to turn, when suddenly drawing back his right hand, he blindsided her over the head with the butt end of Sandy's weapon.

"Sorry, ladies, but I can't have you getting in the way of my plans," he muttered under his breath, while looking back over his shoulder to make sure Cory hadn't heard the struggle.

Unfortunately, having to use the chloroformed rag on Sandy, he had to resort to plan B.

Meanwhile, over at stage three, Max and the others were still busy checking things out while Angela was so preoccupied watching Cory's book unfold right in front of her very eyes.

"Darn," she spoke up, looking around, "Cory and the others should have been here by now!"

Getting to her feet, she headed for the stage door to go back over to the other studio. "Sid…" she called out, "tell the guys I'll be right back."

"Where should I say you're off to?"

"Back to Studio One to check on Cory and the others," she returned hurriedly.

"Sure will, but shouldn't she have already been here by now?" he asked, looking at his watch.

Hearing Sid's concern, Mike cut her off, before she could get to the stage door first. "Hold up there!" he called out, taking her arm. "Where are you going in such a hurry, and why aren't Cory and the others with you?"

"I was just on my way over to check on them. I would have thought they would have been here by now!"

"What do you mean by that?" Max growled.

"They're not alone, there's a guard with them."

"That doesn't matter," Mike yelled. "They were all to have stayed with Sid and the cast, in case Ted showed up!"

"Yes, but you should know by now how she is! She insisted that she would be all right! And the others were going to be hiding off in the shadows, in case he was to show up, to catch him. We really didn't think they would be this long! She just had a few pages left to do."

"I don't like the sound of this, Mike," Max interrupted, "I have a real bad feeling that she is in some sort of trouble."

"Angela, stay here and have Sid call for backup," Mike ordered, just as they took off out the door, heading for one of the security jeeps to get them to the studio in a hurry.

"Yes, sir," she called back, feeling bad for having left Cory and the others to deal with it alone. *'Why didn't I just go and tell the guys when I first got here?'* she thought, scolding herself for what she had done.

Just then, Sid walked up with some of his crewmembers, after hearing the rest of her story. "Come on, guys, Cory Spencer may be in trouble!" he ordered, heading out to his own jeep, while pulling out his cell phone to call the lots' security.

Meanwhile, over at the other studio, she was just about to close the script to leave, when she began hearing scuffling sounds from overhead. "Hello!" she called out. "Is someone up there? Max...? Kate...? Is that you?" Though, startled to find there was no answer, she began to feel frightened. "Oh... Max... where are you...?" she cried softly, while turning back to pick up the script. At that moment, she heard the noise again. Looking up, she suddenly became aware of a large stage light swinging above her head. "Oh, my God_____!" she screamed loudly, as it suddenly came crashing down toward her. Frozen to the spot, she continued screaming, while covering her head.

Just at that moment, the stage door came flying open, when the three men came rushing inside the semi-darkened area.

While trying to focus on their surroundings, Max suddenly saw the lighting equipment come crashing down toward his love. "Cory_____!" he cried out, breaking away from the others to get to her first, before the heavy metal contraption could.

Throwing himself into the work area, where she stood frozen in its wake, he grabbed her to pull her out of the way, before the large fixture could reach them.

Fortunately for them, it missed by a fraction of an inch.

"Cory_____" he called out again, rolling her over into his arms to check her for any possible injuries, "are you all right?"

"Max...?" she cried.

"I'm here!"

Wrapping her arms around his neck, she continued to cry, "Oh, God, Max... w...what happened...?" she asked between sobs.

"Gees, Cory... I'm sorry... I should have told you...!"

"Told me what?" she asked, while the others went immediately in search of Ted, not knowing that the others had been detained earlier.

"Mike! Over here!" Sam called out.

"What is it?" he asked, running over to see what Sam had come across.

"The guard," he announced, kneeling down to check him over. "He's been…"

"Killed?" Mike asked, reaching his side.

"No, just knocked out. He's all right though."

"Well, if that's the case, then where are the girls?" he asked, while looking over the area worriedly, now that their eyes had gotten adjusted to the lighting.

"You tell me. They should have been here!" Sam grumbled.

"I don't know, but let's split up and go and find them. I want to know what had happened here."

"That makes two of us."

Before they went anywhere, they all heard that same sadistic laugh of Ted's.

"I'm coming back for you, Cory! You hear me? I'm coming back for you…" his voice echoed throughout the studio.

Just then Sam spotted the source of where it was coming from, while Cory cried, while covering her ears.

"Oh, God, no_____! No_____! Please_____ make him stop_____!"

"Cory_____" Max called out, taking her back into his arms, "for God's sake, come back home with me, now…! Please…, before one of these attacks does get you killed…!" he pleaded, while pulling away to look down into her frightened eyes.

"I can't…! I have to see this thing through…!" she sobbed tearfully.

"Even if it kills you?" he asked, a little too harshly.

"Oh, Max, I can't think of it that way! You know what this movie means to me...!"

"Yes, but you may not make it that long. Darn it, Cory, he is out there, and he isn't going to stop until he kills you, or until we get to him first, if we're that lucky. Besides, I thought you loved me!"

"Max... how can you say that? I do love you."

"Then come home with me, or simply just stay at the hotel, until we can catch him," he was begging, when hearing Mike calling out to them.

"Max...! Cory...! Can you hear me?"

"Mike... we're over here...!" he called out, while studying her a moment longer, before shifting his weight away from her. "Please... Cory, don't let Ted take the only thing that keeps me going, away from me."

"Oh... Max... I'm so sorry...!" she was saying, when Mike and the others ran up to move the lighting equipment away.

"Are you two all right?" Mike asked, while helping them to their feet.

"Yeah, but what about Ted?" Max asked.

"Max," Sam spoke up, when walking up with Kate and Sandy at his side, while looking somewhat dazed, after their own ordeal.

"Did you find him?" Max asked.

"No. However, he did leave us this!" Sam explained, while holding out the recorder.

"That must have been what we heard coming from the sound booth, before we were..." Kate started to explain, when her head began to throb.

"Kate, you all right?" Mike asked, when seeing her reach up to rub

Yeah, just a headache from where I had gotten clobbered," she moaned, when discovering a nasty goose egg at the back of her head.

"Sandy?" Mike turned.

"Ted must have used chloroform on her," Sam explained. "I picked up on the scent when I found the two ladies coming around over near the sound booth."

"Sandy...?" Mike asked again.

"I hit my shoulder in the fall, is all. I'll be fine."

"Fine, hell!" Sam growled. "You two could have been killed by this lunatic. Why the hell didn't you call us?"

"We felt we had it covered!" Sandy returned, wishing all along she had called them.

Soon they heard other voices come running in to see if they could offer their services. Sid being the first to arrive with his crew and extra security, not to mention, Angela, who went right up to check on her friend.

"Cory, you're hurt!" Sid announced, taking out a clean handkerchief to tend to her hand.

"It isn't much," she returned, feeling lightheaded, when they helped her over to a nearby chair to sit down.

"You will still need to have it looked at," Mike replied, when looking it over with Max standing nearby. "That goes for the two of you, as well," he ordered, when turning to Kate and Sandy.

Seeing her face turning white, Sid called out to her, "Cory! Cory!"

"We've got to get her back to the hotel," Max ordered, while moving in to lift her up into his arms.

"Are you sure you can get her?" Mike asked, while offering to help.

"Yes, I'm sure. Besides," he turned to look down on her sweet face, with a sheepish smile on his own, "I have to start practicing anyway for when we get married!" *'I just pray that it won't be too late,'* he thought quietly to himself.

"What of this Ted?" Sid asked.

"Have security look for him, or any signs of his having been here," Sam ordered, fanning his arm out over the area. "He may still be lurking about to see if he succeeded in getting her."

"You heard him!" Sid called out to the others.

"Yes, sir," one guard said, turning to the others, "Let's go!" he pointed off in different directions to go in search for her ex-boyfriend.

"Max?" Cory spoke up softly, on their way out to the limo.

"Yeah?"

"I am so... tired!"

"We will be at the hotel soon," Mike assured her. "Just try and take it easy. It won't be much longer."

And it wasn't. As the limo pulled up in front, and the men were out and watching for any signs of Ted, as Max went to help Cory out.

"Can you walk?" he asked.

"I think so!"

"Just in case you need me, though, I'll stay close by."

Stopping to look up at him, she had tears in her eyes. "Max, I will always need you," she cried, while putting an arm around his waist for support.

Walking into the lobby, the manager walked up to meet them. "Is she all right?" he asked, sounding concerned.

"She will be just as soon as we get her up to her suite," Sam replied, while Max and Cory went on ahead of them.

"Sir! Sir!" the manager cut Mike and Sam off. "I need to see the you two for a moment."

"What is it?" Sam asked.

"We received a call earlier from a man. He wouldn't leave his name, but..." The young man looked around them then.

Seeing his concern for privacy, taking him off to one side, Mike asked, "What did he say?"

"He said; and I quote. 'Tell Max to enjoy what little time he has left with her.'"

"Ted!" both Mike and Sam growled.

"Anything else?" Sam asked.

"No. He hung up."

"That doesn't sound good," Mike commented, shaking his head.

"No, it doesn't!"

Heading for the elevator with Mike following close behind, the two went up to fill Max and the others in on what they had just learned.

"Sam?" Mike spoke quietly on their way up to her suite, since not being alone.

"You're wondering what went wrong!"

"Yeah, I thought they had him locked away!"

"They did! And when we get back to our suite, I'll call and find out just what the hell happened, before stopping over to talk to the others."

"Good. I'll pass the word on once I get there."

Just about that time, the doors opened to let the other few people out, leaving Mike and Sam to ride the rest of the way alone.

"Angela," Max spoke up, "will you take Cory on into her room?"

"Sure!"

"Max, I'll be fine, really!" she protested.

"I know, but humor me, will you? What took place today was too close a call. And yet I would still like to have a doctor check you out. The fall could have done some damage to your shoulder."

Giving in, she went off into her room with Angela and Sandy, while Max went to put in a call to a doctor Sid had recommended.

Waiting for him to finish, Kate stood by patiently, until hearing his last words.

"Thank you, we'll be waiting to see him."

"You don't think she'll have to go back into the hospital, do you?" she asked worriedly.

"No, but still, I would rather make sure she's going to be all right."

"Yeah, that goes for the rest of us," she agreed, rubbing her head.

"How about you? Are you all right?"

"Yes, just a headache."

"When the doctor gets here, we'll have him check you out as well."

It wasn't long before a doctor had shown up. Once he had been cleared and allowed in, Max showed him to Cory's room, after looking both Kate and Sandy over.

"I shouldn't be long," he replied, "if you'll wait out here."

"Fine," Max spoke firmly.

Not trusting any stranger with his woman, he turned to Kate.

Nodding her head, she turned back to the doctor. "Doctor Sutters, if you'll excuse me, I'll be going in with you," she announced, "for security reasons, you understand?"

"Of course," the man in his late fifties nodded, as he went on in behind her.

With all three women in with Cory and the doctor, Max began to relax somewhat, when the phone started to ring. "Great," he grumbled, picking it up on the second ring so not to disturb the others. "Hello!" his voice sounded tired, yet gruff.

"Max…?" Rose's voice sounded so clear on the other end of the line.

"Rose?"

"Yes, is everything all right?" she asked, while surprised to hear his voice.

"Yeah! Where are you?"

"We're still at home! How is Cory doing? Is she keeping busy?"

Not answering right away, she began to worry. "Max…?"

"No, I mean yes. Yes, of course, she's been working pretty

hard at wrapping things up here. You would really be proud of her!"

Shaking his head in defeat, he knew Rose wouldn't buy into that, or at least not all of it.

"Max, what's wrong?" she asked. "You know you can't fool me. You've tried that on me too many times in the past, and still you can't pull the wool over my eyes. So out with it."

"She just had a scare, that's all. No big thing. Besides, Mike's got his old friend here, on the police department, helping out. Not to mention, all the security over at the studio! Now," he went to change the subject, "what's going on with the cabin? Is Roger getting it taken care of, and what about the pond, is it…"

"It's coming along quite nicely," she laughed at his nervousness. "I just called to let you know that we will be coming sooner than we had planned."

"Great, she'll be happy to hear that!"

"Now, what about you? You sound tired."

"I am."

"Max… you're still overdoing it aren't you?"

"Rose, you know I can't let up. So, please."

"All right."

It wasn't long, before they wrapped up on their conversation that he headed in to check on Cory.

"Angela," he spoke up, meeting her outside Cory's room. "How is she?"

"She'll be fine. The doctor gave her something to help her sleep."

"Good."

Just about that time, they heard the door to the suite open.

"Max," Mike called out, walking in. "How is she?"

"She's about to go to sleep, and Rose just called to let us know that they are on their way," he explained, while going over to get a cup of coffee, before taking a seat on the sofa to remove his boots.

"Wow, so soon?" he asked, while going over to get himself a cup of coffee, too.

"Yes."

Bringing his cup over to have a seat, he laughed, "I guess that means Roger will be staying with us?"

"Yep, some things just never change!" he laughed, shaking his head. "Now, tell me, what did the manager want?"

"He had a phone call," he replied, watching Max's expression closely.

"Oh... who was it?"

"Ted!" Sam spoke up, when coming in to pour himself a cup of coffee, too. "The message was for you!"

"What...?" Max looked up from the sofa, while gripping his cup.

"Yeah, he said to tell you to enjoy what little time you have left with her," Mike informed his friend.

"Damn him..." he swore. "He isn't going to get anywhere near her. Opening night is coming up soon. Kate! Sandy!" he turned to the two female officers who were just walking back into the room.

"Yes!" they both responded.

"Our mothers will be getting in sooner than we had expected."

"That reminds me, just when are they getting here?" Mike asked.

"Around seven this evening. And until then, I want Cory to get as much rest as she can."

"Oh... but what about tomorrow?" Angela spoke up disappointedly. "She was wanting to go shopping for our dresses!"

"That won't have an effect on how tomorrow goes. No," Mike offered, "we'll take care of that. You ladies will get your dresses for opening night."

Knowing how important having them was to her, Max agreed. "Now, if you will excuse me, I'm going in to be with her. Oh, and Mike..."

"Don't worry about a thing. I'll wake you in time for supper."

"Thanks, buddy," he replied. Going on in, he closed the door behind him.

"Wow, he is really protective of her," Sandy commented, to the others.

"With good reason," Mike put in. "They have a history, those two."

"Yes, she told mom and I all about him, when she stayed with us."

"Yes, and if she hadn't gone off to New York in the first place, she would have never met Ted," Angela commented bitterly.

"And if she hadn't," Mike spoke up, "Max told me this book of hers would have never come to this."

"The movie, you mean?" Sam asked.

"Yes, and aside from that, he is really proud of her, as well as her father was, just before he died. People, we can't lose sight of that. It's for her father now."

"You're right," Angela admitted heavily. "And Cory is really missing him pretty bad right now."

"Yes, I can only imagine," Kate put in, "with the wedding coming, and all."

"Especially the wedding," Angela added sadly.

"Well," Sam spoke up, "how about we get ready for dinner!" he suggested, while setting his cup down to head back over to the security suite.

"Yeah, sounds good!" Mike agreed, while doing the same. "Do you think I'll have time for a quick nap, since Max will be out for awhile?"

"Yeah, a quick one!" he grinned, turning back to see the humor written on Kate's face. "In fact," he turned back, laughing, "I'll even put on an extra man to keep watch over you. You

know, in case someone was to try something like what had happened earlier."

"Funny!" Mike laughed, while heading for the door. Stopping, he turned back to see a smile on Kate's pretty face. "You wouldn't?"

"Me…?" she smiled innocently, as he went on out, closing the door behind him.

When dinnertime rolled around, Cory had already been up, covering Max with an extra blanket, before heading for the door.

"Cory!" he called out, throwing off the blanket, as she was about to open the door.

Hearing his sleepy voice, she turned back. "I'm right here," she replied, going back over to him.

"Hi there…!" he smiled, while stretching out his long handsome body. "Mmmm… what time is it?"

"It's time to get ready for dinner. Are you hungry?"

"Hungry enough to eat a bear!" he laughed, getting up off the couch that her room had to offer.

"I had better be getting dressed then," she replied, scooting him out of her room.

"All right! All right!" he laughed, as he went out, closing the door behind him.

"Well, if it isn't Sleeping Beauty!" Mike greeted his friend with a fresh cup of coffee, when Max looked up to see his fresh smiling face.

"What's everybody doing?" he asked, taking his cup.

"They're all getting ready for dinner. How was your sleep?"

"Pretty good, and you?"

"The same," he agreed, while looking across the room to

where Kate was now, having just come out of her room, along with Sandy.

"What?" Max asked, following where his attention had gone off to.

"Our Kate, there," he laughed. "Since she didn't disturb me, it was pretty good!"

Smiling too, Max downed his coffee, and headed for the door. "Well, I better be getting ready then."

"Yeah," Mike agreed, turning his attention away from Kate, when she came over to get herself some tea that was brought up, while getting herself ready for dinner. "Hey, Max!" Mike called out, joining him in the hallway. "Wait up!"

Going off with him while he got himself ready, it wasn't long before everyone was set to head down to the hotel dining room.

While there, security was at an all time high, but not only to watch for Ted in the crowd, but to keep the news media away from Cory and her group.

Having learned of the studio accident that nearly took the famous writer's life, it was considered hot news, because of the Broadway play that was coming out, followed by the movie to her book.

"This is crazy!" the men complained, while shielding Cory from the swarm of flashing cameras and screaming reporters, all wanting to know when she was going to get another big hit out, and if the man who tried to kill her was going to show up during the show to try it again.

Spotting the Manager, Sam got his attention, and arranged to put them into a private dining room, with a back way out, so they could get to their suite without too much trouble.

"This way," he suggested, when soon they reach a more quieter area, while leaving a few officers at every exits.

"Is this how it's going to be on opening night?" some of them asked.

"From what Sid tells me," Cory grumbled. "Yes."

"That's not good," Max and Mike agreed with each other.

"No, but this is New York," Sam reminded them. "And she is the most current hot commodity, until someone else comes around to steel her lime-light."

"Steel away," she commented, while looking over the menu, until their server came in, which was one of Sam's people, along with a regular waiter.

"Frank," Sam called the man over to his side of the table.

"Yes, sir."

"What's the word on getting the reporter out of here?"

"It's being handled now."

"You are keeping them from going upstairs, aren't you?"

"Yes, as you have arranged, the extra guards have been put in place all around the Hotel and parking garages on all sides."

"Good. As for the rest of you, what are you interested in eating?"

Getting their orders put in, the food wasn't long in getting back to them, that they sat talking and enjoying their meal.

After dinner, everyone was getting ready to return to their suite, when the all clear was given about the reporters having all left the lobby. Coming out, feeling full, just as they were heading for the elevator, the hotel manager came around the counter to let them know Cory had company.

"Max?" She turned, tightening her grip on his arm.

"It's all right!" he returned, when looking down at her pale expression.

"Strauder, who is it?" Mike asked Sam's man, who was there to cover the evening shift.

"It's your mothers!" he explained, looking to Cory apologetically. "Along with two other friends of yours from home," he added.

"Mom is here?" her eyes lit up excitedly.

"She sure is…!" Max laughed. "I almost forgot they were coming!"

"Well," Mike put in, while going over to the elevator, "what do you say we go and see them?"

Happy to hear that her mother had arrived earlier than expected, Cory had almost forgotten about what had happened earlier.

Meanwhile, arriving back at the suite, they all had a warm reunion awaiting them.

"Mom…" Cory cried, going over to greet her. "I am so glad you guys were able to get here earlier! We have so much to do to get ready!"

"So I'm finding out," Rose smiled, while giving her daughter a gentle hug, when a tear found its way to the surface. Wiping it away, she looked up at Max, when seeing his saddened expression, just as she tried to smile.

Meanwhile, the others went over to take their seats, while the conversation went on about how the movie was doing.

"Oh… Rose," Angela cried, "it's really gory, with how they have the old Scottish castle set back up on this dark and wooded mountainside."

"And those young girls…" Kate started up, when Cory cried out hushing her.

"We can't tell them everything! The Broadway play is just a day away!"

"Well, you're right about that," Mike piped in, when seeing some tired faces. "Have you seen your suites yet?"

"We sure did," Mary replied. "They're beautiful."

"Well, on that note," he went on, "seeing how late it's getting, how about if we continue this talk tomorrow, while you're all out doing your shopping to get ready for this grand finale?"

"Sounds good to me!" Roger returned, while getting to his feet.

"Yes, you're right," Rose agreed, taking his hand, when offered to her. "We'll talk tomorrow, dear," she turned and smiled.

"O…Okay…!" Cory returned, feeling lost.

Seeing how her daughter was beginning to feel, Rose pulled her hand free of Roger's, and went to give her a warm, loving hug. "Don't worry, I'll be back in the morning," she smiled thoughtfully. "Now, get some rest, it's getting late."

"All right!" she returned. "Goodnight, everyone!"

At that time, Mary turned to Jenny, "Are you coming with us, or staying here?"

Looking at the others, Jenny looked apprehensive at first.

"We have room," Sandy spoke up, seeing how she felt at a loss without her friends.

"Sure!" Angela put in. "Our room is the largest. We can even get a rollaway bed brought in for her."

"Max?" Cory turned.

"I'll call it in now," he smiled, going over to the phone.

After making the call, he turned back to see the look of puzzlement on her face, when everyone had gone.

"What's wrong?"

"Oh… it's probably nothing!" she fibbed, thinking about her mother, and Roger, just then.

"Well, we should be getting some sleep. Tomorrow is going to be another long day for everyone."

"Yes, you're probably right. What about you? Where are you going to be staying?" she asked with a slight hint of fear in her voice.

"I'll be out here on the couch, in case you need me," he returned, while going over to get comfortable.

"Oh?" she smiled timidly, while leaving the room.

After going in to change out of her dark blue, calf length dress, she returned to the main area of her suite to find him stretched out on the couch with one hand tucked in behind a pillow, the other across his chest, and his eyes closed.

Standing perfectly poised in her long white linen nightgown, she spoke softly, "Max?"

Opening his eyes to see her standing there, he was reminded of her last visit to seeing him in the hospital. And now, standing at the end of the couch, she still reminded him of that angel, in the soft dim light of the gas log fireplace, most of the suites provided.

Smiling her sweet smile, with her soft brown hair shimmering in the light, he whispered, while feeling a lump at the back of his throat, "Cory…"

"I couldn't sleep!" she replied, fidgeting shyly with her gown. "Can we…"

"Come," he got up to make room for her on the couch next to him.

"I don't want to disturb you! You must be tired, too!"

"No, I'm all right. Would you like to talk?"

"Can we?" she asked, while feeling an involuntary shiver come over her.

"Yes, but first, let's get you covered up," he suggested, while pulling a blanket he had at the end of the couch to cover her with, while covering himself, as well.

Feeling the warmth of her body up next to his, he could only imagine that she wasn't wearing much under her gown. But this time it seemed different somehow, and just the thought made him ache inside, as she turned to wrap her arms around his waist to get warmer.

'Oh, God, why does she have to feel so good sitting here next to me?' he groaned, placing his own arms around her.

"Mmmm…" she cooed, while taking in the warm scent of his cologne.

"This isn't really safe, you know?"

"Why?" she asked, looking up to see something in his eyes that she had never seen before.

The look was now more intense, as the feel of her body pressing into his side made him want her even more.

"I...it's nothing," he lied, not wanting her to leave him just yet.

Taking that moment, he gazed into her sparkling eyes, while running his hand softly over her injured cheek. Doing so, the feeling of his desire for her just kept building to an astronomical temperature.

Feeling it as well, she found herself leaning up to meet his lips just as he lowered his hand down to capture her chin. "Oh... Max," she softly moaned, as their need had then increased, and when it did, so did the heat of their passion, when all of a sudden, she felt her body slowly being drawn down onto the couch, where his weight slowly covered her.

At that moment, finding his hand going down to capture one of her breasts, he stopped himself to look down into her wanting expression, "I can't do this to you, it's not right," he groaned.

"Max..." she cried softly, wanting him.

"God, girl, I want you so bad," he groaned yet again, while feeling that one part of him building to a point that he had to shift his weight slightly so that she wouldn't notice.

"Is this how it's going to feel when we're about to make love?" she asked, while feeling all sorts of emotions pouring through her, as well as something she'd never experienced before.

Studying her for a moment, he wondered before going on; *'Had she felt that?'* He groaned, "What are you feeling?"

"Heat, desire, and..." She stopped to look down between the two of them.

"You felt that?"

"Just before you moved!" she smiled shyly.

"Oh... Lord, I was hoping to avoid that. I'm really sorry."

"No. It was..."

"Different?" he grinned sheepishly.

"Yes, but at the same time, I…"

Unable to help but smile at her difficulty in finding the right words, he tried hard not to laugh, knowing he would have been her first. Instead, shifting his weight around, he brought Cory to lie on her side facing the fire.

"What are you doing?" she laughed quietly, so not to draw attention from the others.

"I'm fixing it so that we can cuddle, while watching the fire all at the same time!"

"Oh!" she smiled, feeling her backside resting up against him, while facing the warm glow of the fire.

Afterwhich, Max pulled the blanket up over them both from the back of the couch, after having tossed it when things had started to get a little warm between them.

"How is that?" he asked tenderly.

"Mmmm… nice!" she smiled even more, while resting her head on his arm, while his other hand went around her waist to hold her in place. "Max?"

"Yes?"

"I l…love you!" she yawned just as they started to slip off to sleep in each other's arms.

❧ *Chapter Twenty* ❧

Early the next morning, Max woke to find Cory still snuggled up against him, looking like a soft little kitten. Admiring her soft gentle features, he smiled down on her, before carefully lifting himself up over her to slip off quietly into the bathroom.

"Mmmm… Max?" she cried out softly.

"Right here."

Rolling over onto her back, she gently rubbed the sleep from her eyes. "What time is it?"

"Five-thirty, why?"

"I should be getting back into my room, before our mothers see us out here together."

"You're probably right," he agreed, while she attempted to get up.

Doing so, a sharp pain came wincing through her left shoulder. "Ahhh…" she cried out, bringing him back over to comfort her.

"Cory…!"

"My shoulder!" she exclaimed, finding it in herself to let out a little laugh.

Shaking his head, he grinned, "You didn't take your medicine last night, did you?"

"No, it kinda slipped my mind!"

"Where is it? Your dresser?"

"The bathroom."

Getting up, he went off to get it for her, along with a glass of water, while she sat, rocking back and forth, wishing the pain would simply go away on its own.

"Here you go," he offered, coming back to take a seat on the right side of her.

"Mmmm…" she moaned, taking the little white pill with shaky hands.

"Is it that bad?" he asked, while giving her the water.

"Uh huh!"

"Here," he offered, taking the glass from her to set it down on the coffee table, "why don't we just sit here for a little while longer to let the medicine kick in, before you go back to your room?"

"Oh… that sounds good to me…" she shivered, as he went to carefully place an arm around her left shoulder.

"Cold?"

"A…a little!"

Reaching over with the same hand, he grabbed the blanket and covered her with it. However, bringing his arm back down, she tried to muffle a cry when it jarred her.

"Damn, I'm sorry!" he swore, moving back away from her.

"No, it's okay! Please, don't stop holding me!"

"But I don't want to hurt you!"

"You wouldn't if you put your hand around my waist, silly!"

"Mmmm… I can do that!" he grinned. Only instead of it being his left hand, he placed his right there and claimed her lips lovingly, while using his left to run through the slight tangles of her once soft hair.

"Oh, Max… you dope…!" she laughed, placing her left

hand painfully up to his cheek. Though the pain easing up somewhat, it still reminded her to take it easy.

"Well… your lips looked so inviting, just then!"

"Ah huh…" she smiled, while bringing his lips back down to kiss her again.

"Oh, no you don't, you mean little brat! It took all that I had last night to fight off the urge to have you for my own."

"Mmmm… and it was wonderful too!"

"I just bet it was," he laughed lightly, while getting up off the couch to help her to her feet. "And God help me when we are married."

"Oh, are you getting worried?"

"Should I?"

Taking her into her room, he tucked her into bed, and smiled down on her, before leaving the room.

"Max?"

"Get some sleep, meanness," he grinned. "I'll wake you in time for breakfast."

And wake her he did.

After breakfast, the women had all gotten together to go shopping, with the men following nearby for security's sake.

Having nearly forgotten about Ted's posing threat, Cory and the others were actually having fun.

"Wow, look at this dress. Isn't it beautiful?" Angela asked, while holding up a beautiful white wedding dress. "Wait…" she cried, recognizing it from the catalogue Cory had shown her on the plane.

"Yes, Angela," she smiled, while looking to see that Max's attention was elsewhere, "it's the same one."

"Oh, my, gosh… it's beautiful!" they all gasped, but Rose.

"I had thought so too," she smiled.

Looking to find a sales clerk, Cory spotted one, "Miss!" she quietly flagged her down.

"Yes, ma'am!" the young blonde walked up, smiling.

"Do you have this in a size seven?" she asked.

"Yes, we do! Can I get it for you?"

"Yes, will you?" she whispered.

"Are you going to try it on?" Mary asked, while waiting for the sales girl to return.

"I want to, but..."

"Cory… what is it?" Jenny asked, while caught up in all the excitement.

"I think I know!" Kate put in. "It's Ted, isn't it?"

"You could say that. I mean after all it's hard not knowing what the future is going to bring if the past won't leave me alone!"

Feeling her daughter's pain, Rose went over to hold her.

Meanwhile, out in the Mall, close enough to see Cory and her party, the men watched closely.

"Max," Mike spoke up, seeing his look of concern, "what is it?"

"Look at her," he said, indicating worriedly with a nod of his head.

Doing so, not only Mike, but Roger too, saw the emotional embrace between Cory and her mother. "That doesn't look good," Mike replied. "Something's wrong!"

Meanwhile, watching a suspicious man a couple of shops down, Sam turned to see what was going on inside the bridal shop. "What are we talking about?" he asked.

"She looks so sad," Roger returned.

"You don't think she's worried about Ted, do you?" Mike asked, when Sam turned back to see that his mystery man had disappeared.

"Damn it…!" he swore.

"What?" the others turned to see what he was talking about.

"Frank!" he called out over his hand radio.

"Here!"

"Our man. Where did he go?"

"He's on his way out of the Mall!"

"Sam?" Max spoke up.

"We had a visual on a suspicious looking man."

"Why didn't you say something?" he growled.

"Because it was you he was watching!"

"Sam?" Mike then spoke up.

"Yeah," he returned, seeing Max's questioning expression. "Sorry, Max, but it looks as though you're his next target."

"Why?"

"Because you're in his way!" he growled.

"Great!" Max, Mike and Roger grumbled.

Meanwhile, taking their minds off what was going on inside the shop, the sales clerk returned with Cory's gown. "Ma'am!"

Looking it over, she turned away sadly.

"Honey, why don't you just have her box it up for now, and we will just take it with us." Rose suggested, while standing in behind her daughter.

"Miss, would you mind?" she asked, while looking back over at the dress.

"Yes, of course! Will there be anything else for you?"

"Yes, I think we'll take these dresses and anything else they will be needing," she returned, pointing out the dresses they had picked out.

"Cory, are you sure?" Kate asked surprisingly. "These dresses are so expensive!"

"Yes, I'm sure."

"We can always wear them to her wedding! That is once we're done with them after opening night!" Angela suggested.

"Cory...?" Jenny spoke up hopefully.

Feeling a sense of doubt with Ted still out trying to get

to her, she threw a bit of rain on their parade, when she questioned whether or not there was going to be a wedding.

"Cory, stop thinking that!" Rose cried.

"Mom, I'm sorry, but how can I not? He isn't going to stop trying, until he can finally succeed. Why won't you see that...!" she cried. "It may even happen on our wedding day. And if he does..."

"Cory," Mary jumped in, "we know you are scared, but you can't let this man ruin what you and my son have for each other. Now stop letting him get in the way!"

"Mary's right," Rose added. "Honey, you have loved Max for years. If you don't go on with your life, then Ted has already succeeded in hurting you."

"And what if Ted comes after me, and kills Max in the process? How am I going to live with that, knowing that my mistake caused the life of the man that I have loved most of my life?" she cried, walking out of the Bridal shop, once everything was paid for.

"I'm not dead yet!" Max spoke up, when he and the others joined them.

"Max!"

"Come on," Mike suggested, ushering them into a nearby coffee shop to get the two out of the open, "let's go in here and talk this out."

"You're right," Max agreed, remembering what Sam had told him.

Arriving at a secluded table, Max turned to the waitress, "Miss, coffee for me, and apple cinnamon tea for her."

"Yes, sir," the waitress replied, before turning to the others.

"Coffee," Sam, Roger and Mike announced, while taking the outer seats to safeguard the others, while the women ordered hot tea and hot chocolates.

"Max," Cory went on, while trying to hold back her

emotions, "I couldn't live with myself if something were to happen to you."

"Cory, I know how you feel, really I do, but I don't want to put this marriage off any longer."

"But, Max…"

"No, Cory. I want to marry you as soon as we get back, and that is all I will say on the matter. You got that? No more."

"No… I can't… I can't think about that right now! I don't dare to hope for something that may never take place!" she cried, getting back up to push past the men. "Kate! Sandy!" she called back. "I want to go back to my suite. Mom! Mary! Angela!"

"We're coming, dear," Rose returned, looking over at Roger and the others.

"We'll take care of things here," Roger replied. "Go."

"Cory…" Max called out, nearly knocking into Mike and Roger to follow after her, "what are you saying?" he asked, reaching out to stop her just outside the shop.

Not meaning to grab her bad side, she winced, at the pain, "Ahhh…"

"Damn it, Cory…!" he cried, raking his hand through his hair.

"Max…"

"No…" he cut her off, begging her not to call off the wedding, "please, tell me you're not doing that."

"I don't know…!" she cried. "Oh, Max… I just don't want to see you get killed because of some sick jerk that won't leave me alone!" she cried, seeing the hurt in his eyes.

"Gosh darn it, Cory!" He stopped to look around them, when seeing they were drawing a crowd. Taking her good arm, this time, to pull her aside, "I'm not going to just let you walk out of my life like this. I will fight him to keep you. God help me, I will fight him."

"Max, he will kill you!" she cried, curling her fists up against his chest.

"No, he won't!" Mike spoke up after canceling their order. "I think I may have come up with a plan that just might work. Let's head back to the hotel where I can fill you in," he explained, while leading them all out to the limo.

Once back at the hotel, Mike and Sam took Max, Kate and Sandy into the security suite, where Sam had been working on the plans for opening night. Back in Cory's suite, Cory went off into her room to cry herself to sleep, while leaving the other to talk amongst themselves.

"Before we get started," Max spoke up heatedly, "what the hell happened back at the jail? Have you heard anymore about it?"

"Yes," Sam returned. "Ted switched clothes with an inmate who looked a lot like him."

""Max," Mike cut in. "They had no idea it wasn't him they had locked up, until much later.

"When she and the others were attacked at the studio! Damn it, when is this ever going to end?" he growled bitterly. "I love this girl, and I want to marry her, damn it!"

"And you will," both Mike and Sam said assuredly.

"Now, back to why we're here," Sam went on.

After an hour had gone by, Max returned to Cory's suite to check on her, "Mom," he quietly asked, walking in, "where is she?"

"In her room," she gestured with a slight nod of the head.

Heading that way, Rose called out, cutting him off, "Max, take it easy on her, she's pretty scared."

"I will. I just can't let that maniac get in the way of our plans," he returned, while tapping quietly on her door, before going on in.

"Come, Rose," Mary took her arm, while Roger went to pour them both some hot tea, "let's just have a seat over here on the sofa, while the others are out. Maybe they will come up with the perfect plan to stop Ted for good."

"And they will," Roger spoke up, handing them their tea, "because Max isn't likely to give up."

In the confines of Cory's room, seeing her lying so quietly on her bed, with her hair laying in soft wisps over her pillow, he went over to join her. "Cory," he called softly. Seeing she hadn't moved, he sat down carefully next to her. "Oh, girl…" he groaned, reaching out to touch her hair, "just how many times am I going to have to say this? I don't want to lose you, not now, not when you have come to matter so much to me. And if telling you that can't cut it, how about the fact that you have gotten my heart twisted so tightly that if you were to call off this wedding, Ted might as well have killed me."

"Oh, Max…" she cried quietly to herself, while feeling the hot tears rolling down onto her pillow, when turning to reach up for him.

"Cory…" he cried holding her.

"Oh, Max… I don't mean to sound like a broken record. I want to be stronger about this, really, but I am just so scared…! What if he were to get to you first…?"

"Let's try not to think about that," he grinned nervously, while running a hand up under her hair.

"Oh, what I would give not to," she sighed, "when he could just as well stop us before you can even slip the ring on my finger."

"Not a chance."

"And you know this, how? Because, unless you have some trick up your sleeve that you haven't told me about."

"We just might have, but we won't know until they get through with the final touches." "But you were there, while they were going over them."

"Yes, but I had left, to come over here, to see how you were holding up, while they were making a few last minute calls! So, you little brat," he teased lightly, while giving her nose a tap with his finger, "I can't say until they have finished."

"What can you say?"

"Just that it is sure to top everything we have done thus far!" he smiled, when there came a knock at her door.

"Max..." Mike interrupted, "it's me!"

"Yeah, I'll be right there," he called back, looking to Cory, "You ready for this?"

"But..."

Holding up his hand, he turned back opening it. "Mike!"

"Hey," he smiled, stepping just inside to see Cory sitting there quietly, while now hugging a pillow. "Sid's here. He wants us all to have dinner with him and the cast down in the private dining room so that we can maintain some sense of security."

"Oh, I didn't know that was part of the plan!" he commented puzzledly, while looking at his friend. "What about..."

"It's covered," he grinned mischievously, before turning to Cory. "Oh, and Cory, Sid wants to see you for a moment too. I think. No, I know you will want to hear what he has to say. And you too, Max. Everything is going to be all right, you'll see."

"I so... wish I could believe that," she groaned, shaking her head, as she slowly began to get to her feet, "I'm telling you guys, know him, he isn't going to just simply give up. You've seen that already!"

"Well, no, I expect he isn't. But now he is sure as hell up against a lot more of your fans than he ever expected to be. So why don't you come on out and hear what the man has to say. Max...?" Mike turned.

"Give us a moment, we'll be right out."

"No problem. I'll be just outside the door here, until you're ready."

Getting herself up, Cory felt the room begin to spin around her, as she went to stand. "Max…" she cried out, when finding herself about to fall back.

"Okay!" he laughed, leaving Mike standing in the open doorway to go and give her a hand, until she could get her bearings. "Are you okay now?"

"Yes, I just got up a little too fast, is all," she returned with a blush, while heading for the bathroom. "I shouldn't be long, I just want to wash up a bit, while the two go on talking," she smiled, while seeing how Mike looked like he had more on his mind.

"Mike," Max waited until the bathroom door closed, before quietly going on.

"Max, before you say anything, just let me tell you. It's a shoe in."

"What?"

"Yes, Sid is here and he has a brilliant idea."

"I sure hope so, because I don't know just how much longer we can keep this up, with all the stress of Ted, this movie, and our wanting to get married, not to mention, she is still worried how she is going to look once these stitches are out. Man… it's going to be the death of us yet, if we don't get something done, and soon!"

"Just hang in there, Max. Remember what the plan is for opening night, and it will work. It is certain that we will catch him."

"We had better," he was saying when she came walking back out to join them. "Are we ready now?" he asked, seeing her now in her soft, green, cowl neck sweater, and how it enhanced her eyes even more.

"Sure…!" she smiled, taking his arm.

Once in the living room, where the others were waiting, Roger greeted her first, "Hey there, little lady!" he smiled, while going up to give her a fatherly hug.

"Cory," Sam spoke up, getting to his feet, from a low back

chair, he was offering her, "come and have a seat. There is so much for you to hear. And Max, you will want to hear this too."

Going over to take her seat, Max hung back with Mike and Roger.

"Young lady," Sid bowed his head confidently, while walking over to sit across from her on an overstuffed chair. "The doctor says your stitches are ready to come out. So I took the liberty of bringing a medical technician with me to do just that. And so, by the time it's all said and done, *you*, my dear, will never know you had ever been injured."

"And at this Broadway show," Sam went on, "Kate and Mike will be going in as you and Max."

"What...?" she asked, looking to him in surprise.

"That part I knew," Max laughed.

"You see, Cory," Mike jumped in, grinning, before she could say anything, "we want the two of you to go in undercover."

"Cory, Max," Sid spoke up again, pointing to a studio makeup artist. "This is Roxie. She is our number one artist. She is going to do the two of you up for tomorrow's event to look like Kate and Mike. That way, if Ted shows up, he won't know the difference."

"Miss Hall," the woman, seeming to be in her mid-thirties, spoke up, "knowing just how much your long hair means to you," she explained, while running a brush through it, "putting it up in a shoulder length wig will do nicely. Maybe even go a little lighter to match Kate's hair. As for your eyes, we can go with blue-green contacts. And for you, Kate," she turned to look over her hair, "I have a wig that will do nicely for you, as this Ted will never know the difference once you both are finished. And Mr. Brummet," she turned, "black hair and icy blue eyes would work nicely for you. And are you planning to wear a tux?"

"Yes, we all are!" Mike spoke up.

"That's good, then. In that case, this will look perfect with your attire!" she exclaimed, while holding up a 24 karat gold chain.

"And after she gets done with the four of you," Sam added, "I have these pins to put on all our security people. Cory," he turned, "I want you to wear this cameo so if you spot him in the crowd, you can let one of us know."

"Gentlemen," Sid spoke up, "why don't we try a practice run, shall we?"

"Well," Mike laughed, looking at Kate, "I'm game!"

"Sure!" she agreed, smiling.

"Roxie," Sid instructed. "What do you say we get these people into costume for tonight's dinner?"

"Yes, sir!" she returned. "Mr. Brummet! Mr. Jones! Shall we?"

"Mike…" Max looked at Cory, whose face lit up in a nervous, but brilliant smile.

"Sure, I'll go in first," he offered, knowing that Max would want to be there with her when the stitches came off.

"Thanks."

Taking that moment to turn and face the technician, everyone else stood back with bated breath, while he worked carefully to remove each stitch one at a time.

"You're doing fine, Miss Cory," Sid smiled, while coming around to observe the work, when then seeing a tear leave her eye.

"Are you in any pain, ma'am?" the technician asked thoughtfully.

"No…, just scared…!"

"You'll be fine. The scar is barely visible now," he offered, while taking the tweezers to another stitch, and then another.

Soon he was finished.

"Are you ready?" he asked, while handing her a mirror.

"Mom…!"

"Right here!" she called back, while coming up to be near her.

"We're all here," Angela put in, while coming around to reach across the table to take her free hand.

Lifting the mirror slowly, with her back to everyone, she looked into it, as her mother stood by praying, along with Max and most of the others.

"Oh, Lord…!" Cory cried, holding the mirror to her breasts.

"Cory…" Max groaned, unable to stand it any longer.

With all eyes on her, she slowly went to turn around. As she did, she smiled as the tears began to fall freely now.

"Oh… yes…" he cried, going over to take her into his arms. "My beautiful little brat, you're back," he whispered thankfully.

"Oh, Max…!" she smiled even more, while wrapping her arms tightly around his neck.

"Good job," Sid spoke up, turning now to the others. "Okay people…we are in business. Now let's make this changeover happen. Ms. Roxie, when you are through with the men, take the women in, and do your magic," he ordered, when she made her appearance from the larger of the two bedrooms, with Mike still waiting inside until all was done.

"Yes… sir!" she smiled, reaching out an arm to Cory and Kate. "Mr. Brummet," she turned, "my assistant will finish on you and Mr. Jones, while I do these two."

"Sure," he replied, turning to a short middle aged woman, standing next to him with short brown hair.

"Shall we?" she smiled up at him.

✤ *Chapter Twenty-One* ✤

By the time she had finished, they returned to the living room one at a time, with Kate being first.

"Kate…" Rose cried, seeing the strong resemblance to her daughter in Kate's face, "is that really you?"

Smiling, she nodded her head.

Then came Mike, looking so much like Mary's son that Mary couldn't quite get over it. "Mike…" she too cried with an unbelievable look on her face, "it's uncanny!"

"That's the whole idea!" Sid exclaimed, when Max and Cory walked out, to join them.

"And now for the real test," Sam cleared his throat, "Kate! Mike! Let's see if you can copy their passion for each other."

"Sir…" Kate looked as though she were a doe caught in a set of headlights, "just what did you have in mind?"

Knowing exactly what he was suggesting, having no more than gotten the words out, Mike pulled her up into his arms to claim her lips for one long passionate kiss. As he did, bringing his right hand around to the small of her back, he brought her up even closer. Though doing so, their kiss went farther than either one of them had planned, when he finally had to break it off.

"Well now, Officer Martin," Mike smiled down into her baffled eyes, "was that better than before?"

"M...much better, sir," she replied, looking up into his own, somewhat confused eyes, as the two tried to control the unexpected reaction the kiss had left on them.

"We should be going, then," Sid announced, breaking up the happy moment. "I told the others we would be down by seven."

"Well, let's go, then. It's show time!" Sam announced, while heading for the door.

"Miss Cory!" Mike teased, still smiling down at Kate.

"M...Max!" she trembled nervously, taking his hand.

"Kate?" Max himself turned to his Cory and smiled.

"I don't know if I could ever get used to calling you Mike."

"Or me, not wanting to hold you in my arms!"

"It's going to be rough, you two, but try and maintain some dignity, shall we?" Mike teased.

"Not a chance," he laughed, when stopping to pull Cory up into his arms to kiss her.

"Mmmm... Max...!" she cooed, taking in one more kiss, before it was time to go.

On their way down to the private dining room, Sam filled everyone in on what they were to do. "Kate," he continued, "I want you and Mike seated next to Rose and Mary, while Max, you and Cory sit next to Sid and myself, as well as a few of the other cast members that will be joining us."

"And where do you want the rest of us?" Sandy asked, just as the elevator doors began to open onto the main floor.

"Fill up the rest of the vacant chairs."

Nodding her head, they exited the elevator, and were shown to their private dining room, where everyone was soon seated. At that moment, not noticing how there was an extra waiter helping out, it didn't take long before the hair on the back of Cory's neck began to prickle.

Looking up, she saw him standing there, looking Kate over angrily. *'Oh, my God...'* she cried, looking down at her pin, *'I have got to warn her!'*

Remembering what Sam told her, she ran her fingernails over the delicate jewel to create a sound of static, which caused them all to flinch, when they looked over to see her frightened expression.

"What is it?" Max whispered, when feeling her hand tighten around his, at the same time.

"He's here!"

"What..." he growled quietly, just as an undercover officer, posing as a waiter, approached Sam.

"I know who it is, sir. What do you want us to do?"

"Kate, Mike," Sam spoke quietly, with his hands clasped together in front of his mouth, though just enough for the pin on his lapel to pick up his voice, "it's time to put on a little show for our uninvited guest."

"You got it!" Mike nodded, when turning to Kate to place an arm around her shoulder. "Cory?"

"Hmmm...?" she looked up into his eyes lovingly.

"You realize that we only have one more week before I can really make you mine?"

"Mmmm... and I can hardly wait!" she returned with trembling lips just as he went to kiss them.

Returning his kiss with an equal amount of love, the others saw just how angry they were making Ted, when Mike just had to add one more nail to Ted's already mounting anger. "Oh, Cory..." he went on.

"Yes?"

"Why wait, when I want you so... bad?"

"Oh, Max... I..." she began, but then was cut short, as he brought up a finger to silence her.

"I don't want to wait. Let's just take the first flight out after the show, and get married right away."

"B...but..."

"But nothing!" he went to claim her lips once again. Only this time he allowed the kiss to linger a little longer than before.

"Mike… what are you trying to do…?" Max groaned, warning his friend that the look on Ted's face had just turned very lethal, as he moved slowly around the room to glare even harder at her.

"Yeah," Sam agreed, warning his friend as well, "he sure the hell isn't too happy to see that."

Picking up on their concern, Mike backed it off some to act as though they had been caught making love. "Oh… gosh…" he looked at the others, acting all red-faced, "I'm sorry, it's just that this wait is really starting to get to me!"

"That's obvious!" Roger teased, seeing that it was beginning to be more than just a pretend kiss between the two.

Hiding her embarrassment, Kate buried her face in Mike's shoulder just as Sam turned to tell the undercover officer to get the others together. "I want him caught this time. You hear me?" he whispered severely. But then, seeing Ted coming around to their side of the table, he abruptly changed the subject. "Oh, and please, make sure the food is done right this time!"

"Yes, sir! I'll get that order taken care of right away," he returned, knowing exactly what he meant by that.

Just as the officer went to move away, Ted stepped right in behind the real Cory, making her even more frightened than before.

'Oh, God…' she cried, squeezing Max's hand even tighter, *'please… go away…!'*

"Take it easy," he whispered ever so quietly, "we're working on it right now."

"I can't…! He's…"

"Uh huh," he returned, when fortunate for her, Ted started toward the door to leave. "Sam…" Max growled under his breath. "Don't let him out of here…!"

"Hang in there," he returned, when turning back to call the waiter, before he could get away. "I'm sorry, but will you please refill our coffee before you go?" he asked, while signaling the others to be ready to close in. Then, with a nod of his head, he turned to Sandy.

"Yes, sir!" she nodded quietly.

"Max..." Sam turned quietly to the real one.

"I know." he too nodded, when turning to the women. "Ladies," he spoke, using a higher pitch to his voice, while causing most of them to laugh, as he went to get up, "I'll show you where to find the powder room, while we're waiting for our meal."

"Wonderful!" some of them put in, getting to their feet to follow.

"I don't know about most of you, but I for one, really need to go," Angela cracked up just then, while bringing the room to a roar, as they filed out one by one.

Watching Kate leave the room with the others, Ted glared at her, as she stopped and bent down to kiss Mike one last time, before whispering in his ear, something that Ted could not hear. "Be careful, love, I have come to rather enjoy your kisses."

"Mmmm... same here," he smiled, while getting up to walk her over to the door, with a slight limp as if he were Max.

Just as soon as they were out, Sam turned to Sid and motioned for him to take his own people out.

"We'll be right back, as well," Sid announced, bowing his head ever so slightly, as he was about to walk past Sam. Stopping, but only long enough with his back turned to Ted, he whispered to Sam a warning message, "Be careful, my friend, he doesn't look at all happy."

Nodding his head, "I will," he turned, closing the door after more undercover officers came in, posing as waiters, while bringing in their salads.

"If there isn't anything else, I will take my leave now," Ted bowed his head, while heading for the door, with the half empty pot of coffee in hand.

"Oh, but I don't think so," Sam announced, just as he motioned for two other officers to move in, while closing off his escape. "Ted Harden," he went on, while pulling out a set of handcuffs, "you are hereby under arrest for the murder of a New York private investigator, and the attempted murder, and repeated attacks on Ms. Cory Spencer. Now, be a good boy and slowly put the coffee pot down."

Looking bitter, he acted as though he were about to do just that. "How did you know?"

"We were alerted of your being here. Now, don't be stupid, we're all officers here," he explained, seeing the slightest shift in Ted's movement, as he turned to look back at Mike.

"Oh well, I may not be able to get Cory," he yelled, throwing the pot back at Sam, while at the same time pulling a gun out of his white waiter's jacket, "but I can get you...!" he sneered, aiming the nine millimeter at whom he had thought was Max.

At that time, the others pulled out their guns as well, but before Sam or Mike could get in a good aim, Ted fired off a shot, hitting Mike in the shoulder, while causing him to be propelled back onto the floor from the impact of the bullet hitting him.

"No...!" Sam yelled, as the other officers overpowered Ted, while taking his gun away. "Do you have him?" he shouted back over his shoulder, as he went rushing over to check on his friend.

"Yes!" one of the officers answered.

"How's Mike? Is he…" another officer was just about to turn and ask when Ted went for the officer's gun.

"You tricked me...!" he yelled, aiming the gun again, but before he could get off a shot, Sam turned, suddenly, and rushed him, while tackling him to the floor.

The next thing they all heard was the sound of the gun going off.

At that moment, the double doors opened, and more uniformed officers came rushing in, as Sam looked to see Ted's face go blank. "Take it easy, we'll have an ambulance here for you, and then you can spend the rest of your life in prison."

"N...no, I...I w...won't," he gagged and choked on his own blood, "b...but will you t...tell Cory I...I'm sorry, I...I r...really did l...love her?"

Without warning, Cory appeared, standing over him. "How can you call that love?" she cried.

"I...I'm s...sorry. I just wanted you to l...love me..."

"No, what you did wasn't love. You don't even know the meaning of the word! You raped me, Ted! And then you tried to kill me!"

"C...Cory, I..." he choked one last time, and with that, he was gone.

Just as Cory felt as though she were about to pass out, her mother came up behind her. "I got you, honey," she said, comforting her, when shortly thereafter, Kate came walking in.

Not seeing Mike's face in the crowd, she cried out, "Oh, God...! Mike...! Mike...!

"Kate," Sam spoke up, getting to his feet to take her over to him, "he's over here."

"What?" Max asked, while walking in with Roger, when they looked over to see another man down, besides Ted, who was being covered with a white linen tablecloth.

Meanwhile, going on over to hold him, she pulled off her wig to let her own hair down, as she fell to her knees. "Oh, Mike!" she cried, seeing him lying there in pain.

"Hey... pretty lady!" he whispered, while trying to smile up at her, when both Max and Roger joined them.

"Mike, where were you hit, buddy?" Max asked, while kneeling down to look him over.

"My left shoulder," he groaned, while gritting his teeth, when attempting to sit up.

"Mike, no...!" Kate cried, stopping him. "What do you think you're doing, you dope...? You shouldn't be trying to move...!"

"Yeah," Roger laughed, "it looks as though he just missed your heart! Had it not been for you wearing your vest, and had he had been a better shot, you wouldn't have been here right now."

"You're right about that," he agreed. "As for my heart," he exclaimed, looking up at Kate, while reaching up to touch the side of her face, "I think I lost it the other day!"

"Oh... Mike," she whispered softly, taking his hand.

"Pardon me, Miss," a medic replied, as he and another technician moved in to get Mike ready to go, "we need to get him to the hospital."

"Yes, of course," she stood up with Roger's help, while they moved in to get him onto a stretcher.

Going with him, she continued to look worried.

"Sam," Max spoke up, getting to his feet, "what's the word on Ted?" he asked.

"Ted Harden?" one of the two medics interjected.

"Yes."

"He didn't make it!" the other one announced, when getting Mike strapped on and ready to move.

"What...?" he growled, looking over to see Cory standing there with their mothers. Seeing the look on their faces, he went right over to be with her.

"Max..." she turned, feeling his arms closing around her, as he held her close to him, "he...he..." she looked up with tears in her eyes. "He's dead!"

"Yes, I know, and he won't be hurting you anymore, either."

"And Mike," she asked, hearing what had happened. "What of him? Will he be all right?"

"Yes," he groaned, pulling her around to look down into her face. "How about I get you out of here, and back up to your suite?"

"Please…" she cried, when turning to leave with their mothers and the others following behind.

Arriving back at her suite, they were all surprised to see that Sid had taken the liberty of ordering up food for everyone.

"Mr. Brummet," Sid walked up, "how is she?" he asked, while Max closed the door behind him.

"She'll be all right."

"And this Ted Harden? Has he…" one of the cast members spoke up.

"Dead?" he said, looking numb. "Yes."

"Young lady," Sid took her from Max to walk her over to the couch, "it's all over now. You can start concentrating on more happier things."

"Yes," Jenny chimed in, while trying to cheer up her friend.

"And Aunt Cory…" Sandy walked up to kneel down in front of her, "I'm just so glad you're safe now!"

"Oh, Sandy," she smiled painfully, while placing her arms around her adopted niece. Unable to express what she wanted, she just cried into the girl's shoulder, as the others all came around to offer their support.

Moving aside, Sid got back up to instruct the waitresses, as to where to put everything. "Ladies and gentlemen," he turned, "if anyone here still has an appetite, why not try and enjoy some of this fine food, before it all goes to waste."

Doing so, they all went on talking about the next day's event, hoping against all odds to get their minds off the horrible incident that had taken place a short while ago.

However, their conversation was cut short, when Sam walked in to announce some good news. "I just got off the phone with the hospital. Mike is going to be all right! It looks as though the impact of the bullet did some serious bruising to his left shoulder. So he will have to wear a sling for a while, until it can heal. But I was assured that his nurse, Miss Kate, will be staying with him tonight to make sure he behaves himself."

"Staying with him?" Max questioned with a broad smile. "Just where are they staying?"

"In another suite," he smiled. "Mike had me get it for him before I got here."

Smiling even more over the news, Max looked at Cory, when seeing her own smile. Though he could tell there was something else plaguing her mind, he didn't have to ask what. "Sam," he turned, "what of Ted?"

"Luckily we had it all on video tape, thanks to Sid and his cast members here," he pointed. "All I have to do now is go down and finalize it."

"Oh, but you will be at tomorrow's opening night performance with us, won't you?" Cory asked, sitting on the sofa next to Max.

"After all we had to do to get you here, I wouldn't miss it, Miss Hall," he replied, heading for the door. "I'll see you all tomorrow."

"Make sure you're here early! We will all be getting together to have breakfast," Mary announced with a friendly smile.

"We sure will," Max smiled, looking back at Cory's sleepy face. "As for now, I think we have someone who needs some sleep here."

"We sure do," Rose agreed.

"That sounds like our cue to go!" Sid smiled. "See everyone in the morning?"

"All right," Cory smiled up at him.

After they had all gone, Max got up to walk her to her room. "You do look tired," he went on.

"I am."

"All right, I'll see you in the morning then," he replied,

tiredly as well, while leaning down to give her a kiss goodnight.

With a lazy smile, she took his hands into hers to give him one more kiss, before he went across the hall to his room. "Goodnight," she whispered wistfully, just as their lips brushed lightly over each other's.

"Mmmm… and it sure will be."

❧ *Chapter Twenty-Two* ❧

By the next morning they had gotten word that Mike and Kate would be there, in time for Cory's opening night's performance.

"I sure hope so!" she replied worriedly, while running a brush through her hair. "Mom?"

"Yes, dear," she replied, looking up from the sofa.

"Would you mind if we ate out on the terrace this morning?"

"Do you think it will be large enough for everyone to eat out on?"

"Oh, yes. It'll only be the eight of us here. Not to mention, I've called Helen to join us!"

"Mom's been really looking forward to this day," Sandy mentioned, when walking out of the other bedroom, with Angela following behind, while pulling her hair back into a loose ponytail, and Jenny fusing with her shirt collar.

"I'll be so glad to see her, how has she been?" Cory asked.

"Busy, now that you have made a big name for yourself at our rooming house!"

"Hey, she said she needed the business," Cory teased,

while going back into her room, when both, Max and Roger walked in.

"Good morning, Mom!" Max called out cheerfully, while closing the door behind him. "Where's my little brat this morning?"

"She just went back in to get dressed."

"Oh, and before I forget," Rose announced. "She wants to have breakfast out on the terrace this morning, if you wouldn't mind."

"Sure, that'll be fine with me!" he agreed, when going over to the phone to place the order for everyone.

"Oh, and there will be one more joining us," Rose added.

"Oh?"

"My mom," Sandy offered. "She's been dying to meet you."

"Good. Feelings the same!" he grinned, hearing about Cory's stand in mom, while she was gone.

After getting the order turned in, he and Roger took their coffee and walked out onto the terrace to have a seat, while waiting on the others to join them.

"Well, it won't be long now!" Roger was saying, when turning to Max.

"No, and am I glad," he groaned, shaking his head.

"Oh…?" Cory teased, seeing the look on Max's face that he had tried to hide, when looking up to see her standing there, wearing a soft blue spring-like dress, with her hair tied back, when using a soft blue satiny ribbon to match.

"Hey there, I didn't hear you coming out!" he smiled sheepishly.

"Uh huh, and what are we talking about?" she asked, greeting him with a warm hug.

"Oh, nothing!" he fibbed, changing the subject. "Are you getting nervous?"

"I sure am! It's my first Broadway hit!" she replied, excitedly.

"And you're going to do just fine!" Roger exclaimed, while coming over to give her a warm fatherly hug, before offering her a chair, when all the others started showing up.

After breakfast, the men went back over to their suite to get into their tuxedos, while Sid left to see to his masterpiece, while leaving the women to get ready as well. At that time, the suite was soon filled with so much laughter, while Helen told stories of Cory's earlier days when she had first gotten there.

Meanwhile, across the hall, Max was having a hard time with his prosthesis, "Damn!" he grumbled, trying to get it readjusted to his stump.

"What's wrong?" Roger asked, coming to his rescue.

"This damn leg of mine," he growled, hitting the valve at the side. "This blasted thing gets hung up once in awhile."

"Shall I call Cory over to give you a hand?" he teased, checking the valve out for himself.

"Keep it up, she'll be giving me a hand soon enough."

"Well, in that case, I guess I can help you this one last time," he grinned, getting to his feet to go into the bathroom.

It wasn't long before he returned.

"Here we go, my friend!" he called out, with a bar of soap in hand. "This had helped before. Let's hope it'll do the trick again."

Applying the soap to the valve at the side of his prosthesis, Roger worked it in for a few seconds, before Max slipped it back in its place.

"How is it now?" he asked, while handing Max his pants.

"Better. Let's just hope it doesn't act up when I get married."

"Yeah, let's hope!" Roger was saying, when the door to their suite opened, and in walked their friend, Mike.

"Hey there, you two aren't going to this thing without

me, are you?" he asked, closing the door after having left Kate with the women to get ready.

"Of course we wouldn't!" Max laughed, greeting their friend. "It's good to see that you made it!"

"Well, I can't let Cory down now, can I?"

"No, she would be pretty unhappy if the two of you didn't make it to tonight's grand finale. She's nervous enough as it is!"

"That she is," Roger went on, while holding out a tuxedo for Mike. "Hey," he asked, "with that sling on your arm, will you still be able to wear this?"

"Sure, but I'll need some help putting it on!"

"Sure, no problem," Max laughed. "Should we get your nurse to help you?"

"No," he laughed along with him, "but I should warn you, you're not the only one getting married."

"What...? The man who swore that he would never say '*I do*' again!" he roared, while he and Roger went to congratulate him.

"Well, I guess that means we're now going to have to work on Roger now?" Max added.

"Maybe not," Roger replied with a grin.

"What...?" they both cried, looking at each other, then at Roger with a look of surprise on their faces.

"We didn't want to say anything yet, with everything that has been going on and all. It's just that Rose and I..."

"Rose...? As in, our Rose?" Max asked, shaking his head, while tying his tie. "I should have known."

"Max, I'm really fond of her. We're just not sure how Cory would take the news, with her father only having been gone a year and all," he explained, while looking away sadly.

"Yeah, well, I can understand how she feels, but how does Rose feel about you?"

"The same, I think...!" he explained, questioning her feelings for him, when not all that sure himself.

"Don't you know?" Mike asked, with a hint of concern, while fussing over his own tie.

"Well, sure I do...! We've talked about it!" he was saying, while going over to give Mike a hand.

"Then take it a day at a time!" Max suggested, while taking that moment to look them over. Seeing how they looked all right, he asked, "Are we ready?"

"Yeah," Roger laughed, as Max led the way across the hall, "they're probably wondering what's taking us so long."

Walking in, they saw Sam sitting on the sofa.

"Hey there, what took you so long?" he asked, smiling up at the two of them, when then he saw Mike walking in behind them.

"Well, we had to help this poor cripple with his tux!" Max laughed.

"It's a guy thing, you know?" Mike laughed, when at that time they turned, hearing the bedroom door open.

Seeing Rose coming out first in her long, dusty blue evening gown, followed by Mary in a simple light green number, the guys wooed. And then came Angela, wearing an emerald green formal, followed by Jenny, in her long, black satin sleeveless dress. Then the time had come for Kate, when Mike's eyes lit up, seeing how beautiful she was in her long, pale blue satin evening gown.

"Kate..." he smiled, "you're beautiful!"

"Thank you," she returned, while going over to join him, when everyone turned then to see Cory make her grand entrance.

With Max holding his breath, while waiting for that moment, standing there, now, in the doorway of her room, was Cory, wearing a long white formal, with her shoulders bared, she was wearing a cameo necklace given to her earlier to show off her beauty.

"Oh, my God..." he remarked, walking up to her. Not once taking his eyes off her, "you look like an angel standing here, my angel," he replied, with tears welling up in his eyes, as he ran his fingers along her delicate cheek, whereas the remains of her injuries were barely visible.

"That's what daddy used to say to me," she replied, fighting back her own tears that had threatened to come.

"Yes, and now you're mine, as well," he told her, while taking her hand into his.

"Shall we go?" Sam spoke up, standing at the open door.

"Well?" Max grinned.

"Yes."

Arriving at the Broadway Theater, Cory and her group were ushered right up to their very own private box seats, where they could view her book without any disturbances.

"Wow," Jenny cried, looking around the old theater with all its artistry, "this place has sure been around for quite some time!"

"More than we could ever imagine," Cory whispered, while taking their seats just as the curtain went up.

Placing an arm around her shoulder, Max took her hand as well. And a good thing he did, for what they watched at times had gotten pretty scary, even to Cory, who had written the book herself.

Just then, there in front of them, a young girl ran out of a dark and desolate Scottish castle into the rain, only to be met by a shadowy figure towering over her, with hands outstretched.

"No_____!" the actress cried out in one horrifying, bloodcurdling scream, as the figure covered her in his black cape, before vanishing in the night.

"Ahhh…" almost everyone jumped in his or her seats.

And yet as another scene began to unfold, Angela, Jenny, Kate and Sandy all covered their eyes. As for Rose, Mary, Roger, Mike and Sam, they cowered off sideways in their seats, anticipating the worst, when sitting back laughing at them, Cory knew all along the scene was going to change to something totally unexpected.

"Of course you would know better, wouldn't you?" Max grinned down at her.

"Uh huh!" she smiled.

And as she did, the scene in front of them changed to the stables just on the edge of an old Scottish town, dated back in the early sixteen hundreds, where a horseman was about to mount his steed to ride off to the castle, where his own younger sister was about to meet her demise.

Lord Mac Raven's Castle

Running through the castle, the young girl and her friends were attempting to flee the ogre who had died there, years ago, when found guilty of beheading hundreds of innocent young girls and women.

"Oh, my… God…!" several guests in the audience were screaming, when seeing the man's ghost-like face, having been eaten away by worms and other earth-roaming creatures, all but his eyes. The glow of the aberration's eyes was green, and all so eerie to look into. When one did, one felt she would soon be engulfed, and never heard from again.

"This is really creepy, Cory!" Jenny reached across to whisper to her friend.

"Oh, but it gets better," she smiled.

And better, it did.

As the brother went riding off to rescue his sister, along the way he was met up with others looking for his or her loved ones, sisters, daughters, and even friends of their sisters and daughters.

Arriving at the castle, Emily's brother, big and brawny as he was, jumped down off his horse, while running toward the front castle doors, just as the wind began to howl, and in it, the sounds of young girls' voices crying out. Just as quickly as it came, the cries along with the wind were gone.

"Oh, my, gosh!" her friends cried out, covering their eyes, while the guys sat back shaking their heads.

"Where did that come from?" a father cried out in anguish. "Justine... Justine..." he continued to cry out in total agony.

As the play went on, the crowd was getting more and more frantic over their missing loved ones, when soon, several men cried out before vanishing themselves.

"No way..." Sam groaned, roaring in his seat, along with the other guys, as well as Cory. Though, the others found nothing to laugh about, they watch as the scene went on, nearing the end of act one.

Once the curtains had closed, most everyone got up to stretch their legs, while the guys went off to get the women some refreshments.

"What do you think?" Cory asked the others, smiling.

"What did we think?" Mary cried, rubbing her arms to ward off the shiver she felt creeping up on her.

Having been with her most of the way through her writing, Sandy and her mother knew what to expect, but still, seeing it, they were thrown by its intensity.

"Well," Helen began, "I think it's great for a horror flick."

"Yeah, but…" Kate was about to say when the guys came back.

"What are we talking about?" Mike asked, while grinning knowingly.

"The show," Jenny laughed. "It's so gruesome!"

"Well, what did you expect?" Angela teased, taking her drink from Roger.

"Well, I'm proud of you, little lady. You have really out done yourself."

"Hasn't she though?" Rose spoke up, shaking her head all along, knowing how long her daughter used to hide up in her room, writing for hours on end. It was just a matter of time before she would take it to this point. Doing so, Rose was proud of her. Not to mention her father, too.

"Well, it looks like they're ready to start again," Max announced, while taking Cory's arm to find their seat.

When opening night was about to come to a close, Sid asked for Cory to come down to the stage, "Ms. Spencer, if you will please join us!"

"Max?" she turned for his loving support.

"I won't be far," he smiled proudly.

With the accompaniment of her friends, she was on her way down, while Max led the others in a standing ovation to applaud her success.

Reaching the stage, she was greeted by none other than Sid, who reached out a hand to take hers. "Ladies and gentlemen…" he called out across the audience, while waiting for their silence. As it came, he turned to the lady on his right, who by this time had tears streaming down her cheeks, "I'd like to present to you, Miss Cory Spencer, the writer and creator of 'The Ghost of Mac Ravens' Castle'. Miss Cory," he smiled, when turning back to the audience, as the whole cast and crew bowed, when the audience had once again started up their applause.

Afterwards, flowers were brought up to her. However, in place of the usual delivery boy, it was Max who handed her the large bouquet, as Sid then went to hand Max the microphone.

"Cory," he began, as there came a hush over the audience, by means of Sid's insistence, when raising both hands to quiet them. "The flowers are from everyone here who loves you. As for why I delivered them," he smiled, just as he went down on his left knee. "A little while back I asked you to marry me. And now, I am here in front of God and all these wonderful people to ask you once again. Will you, Cory," he stopped for a moment, as she covered her mouth to keep from crying. "Will you be my wife? Will you marry me and have my children?" he asked, while looking up into her eyes with so much hope and love in his own.

"Oh, Max, I have loved you for so... many years," she couldn't help but cry. "I couldn't bear another moment without you in my life." And then the audience became even more silent, when finally the words slowly came out, "Oh... yes," she began, as he attempted to get back up with Sid's help, "yes, I'll marry you, and have your children!" she cried even harder, when Sid went to take her flowers so that Max could wrap his arms around her. "Oh, Max Brummet," she had just gotten the words out, when he went to claim her lips, as the whole audience got carried away applauding them. Not to mention, the reporters who had been taking the pictures over and over. "I love you, Max, with all my heart, I love you," she repeated, as he went to claim her lips to his once again.

Pulling away, he smiled down at her. "Miss Cory, it's time that I take you home."

"Boy, am I ever ready," she cried, as he turned to lead the way out through the crowd, only to be met by the others outside, right along with security to make sure their departure was safe.

Back at the hotel, she was greeted once again with flowers and gifts, as they headed up to their suite.

"Max, did you know about this?" she asked.

"We all did," Mike cut in, while reaching the elevator first.

"Roger," Cory turned to their friend once they were all inside, "I haven't had a chance to ask you yet, but will you do me the honor of walking me down the aisle Sunday?"

"Oh, little lady, dear," he choked back the tears, "I would love to walk you down the aisle," he replied, hugging her warmly.

"I'm glad, because you're the next best thing to having as a father. Thank you."

Unable to hold the tears back, while still holding her in his arms, he looked over at Rose, while reaching out his hand to hers.

Smiling tearfully, as well, she took it and gave it a gentle squeeze, as the elevator reached their floor.

Getting off, everyone went into Cory's suite, all but Max, who took Cory by the arm to pull her back into the elevator. "I just had to hold you again for a moment longer, before we have to get ready to go," he whispered deeply, as he went to kiss her again. This time allowing the kiss to go on even after the elevator doors had closed, until their kiss was interrupted when the doors had opened again. However, that never stopped him, when he simply pressed the hold button, and continued kissing her.

"Okay, you two, let's get the show in the air. We have a plane to catch, and a wedding to prepare for, you know?" Roger laughed, when he and Mike escorted them off the elevator, and into the suite, once they release the elevator for others to use.

"You don't have to twist my arm!" he laughed, eager to make Cory his own.

With everything packed, the group headed down to the awaiting limo to take them to the airport.

"Miss Cory!" a man called out from the crowd.

"Sid…! James…!"

"I want to thank you, all of you, once again, for all that you have done," Sid explained.

"Not to mention, I will be looking forward to our next project," James added.

"James, I already sent you something in the mail a short while back. Anything else will have to wait until after the wedding," she cried out, laughing.

"Yes, well, after," Max groaned, looking down at his bride-to-be.

"Uh… huh…!" she agreed, looking up into his handsome face, when Sid went on to walk over to give her a hug.

"Good job, young lady," he whispered warmly.

"Thanks, Sid. I…" she started, then stopped, when feeling the pain of all that had happened to her.

"It's all right, in time. Just give it time."

"You will come to the wedding won't you? I know you're a really bus man and all, but after everything…"

Smiling, he bowed his head. "It would be an honor." At that, he took her hand and kissed it, before turning to Max, "Take good care of our girl, here. She is a very special young lady."

"You don't have to tell me that," he smiled, while looking down at her. "But yes, I will."

Shaking the man's hand, they were on their way.

Once back at the cabin, she and the others were busy getting ready for the wedding that was to take place in the next thirty-six hours.

"Well, it won't be long! Sunday is the big day…" Roger announced, turning to Max, "and you know the rules."

"Yep!" Mike stood back laughing.

"No…!" he turned to see the looks that were being exchanged between his two friends. "But we still have tomorrow yet!"

"I know, buddy. But we have our own plans for you, and like Roger said," Mike continued to laugh, while walking up to take Max's arm, along with Roger, "we have got to separate the two of you."

"And when you next see your bride," Roger added with a smile, "you'll both be saying I do."

Stopping at the front door of the old cabin, Max turned back to see Cory's sweet smile. "I guess this means goodnight?"

"Yep, I guess so!" she tried hard to fight back the sudden need to cry, but not for sadness. This time, it was for joy of all the days and nights they will have to look forward together.

"I'll see you soon!"

"Yeah, see ya!"

"Cory…"

Seeing his need for one last kiss, before the big day, she smiled sweetly, just before giving him one he would never forget.

Feeling the heat she was causing him, he pulled back to look down into her smiling face. "You are so mean to me, you know that, you little brat?"

"Uh huh…"

Threatening to even the score, he growled warningly into her ear. "Just remember, you are all mine after Sunday. No more teasing me."

"Wooo… I'm shaking in my sockies!" she laughed up at him.

"We'll see who's shaking in their sockies," he laughed back, as he and Roger walked out with Mike to go back over to the other cabin.

Later that night, unable to sleep, Cory slipped out to go down to the old fishing hole, where there she said a prayer, and a thanks to her father. "Well, Daddy, I kept my promise, I made you! Max and I are getting married the day after tomorrow. And Daddy, thanks for making it possible. I don't think I could have ever done this without you."

"Oh, yes you could!" Max spoke up, getting up off their rock.

"Max…?" she cried out in surprise.

"I made him the same promise," he went on, while walking up to her. "It's just that I had never realized how beautiful my little brat would turn out to be!"

"I'm still that little brat!" she smiled sweetly.

"Oh… yes, you sure are. And after we are married, you will be my little brat," he said, while taking her back into his arms to claim her lips for that one last kiss, before they were to become man and wife.

When Sunday morning had come, the guests were now all arriving. And with Cory and her friends too busy to think straight, Rose called out, "Are you ready, dear?" she asked, while trying so hard not to cry.

"Yes, I'm ready…!" she called back nervously, as her mother walked up to put her veil on her daughter's head.

"Here are your flowers!" Angela announced, while fighting back her own tears of happiness, when she handed Cory her bouquet, just after Mary and her mother turned to walk out to where the ceremony was to be held.

"Shall we go?" Jenny asked tearfully.

"Yes, I guess we should!"

"You do look beautiful, you know that?" Angela cried, while reaching over pastel yellow dress to hug her. "Max is so lucky to have you."

"And I'm so lucky to finally have him!" she cried, while walking out to the top of the hill, which led down to where Max was already waiting at the old fishing hole with the minister. Stopping in the doorway, she looked back on the old structure, remembering as a child all the time she and her parents came there. Even hearing the sounds of their laughter, as it echoed throughout the walls.

"Cory!" Roger called out a few feet away, when seeing the fond look on her face. I'm sorry, but it's time. Your man is waiting for you."

"Yes, he is, isn't he?" she turned and smiled, while hearing Mike and Kate finishing a beautiful song, meant only for her and Max. "Oh, Roger, why does it feel so hard to leave here?"

"Don't look at it that way. Think of it like this: You can always come back to visit," he smiled on her so tearfully.

Just then, Mike and Kate looked up to see her standing there, with the sunlight glistening over her magnificent gown. And then it was Max's turn, when he saw the look on his friends' faces, when everyone stopped talking to look up, as well.

Swallowing hard, the look he had on his face, when seeing the way the sunlight made her look even more like an angel than before, he cried to his friend, when he walked up to join him, "Oh, my God… Mike," his mouth dropped, while slowly taking in her beauty, "she is so… beautiful standing there!"

"Yes, I know!" he grinned, now seeing his own lady, after making a quick departure up the hill to walk down the path ahead of Cory, with her friends. "And just to think," he went on smiling, "she's all yours, pal!"

"She sure is!" he added with his own brilliant smile, while Roger took Cory's hand.

"Well, little lady," he cried sheepishly, "you are all grown up now, and now you're getting married."

"Yes, and thank you, Roger, for being here for me."

"You know, darlin', your father is really proud of you too?"

Looking heavenward, she cried, "Oh, Roger, I know he is. I can even feel him nearby at this very moment, shining down on us," she smiled brightly, while turning now to look at her future husband, standing there in his tuxedo next to Mike and the others. And oh, how he looked so handsome standing there with his brilliant smile.

Just then, being handed his guitar, Mike began the wedding march, when joined by a few more instruments Sid and some others had arranged to play for them, when the time came.

At that, they began their walk down the path. Smiling as they got closer, it wasn't long, before joining hands that the minister began exchanging vows.

Soon the couple kissed, when the minister announced that they were now man and wife.

After the reception, saying their tearful farewells, everyone cheered them on, when Max and Cory headed out to his nicely cleaned out truck, to head for their honeymoon destination.

"Where are we going?" she asked getting in.

"You'll see," he smiled coyly, while putting their things into the back.

The ride itself wasn't a long one, while taking her to their new cabin resort, overlooking Lake Superior. On the way though, they talked of what all they had been doing, while the other was off living their own life.

"I talked to Mike before the wedding. He had some rather interesting news for me."

"Oh? What was that?"

"Are you ready for this? I get to keep my shield!" he smiled greatly.

Turning to study his enthusiasm, she asked puzzledly, "Does that mean you'll be going back to work as a cop?"

"Only when he needs me. His new commander read over the report given by both him and Sam. They told him that I still had what it takes to do my job, and do it well. He told Mike that under one condition will he keep me on."

"Well…?" she asked anxiously.

Smiling, he took her hand. "No, sweetheart, no real dangerous assignments, only backup types of jobs. I guess that means you'll be having me at home pretty much all the time, until Mike really needs me."

"I can get used to that!" she laughed with a sigh of relief in her voice, when it wasn't much longer, when they arrived.

Getting out, she looked up at him in total amazement. "This is beautiful, who does it belong to?"

"It's ours!" he grinned, coming around to take her hand.

"What…?" she cried, while unable to believe what she just heard.

"I bought it after your father died, thinking how you would be able to relax and write your books out here, while I run the camp store."

"Camp store…?"

"Yes!" he smiled at the look on her face. "Roger has been teaching me the trade for some time! As for our cabin, it has three bedrooms, a large kitchen, living room, and plenty of room for our kids to play."

"Did you have all this planned back then, too?"

"No, not until I saw you at the restaurant that day I was meeting our mothers. I wasn't sure it was you at first, but by the way our mothers were acting, I had a feeling. Then, the night of the storm, when mom called and asked me to go over and see if you were all right, I had to wonder why at first. But then it hit me, you were always afraid of storms! When I got there and saw the roof, I was afraid I was too late. That's when I heard you crying out. I knew then you were my little brat, returning to drive me crazy."

"Then I haven't lost my touch?" she teased.

"Oh… no, you haven't, and now you're all mine."

"Yes, I am!" she replied, running her fingers up along his taut stomach, until he pulled her up into his arms to kiss her passionately.

It wasn't long then, before finding themselves in their new cabin, where in their bedroom about to make love, he whispered, "I love you, Mrs. Brummet."

"I love you too, Mr. Brummet," she replied, as her eyelids began to feel heavy, and yet once their heads hit the pillow, they had both fallen off to sleep in each other's arms.

❧ *Epilogue* ❧

A year has passed by now, Cory was seated comfortably in their large living room on the sofa, working on yet another masterpiece for her publisher. And not too far away from her was the little fair-haired baby boy she had dreamt of, sleeping quietly in the bassinette his father had constructed for him out of pine.

"Well, here is my family!" Max called out, coming back in from working over in the camp store. "How's the book coming?" he asked, while peeking down at his son, before going over to join her on the sofa.

"Just about through," she announced, while slipping off her reading glasses to give her husband a kiss. "James says that Sid has been chomping at the bit, waiting for another piece of work to come his way."

"I guess he has been waiting, hasn't he? Will you have to go there to work on it when it's ready?"

"Nope, we're going over it here. No more going away," she smiled, "and he knows that now."

"Mmmm… I like the sound of that!" he smiled, feeling a great weight being lifted from his shoulders.

"And better yet…"

"What?" he asked, while getting up to go into their room to change, while she went over to pick up the baby out of the bassinet to lay him in his own bed.

Coming in behind him, Max turned to face his wife, as she went to help him out of his snap down shirt, before going on to kiss the base of his throat. "Bobby's sleeping peacefully!" she whispered, as Max then went to back her up against their large bed.

"Oh…" he smiled, leaning down to kiss her neck, as his hands went on down to slip her sweater off over her head, "and how about you, are you sleepy?"

"Mmmm… not a bit, Mr. Brummet," she returned, feeling the cool quilt meeting the back of her bare legs, as he brought her down onto their bed to claim her lips passionately. "Mmmm… not… a… bit."